Bill,
The End is Near!

A Society of
Good Men

Richard MacPhie
12-13-06

For Kirsten, Shannon, Heather and Colton;
may you live long and in peace

ACKNOWLEDGEMENTS

I have not intentionally or knowingly used phrases, ideas or expressions other than my own without permission from the original author or creator. Any unacknowledged similarities are logically deduced or coincidental. The characters in the novel are of my own creation and are not intended to represent anyone, living or dead. Any similarities are coincidental or, in one case, premonitional. While I have used Minneapolis as a stage for the novel, I have used poetic license in describing the actual locations and neighborhoods within the city.

The following wonderful people have contributed technical, informational or literary assistance to me, directly or indirectly, during the writing of "A Society of Good Men."

Very Special thanks to:

Azure A. Anderson, Amy Walz, Bob Davis, Mark Levine, Major Reed Bowman (U.S. Air Force), Denise Grady, Brad Mjolsness, Dr. Peter G. Browne M.D., Herón Márquez Estrada, Hugh Jeffries & Leslie Fieger ("The End of the World"), John J. Miller & Ramesh Ponnuru, Gary Bowman, Michael Royce, Ed Lewis, Dr. Bruce Blair, Peter Goodgame, Phil Jayhan, John O. Edwards, Duncan Long, Beth Carpenter, Winnie Schrader, Bruce Beach, Stacey Petersen, Robert Schlemmer, Kim Wagner, and Dainis Noviks.

--Richard MacPhie

PROLOGUE

Babylon
Revelation 17:15-18
And he saith unto me, The waters which thou sawest,
where the whore sitteth, are peoples, and multitudes,
and nations, and tongues. And the ten horns which thou
sawest upon the beast, these shall hate the whore, and
shall make her desolate and naked, and shall eat her
flesh, and burn her with fire. For God hath put in
their hearts to fulfill his will, and to agree,
and to give their kingdom unto the beast,
until the words of God shall be fulfilled.

APRIL FIRST: THE EARLY HOURS

SAN FRANCISCO, CALIFORNIA April 1, 3:07 AM PST

The navy blue government SUV sped through the Telegraph Hill section of San Francisco toward the docks. The Nuclear Emergency Search Team (NEST), a highly secretive federal inter-agency group that held the responsibility for locating and deactivating terrorist nuclear weapons operations, had gotten a "hot" reading from one of their bird-dog helicopters down by the bay. The elite group was hidden behind the cloak of nuclear secrecy and operated under the authority of the Department of Energy.

The NEST personnel operated with special expertise and equipment and were directed by DOE's Nevada Operations Office on authority delegated by Director of the Office of Military Application. All of them fell under the Department of Homeland Defense. The members called themselves "nesties."

Boscoe Williams drove the first vehicle to reach the dock. The thirty-six-year-old Wisconsin native held a Ph.D. in nuclear physics and had been a nestie for two years. The vehicle screeched to a halt. Williams and fellow nestie, Ron LeFebre, hustled out of the SUV and ran to the ocean-shipping container under the bird-dog helo. The helicopter's searchlight shone down upon him as Williams pointed at the container and gestured as if to say *is this the one?* The helo pilot rocked the bird's rotors up and down in the ages-old aviation sign of affirmative. With gamma-ray detectors in hand, they soon established that this was, indeed, the target shipping container.

The terrorists had virtually hundreds of legitimate-appearing businesses and shipping channels so arranging for an ocean-going shipping container to reach port in America was ridiculously easy. There were eighteen million potential delivery vehicles to covertly introduce a nuclear device in the United States. That's the number of cargo containers that arrive in the United States annually and U.S. Customs inspects only a small percentage.

The detonation of a nuclear device smuggled by way of a sea container would have a far greater impact on global trade and the world economy. Even a two-week shutdown of global sea container traffic would be devastating, costing billions. What's more, unknown to the general public was that a federal task force under the command of the

Department of Homeland Defense had interdicted a live nuclear weapon headed for New England on the high seas just days before.

Support vehicles screeched to a halt around the container a few seconds after Williams'. Other vans and SUV's contained the tools of the trade: powerful x-ray machines, a high-pressure water cutting tool which had the advantage of being non-magnetic, a *must* when tinkering with a live nuke. Sensitive passive heat detectors were also used because decaying nuclear material gives off more heat than detectable high-energy particles.

Despite their existence, no one in the general public ever knowingly saw the nesties in action. They were more than discreet. If ever on alert or in training, they blended seamlessly into the population as they performed their holy tasks. Dressed in civilian clothes, they roamed streets with innocuous looking cases in hand. To the casual observer, a nestie might have been a marketing rep on his way to a sales presentation. After the teams identified the suspected area of imminent danger, dozens of team members fanned out along a matrix of the threat region trying to detect the bomb.

Carrying gamma-detectors inside cases to preserve secrecy, the nesties covered the suspect areas on foot, in vans and helicopters; going in and out of structures, abandoned buildings and warehouses hoping to register the tell-tale signals of hidden nuclear bombs. Keeping the public from panic was part and parcel of their job. For all their skills and knowledge, however, the nesties *were not* soldiers; they were scientists and technicians.

Seconds after confirming that the ground element had the target vehicle correctly identified, the helo pilot pointed the nose of the bird down and pulled up on the collective stick in a determined retreat. A

UH-60 Army Blackhawk helicopter swooped across the bay and screeched up to waterfront, thick ropes tumbling out of the cargo doors before the aircraft leveled out to a flat hover forty feet over the deck. Even though a firefight or hand-to-hand combat wasn't expected, a heliborne squad of Delta Task Force members detached to the nesties came fast-roping down onto the docks from the Army bird, quickly searching and securing the perimeter. The Blackhawk then lifted and orbited closely on station in standard operating procedure.

Best intelligence said this was H-Hour. That meant that caution *had* to be thrown to the wind because the package was mere minutes or possibly even seconds from detonation. The dock area was militarily secured, the support vehicles unloaded and the shipping container locking mechanism had been wired with a small standard charge all within three minutes of Williams' and LeFebre's vehicle screeching to a halt. Even if a live nuke were right on the other side of the door, a small conventional explosion wouldn't be enough to detonate it. Besides, the initial reading indicated that the bomb was about 22 feet to the rear of the container, away from the doors.

The charge blew, the doors swung open and the three techs ran inside through swirling smoke into the container. But what would they encounter when they rushed in? A dirty bomb? A missing Russian "suitcase" nuke? A homemade contraption registering 400 kilotons?

There was no cargo in the container. Instead there were several hundred sandbags laid down for ballast. The nuclear device was nestled in the middle of the container like a bird's egg in a nest. The bomb turned out to be a Soviet 250 kiloton unit with a homemade detonating device rigged up to it. It was nothing like the nesties had either seen or trained for: there was no bright red digital clock counting down like in a James Bond thriller. It was simply a crude gadget with wires and explosives gathered around the recognizable head of a nuke warhead. The men seemed to all talk and listen at once.

"What the hell is it?" said LeFebre.

"Modified ICBM nuke warhead," Williams said tersely.

"How do we disarm the damn thing?" said the third technician, a newbie named Dr. Jensen.

"Lemme think. This damn thing could go off any second," said Williams, as he unconsciously bit his bottom lip. Classroom theory was so much easier than making a split-second decision that could cost a hundred thousand lives. Though inwardly terrified, Williams remained calm on the outside. He used the same self-psychology in that he did back in high school when preparing to release a high-pressure shot in basketball: *Don't think about it, dummy, just do it.*

"How long has this container been on the dock?"

"The harbor master isn't sure. Thinks the dock manifest says about 48 hours, but he's not certain," said the newbie. That would make sense because terrorists would have to account for possible delays or any other contingency when planning the detonation. They couldn't depend on the listed date and time of arrival; they would've had to buffer their estimate. Especially in light of heavy Coast Guard offshore boardings that had recently been stepped up.

"Any chance of a heavy lift chopper taking the whole damn container out?" said LeFebre.

"And doing what? Having an engine or cargo-hook failure? Dropping it in the ocean and creating a cloud of radioactive steam the size of Iowa? Or carrying it over the bay and having an air burst over San Francisco?" Williams asked with despair. "All right," he said,

5

having made up his mind a second later. "We don't have time to analyze this thing. I'm making the call: we're going to freeze the bastard."

"Liquid nitrogen?" LeFebre asked.

"You got it," said Williams. Spraying the bomb with liquid nitrogen would hopefully retard the detonation sequence long enough to get the threat out of the city. *Hopefully.* "After that, we'll get six or seven guys in here, carry the package out onto the dock and then have a Blackhawk or a Chinook sling-load this thing northwest. We won't carry the whole shipping container, just the bomb itself."

"Roger that. Up and away from the city," LeFebre nodded.

The Blackhawk was in a close orbit and Williams had to raise his voice. "Yeah, then circle back eastwards out over the wine country and eventually out to the desert," he said before turning to the Delta chalk leader, a Sergeant First Class, and yelling over the rotor wash.

"Sergeant!"

The Delta ran up close to Williams and leaned in to hear him.

"Here's the play: after you check for booby-traps, we're gonna freeze the package and sling-load it out to the desert. Get on the horn. Get two helos here, one as a back up, both fully fueled and make damn sure both have working cargo hooks."

Training taught Williams that the failure of the most innocuous piece of simple equipment could cost … *everything.*

YODER, COLORADO April 1, 6:25 AM MST

The Peterbuilt semi was screaming westwards on Highway 94, American-born Ahmed Abdullah Khan at the wheel. His original mission had been to deliver a nuclear payload into the city of Denver

6

and detonate it, but plans switched to contingency "B" when law enforcement intervened near Yoder. Now the target was Colorado Springs.

Two State Patrol cruisers, cherries lit and sirens blaring, were in hot pursuit after the vehicle failed to stop for a simple speeding violation about ten miles back. Corporal Lance Bellows was in the lead vehicle. Bellows was a thirty-year-old former 82nd Airborne army paratrooper. State Trooper Bill Loeman followed less than two car-lengths behind Bellows and handled radio communications to the dispatcher and officers ahead.

"Roger that, we have a red Peterbuilt headed west on 94, 85-miles-per-hour. Over." He unkeyed the mic.

"Be advised, feds suspect vehicle may be carrying nuclear payload," said dispatch. *Oh, shit!* Loeman thought as his foot involuntarily came off the accelerator for a second before speeding back up.

"Bellows, d'you catch that?"

"Roger. We gotta stop this guy now."

Bellows was all business. Jumping out of C-130s in full combat gear into a black night sky raises a man's fear-threshold for the rest of his life. *"This ain't nothin but a thing,"* he remembered his stick leader saying right before they ever had to do something very difficult or very dangerous. Now he found himself willfully chasing a nuclear bomb down a lonely desert highway.

Ain't nothin but a thing.

He accelerated trying to get around the big truck. Once there he'd wing it, he thought. Maybe he'd shoot out some tires with his service revolver or take a one-handed blast with the shotgun out the passenger window. He took his revolver out of its holster and laid it on the seat next to him, at the ready. If need be, he decided, he'd crash his vehicle into the cab and try to run the semi off the road.

Khan saw the trooper's maneuvering and began swerving to and fro. Bellows lunged and retreated with his cruiser, never quite able to get up to the cab.

"Dispatch, any chance of military back up?" he screamed into his radio.

"Feds have been notified and are aware of situation. ETA 20 minutes, nuclear response team choppers, over," the dispatcher answered in clipped radio-speak. Intel had suggested that Denver was a potential target, so nuke-hunting feds were relatively nearby. Relatively. But twenty minutes is an eternity in the atomic world.

"GODDAMMIT!" Bellows screamed throwing his mic down on the passenger seat. Their route was about to take them past Schriever Air Force Base, why couldn't they help? Emotion detracted his full attention at the same moment that Khan came up with a faulty plan to lose his pursuers: he eyed the cruisers in the big rear-view mirrors and than slammed on the brakes in a hope that the officers would slam into the rear of the trailer. He slammed the brakes.

Being unfamiliar with the nature of big rigs, however, Khan's maneuver sent the road-beast into a violent jack-knife: The rig toppled over in the middle of the interstate. Both cruisers were going too fast to react and skidded into the truck's wreckage at high speed.

Bellows regained consciousness several seconds after the crash but he was light-headed and disoriented. His head hurt and blood was streaming down the side of his face. His smoldering cruiser was mangled and propped up at an angle against the belly of the trailer. He forced open the door. It groaned as if the car itself was in pain. Bellows instinctively reached for his revolver then remembered that he had laid it on the seat. He looked down. It was gone now. Bellows didn't want to spend the time looking for the handgun either so he unracked the shotgun.

The Colorado lawman lumbered out of his unit and stumbled towards the wreckage of Loeman's cruiser; Trooper Loeman was DOA. Still dizzy, he turned his attention towards the big rig and pumped the shotgun, chambering the first shell. His head throbbed and it felt like he was drunk. It seemed to take forever for Bellows to reach the cab of the semi. He cautiously circled around it with shotgun at the ready and then peered inside through the broken windscreen. Khan was in there, conscious and breathing heavily.

"Let me … let me see those hands …" Bellows commanded weakly. Khan just continued staring at him and breathing with labored effort.

"I said, lemme see those damn hands!"

What Bellows didn't know was that Khan's cargo was a crudely built 200-kiloton nuclear bomb built with stolen fissile material and a simple high-explosive detonator. The crash had disabled the payload and prematurely started the detonation sequence. Bellows was about to weakly bark out another command when the HE exploded, killing both men.

But there was no nuclear event.

BOSTON, MASSACHUSETTS April 1, 9:14 AM EST

Dr. John McIvey whispered to God as he leaned into his trade; deactivating a nuclear bomb. This one was unlike any other he'd worked on before. This bomb wasn't a training mock-up, this one was real. Boston elements of the Nuclear Emergency Reaction Team

(NERT) had been on high alert in response to the latest terrorist threat-level announcement.

Police had ticketed an apparently abandoned semi and its trailer left near the intersection of Joy Street and Mt. Vernon. NERT team leader McIvey got wind of the strange traffic situation at about 8:40 in the morning and ordered a team to scan the tractor-trailer and it came up hot for a nuke. The police and feds immediately did everything they could to start evacuating downtown Boston. Luckily it was still early enough in the morning and many commuters were still in their cars. They'd be easier to evacuate than someone already nestled into a cubicle on the thirtieth floor of a skyscraper.

Thirty-one minutes after the positive reading, McIvey found himself at the most critical and defining moment of his life. The package was laid open and a tangle of wires and electrical components hung out of the bomb's body like disemboweled entrails. He could hear the distant and frantic honking of car horns as Bostonians were being ushered out of the city.

"Guide me, dear Lord. Help me do right," McIvey whispered as he labored through his delicate task. The timing and detonating device were homemade but the Doctor of Physics quickly understood the basics of the unit.

"Wipe," he said. Fellow NERT member Jerry Diamond wiped McIvey's brow and face with a cloth like a nurse in an operating room. Diamond also passed requested tools. The men spoke in near whispers as they crouched in the bay of the semi trailer. Several portable work lights were set up around the men's work area as to give them optimal lighting conditions.

"What do ya think, Johnny?" said Diamond.

"It's a messy sumbitch. Some of these wires don't do anything or go anywhere."

"Decoys? Time-wasters?" Diamond asked in a near whisper.

"It would appear so," answered McIvey. "Is everyone else out of the area?"

"Uh, I think they're still setting up radiation detectors around the blast template. Johnson is back at C-2 working up fallout forecasts based on the wind and estimated kilotonage."

"Make sure there are no other team members in the blast radius. It's bad enough that I might take you out with me, buddy. Everybody on the team is valuable, they need to live to fight another day."

"Roger that. There's a helo down in Boston Common, a couple blocks away. I'll tell them to chopper outta here," said Diamond as McIvey intently kept working. Tiny movements. Tiny movements.

"Yeah," McIvey whispered and he untangled wires and snipped. "Yeah, just go out—*OH SHIT!*"

"What?" said a worried Diamond.

McIvey had not erred in his task, the device simply started its five-second detonation sequence on its own.

"OH SHIT!" repeated McIvey with a desperately worried look. *"NO!"* he cried with the anguish of a man who knows he'll never see his wife and children again.

"WHAT'S WRONG?" screamed Diamond. McIvey didn't answer, his face a statue of anguish and despair.

"WHAT'S WRONG?" Diamond screamed in abject horror.

A nano-second later, neither man existed. A brilliant orange mushroom cloud from a 200-kiloton nuclear device blossomed over the city of Boston.

WASHINGTON D.C., April 1, 9:09 AM EST

The morning sun shone brightly over the District of Columbia. The F-16s engaged the Cessna 152 for the fourth time as it approached the nation's capital. Major Dave Gilchrist, call sign Mystic six-one, and Captain Steve Anderson, call sign Mystic six-two, had already shot warning flares across the plane's nose and had failed repeatedly to raise the pilot on the radio.

"Mystic flight, cameras on," radioed Gilchrist.

"Two," Anderson acknowledged.

"Valhalla, Mystic six-one, how copy?" Gilchrist radioed to the AWACS Command and Control.

"Roger, Mystic, this is Valhalla."

"Valhalla, have fired flares, have pushed several different freeqs, no response, target not responding. Vectoring straight into DC. Request permission to fire."

There was a delay of several seconds before the response came; *"Mystic six-one, engage and destroy target, acknowledge."*

"Roger that, Valhalla. Mystic flight is fangs out, engaging target."

Gilchrist armed his sidewinder missiles as the fast-movers circled around in order to come up for a deflection shot on the invading airplane. Anderson armed his weapons and took up wing position. They came up fast from five o'clock and the major got a good missile-lock.

"Fox-two," said Gilchrist in fighter pilot-speak for releasing a sidewinder.

The missile whooshed loudly off the wingtip hardpoint. Within mere seconds, Gilchrist's first missile found its mark and slammed into the Cessna.

"Shack!" he said into the mic, indicating a solid and devastating impact with the target. *"Splash one."*

The flaming wreckage of the Cessna spiraled and fluttered into the middle of a residential street in Wheaton, north of the capital. The major had destroyed the invader with remarkable ease. But there was no nuclear weapon on board that plane.

The nuclear weapon was on board a twin-engine Beechcraft hedgehopping over the treetops of Annandale, southwest of the capital. The pilot, Ali Al-Fulani, leaned on the throttles and the engines roared in response.

The crew of a U.S. Customs Blackhawk saw the aircraft as it approached Arlington. The Beechcraft was moving too fast for the Blackhawk to interdict. The Customs aircraft radioed the AWACS who, in turn, notified Gilchrist and Anderson. They were immediately vectored to the new threat. Other fighters were already wheels-up out of Andrews AFB, but it was too late: The diversion created by the decoy Cessna had allowed the threat aircraft to approach the capital with relative ease.

"Tally-ho, eleven o'clock low," Anderson said as he spotted the target.

"Got him, Two, follow my lead," Gilchrist radioed his wingman. The fighter jocks had made visual contact two miles out and began their attack run. They already had clearance to engage.

"Valhalla, Mystic flight engaging bandit number-two, how copy?"

"Roger, Mystic, acknowledged. Light him up." There was a sense of urgency in his voice.

Gilchrist armed his missiles for the second time that morning. *This is going to be easy,* he thought. Despite the fact that the Beechcraft was more agile than the Cessna 152, the Air Force jets closed fast on the twin-engine plane. Al-Fulani pulled back on the yoke and the aircraft started gaining altitude. He quickly surpassed 1,000 feet altitude and was climbing fast. The American fighters approached firing range. Closer, and ... Gilchrist fired his sidewinder.

"Fox-two," he calmly said over the radio as the sidewinder gracefully arced away from his aircraft.

Al-Fulani saw the American fighter release his ordnance. He held a detonator in his left hand. It was hard-wired to a 400-kiloton nuclear bomb. The chemically propelled rocket closed fast, but never made it to its target. When the Beechcraft reached an altitude of 2,000 feet directly over the American capital city – but before the sidewinder impacted – Al-Fulani detonated his payload.

THE ENGLISH CHANNEL, April 1, 3:37:47 PM Greenwich

A nuclear device detonated in the middle of the Chunnel, the railroad tunnel system connecting Great Britain to the European mainland. The device was on board one of the many freight trains that run through the system everyday. Even though the Chunnel averaged about 140 feet below the channel floor, the event occurred at a point that was only 83 feet under the seabed. The blast effect emerged from the sea like a giant glowing mountain, creating huge violent waves that swamped and sank dozens of ships in the English Channel. Radioactive steam was created from the ocean waters over Point Zero and started wafting over the European mainland.

But, the worst effects were the tremendous blasts coming out of both ends of the system. Much of the blast energy took the path of least resistance and shot through the tunnel itself. Once away from Point Zero, the blast energy was contained and super-compressed by the underground tunnel and millions of gallons of ocean water pressing down from above. The radioactive atomic blasts shot out of the tunnel mouths with a secondary fury never before seen on Earth. Molten material, dust, plasma and gases not only caused destruction, but projected radioactive contamination for miles into the land and air of the French and English countrysides like giant angry fire hoses.

The plan was brilliant: The death, destruction, property loss and economic and environmental impact were catastrophically and titantically disproportionate given the relatively small size of the nuclear device. Scotland Yard could only speculate how the terrorists got a nuclear weapon past the passive detectors that all cargo must go through before entering the Chunnel.

"There are limits, governed by the laws of physics," as one official put it, "to technology for detecting nuclear materials. In broad terms they have to do with sensing radioactivity at a distance and through shielding, and with the balance between false positives and false negatives." There were classified American Energy Department documents that catalogued what one of them called "shortcomings in the ability of equipment to locate the target materials that if known by adversaries could be used to defeat the search equipment and procedures."

In the end, officials simply concurred that the weapon must have been encased in lead – it was the only answer. The twenty-one billion-dollar engineering marvel was destroyed and all three tunnels in the 31-mile system were totally flooded and highly radioactive. Preoccupied with their own troubles, America's good friends, the British, would not be much of an aid during the coming hardships.

OF IRAQ

Because of its repeated flaunting of UN resolutions, the United States attacked Iraq in the spring of 2003. Some people asked for hard evidence of WMD before the campaign started, the implication being that the absence of evidence is evidence of absence. Iraq was bombed concurrent with a rolling ground invasion.

Weapons inspectors visiting Tarmiya, Iraq, found a huge facility containing over a hundred calutrons after major combat operations ended. The discovery was more than surprising because a scientist named Ernest Lawrence had invented calutrons in the early 1940s, and he named them after "Cal," as in the University of California at Berkeley. His brainstorm was to use industrial-scale mass spectrometry on the isotopes of uranium and thereby separate enough U-235 to make an atomic weapon. The calutrons at Oak Ridge, Tennessee had separated enough U-235 by 1945 to make one weapon and his program was a success. By modern nuclear standards, however, they were museum relics.

A bomb based on U-235 can use a "gun style" configuration, and this was considered so reliable that no test was necessary. The first atomic bomb that was tested at Alamogordo, New Mexico, was a plutonium bomb. Such a bomb requires a carefully crafted implosion –

very tricky business – and it was not clear that it would work, but it was tested and it functioned as designed. The uranium bomb built using calutrons, never tested, was first used over Hiroshima and, of course, destroyed the city and much of its population. A few days later a plutonium bomb, identical to the Alamogordo bomb, did the same to Nagasaki.

So why were the Western governments shocked to find calutrons in Iraq? Because the West was too shortsighted to have anticipated them. The inspectors were looking for centrifuges, for laser separation, and for diffusion plants. All the while, nobody guessed that Saddam Hussein would revert to the simplest, most reliable method, the one that had worked for the United States six decades earlier.

Simple people make things complicated, complicated people make things complex, and complex people make things simple.

Iraqi scientists had constructed facilities to build a bomb that required no testing. Official values released by the U.S. Government stated that a critical mass of plutonium of about 6 kg, less than a half a liter in volume, is more than enough to make a bomb. The government knew that Saddam was caught in the process of trying to build an atomic bomb during the late nineties.

Those who were more suspicious of Iraq said that the inspection results of the mid-nineties were the fruits of good detective work by UNSCOM, the agency then in charge of inspections. The inspectors were never allowed to find the nuclear weapons plants Saddam was building – all they could do was get tantalizingly close only to have Saddam throw them out of the country. He ejected the inspectors in violation of UN treaty agreements.

After the humiliating loss of Desert Storm in 1991, Saddam secretly became intent on developing nuclear weapons and releasing them to be used on the West. Western governments procrastinated in dealing with the threat and delays by the United Nations gave Saddam the margin of time that he needed. The regime was able to covertly export the nuclear material and technology through Syria shortly before the coalition attack on the country. It took time, several years, for the package to move across the Middle East and Europe but, in the end, the Iraqi bomb was used to destroy the Chunnel.

"I just wanna have my kicks before the whole shithouse goes up in flames."

-- Jim Morrison

<u>ONE</u>

Nothing lasts forever. I think anyone would agree with that.

My name is Dallas Burnette. I'm a native of Minneapolis, Minnesota. The name Burnette came from the French-Indian side of my family, and the name Dallas? Well, my dad never fully explained that one to me before he died. My mother remarried and had a little girl, Marissa. Then mom up and died in a car accident when Marissa was four and I was twelve. Closed casket, I never wanted to know the details, even now. My mom's sister and her husband took us in. Nothing special, they gave us food and shelter and they never pretended to be anything other than our legal guardians. They got us to adulthood and then we were on our own. My half-sister is married and now lives in Nebraska.

I had been a lifelong bachelor with no kids. I was always, what they call, a loner. The true nature of my solitude came to the fore a few years back when I parked in the wrong spot and had my car towed. The tow lot was in a distant suburb, not very accessible by public transportation. I didn't have a wife, a girlfriend, a family member or even a buddy to take me there to get my personal belongings out of the car while I was waiting for the next payday to get insurance.

I used to think that being by myself was stoic, that it proved my quiet manliness, like the mysterious drifter in an old cowboy movie. But now? Most people have someone to lend them a helping hand if they get in a little hot water. I couldn't scrounge up one solitary personal acquaintance to take me out and get my car. For the first time, my lone-wolf status hit me.

I worked as a salesman for a small abrasives distributor. Essentially, my job was to sell sandpaper and a variety of other abrasive products over the phone, mainly to other businesses and retail outlets. I had a number of regular customers, so lots of my sales were slam-dunks: Taking the order and getting the commission. It was a small office. I enjoyed working with the other people there and the owner always gave out nice little Christmas bonuses of $1,000 non-taxed cash. It wasn't a hard job, but it was boring as hell. It paid the bills, though, and left me enough cash to enjoy the weekends.

My normal morning ritual was to show up at the office at about eight o'clock in the morning and contact my East Coast buyers because they were an hour ahead of us. I'd usually go down to the corner coffee shop at nine o'clock or so and get a tall dark roast coffee-of-the-day to go with room for cream and sugar. The office was in the Uptown area of Minneapolis and the coffee joint was right down the street. On this particular morning, I got wrapped up on a phone call with a big buyer and didn't leave for the shop until about quarter after.

The first of April was like any other spring day. The temperature was pleasant enough but weather was on the dark and drizzly side that morning as I scurried out of the foyer of my 1930's-vintage office building and headed towards the coffee shop. Cars had their headlights on and they cast bright little reflections on the streets.

I've always enjoyed rainy days, even when I was a little kid. My mom used to say I should have been born in England. Through exams – administered under the guise of coursework during my one semester as a psychology major at the U – I learned that I had a slightly depressive personality. Maybe that's why dreary rainy days always felt like such a comfortable old friend to me. I actually considered going to college in Seattle just for the rain, the drizzle and the regional music scene.

I had been to Seattle once. I thought that it was very much as if a giant had taken a colossal ice cream scoop, scooped Minneapolis right out of the earth, added a Space Needle, and plopped it down there right next to the ocean. I really liked that city.

I shuffled up the wet sidewalk and ducked inside the coffee shop. This was the 'hip' part of town, the area where artists and writers tended to gravitate: Trendy businessfolk mingled with the pierced and tattooed denizens of cool. The service people in this part of town tended to be slow and rude. It seemed as though their attitude was, if you came to spend money at the store where they worked, then *you* were interrupting *their* day. Shit.

This place was no different: The girl at the counter was some gum-smacking hipster with gaudy make-up and apparel who barely looked up when interacting with customers. I had dealt with their attitudes long ago and decided that they could live in their own self-made and personal little hells. I wouldn't let them bother me. I stood in line thinking about nothing in particular.

My mind was wandering to the sounds of traffic and car tires rolling on wet pavement, the din of light conversation in the shop, the clacking of coffee cups and the innocuous white noise of a television mounted on a ceiling bracket high over the serving area.

Suddenly the television cut from the sports update to the CNN Special Report placard with the ominous voice-over, "Attention: This is a **CNN Breaking News Special Report.**" The anchorperson reappeared on the screen looking ashen and shaky. He stammered and then read hurriedly from some papers in front of him;

> *"We have unconfirmed ... correction: CONFIRMED reports that a nuclear device has detonated in the city of Boston, Massachusetts. The detonation occurred at 9:15 am Eastern Standard Time. If the reports are true, and they seem to be– "* He ran his hand over his face as he listened into his earpiece. *"Ladies and gentlemen, CNN has learned that a second nuclear detonation is reported in New York City. If true, two major American eastern-seaboard cities have suffered catastrophic nuclear explosions within mere minutes of one another ... wait ... "* He stopped, held his earpiece closer and then spoke. *"A third explosion, apparently cities have suffered simultaneous nuclear attacks. For anyone watching around the country, please follow the instructions of local police or civil defense experts ... "* The anchor was in a state of controlled hysteria and his voice wavered as he spoke. *"The American cities of Boston, New York– "*

Then the TV screen suddenly went to snowy static. That was the broadcast we heard in the 'Wired Koffee' coffee shop in Minneapolis on that sad, gray April morning. There was no more conversational din or coffee cups plunking down on formica tables and countertops. The joint was silent but for the static of the television set. When I was able to summon the strength to look around at the other eight or so patrons and workers, all I saw were muted, open-jawed looks of utter disbelief. When I caught sight of myself in the mirror behind the service counter, I noticed I was wearing the exact same look on my face as well.

It took the assistant manager an eternal three or four seconds to grab the remote control and start surfing for other news reports. All we could get was local news outlets with terrified non-air staffers in casual shirts, clunky headsets and trembling voices doing their best to relay the horror of the end of the world. A couple coffeehouse patrons wondered aloud if Atlanta, home of CNN, had been nuked and we subsequently found it to be true, along with St. Louis. Seven American cities were gone and there was little doubt that the detonations were the acts of terrorists.

I ran out of the shop and back up the street to my office. Civil Defense air raid sirens had already spooled up and were blaring their terrifying and ominous howls of warning. I scrambled through other pedestrians, weaving and inadvertently bumping shoulders. No one, including me, took the time to turn around and say, *"Excuse me."* The news was spreading like wildfire.

I tore through the foyer and standing there was a confused young woman in her early or mid-twenties who was just saying, *"What's going on? What's happening?"* as everyone ignored her. She'd find out soon enough, I thought, just not from me. I ran up the stairs of my office building to the second floor and into the reception area of the company where I worked, Wegman Abrasives, Inc.

"Jesus Christ, what's wrong with you?" said Julie, the receptionist, as I burst breathlessly through the doors.

"Julie! You haven't heard?" I said. "Half the country has been nuked!"

"What?"

"Nuked!" I panted. "A bunch of cities have been nuked. *They're gone.*"

"April Fool's Day to you, too, Dallas. You really need to work on your humor, ya know," she said with a dismissive wave as she kept typing on the computer keyboard.

"I'm serious as a heart attack, turn on the radio."

She had been listening to a CD and apparently none of the other three people in the office had heard of the attack either. It wouldn't matter what station she was tuned into; every single broadcast venue in the country would be on the story by now.

Julie rolled her eyes and shook her head as she indulged my request. She flipped her small boom box over to radio. "If this is some dumb-ass office prank I'll – " she stopped suddenly.

" *–cities of Boston, Washington D.C., New York, Atlanta, St. Louis, Seattle and Los Angeles have all suffered nuclear attacks ...*"

Julie's face went ashen as we continued listening. "My ... my whole family ... lives in Boston," she said, staring at the office wall in front of her.

"Where's David?" I said, referring to the manager.

"Gone. Back soon," Julie barely got out of her mouth, clearly in shock.

"I'm leaving, I've got to get home," I said.

"Uh-huh," she said. A single tear was rolling down her left cheek. Other than that, she looked catatonic. In retrospect I should have hugged her or at least said I was sorry about her family, but I guess I was somewhat in shock myself. I didn't even acknowledge my other co-workers.

I grabbed my car keys and cell phone off of my desk and I ran to my car, which was parked in a lot about half a block down in the pay lot. I wondered if Minneapolis was about to experience a nuclear blast itself. This was, after all, a major metropolitan area. If you included St. Paul, the metro area was just a bit over four million people: that's a juicy target if you were a terrorist intent on killing lots of Americans. My eyes widened and I felt an almost painful tingle in my lower back as I realized the unthinkable possibility that I could very well experience a nuclear explosion first hand. Who knows how many cities the terrorists had targeted for today? *Could this really be happening?*

I started my car and exited the lot. Though the news was still new, traffic was already starting to congest. Horns blared as office workers ran down sidewalks to their cars or public transportation points. Most people had a cell phone pressed to an ear as they frantically tried to contact *whoever*. I weaved slowly through the building mid-morning traffic jam and my mind was thinking a thousand thoughts.

On the right, I saw a gas station and pulled my car in quick. I was down to a quarter tank and I was pretty sure that there would be huge gas lines before too long. Using my debit card, I topped off the car and then filled the five-gallon can I kept in the trunk. As I got back into my vehicle I noticed a line of cars already building out into the street. I collided with a red SUV quarter-panel to quarter-panel while leaving the parking lot. The damage was light and neither of us got out of our vehicles to inspect; the other driver just looked at me and gave me the *whatever* gesture and we drove our separate ways.

Next stop was the bank. I was itching to get home but I had the feeling that I needed to withdraw my money *right now*. Again I beat the rush but there was only one teller on duty, the manager, so there was a little bit of a wait. Almost everyone was frantically talking into cell phones. Most sort of had pallid faces, worrying about family and such I would guess. Soon it was my turn at the counter. I withdrew a total of $4,354.98 from checking and savings combined, closing both accounts.

"Your money may not be worth anything tomorrow," the manager said.

"Good luck to you," I said as I stuffed the cash into my coat pockets. I don't know why.

"God bless you, sir," she said sweetly. "Good luck to you, too."

I thought about stopping at the grocery store but raced home instead. I had already had common sense enough to stop at the bank and the gas station; the groceries would have to wait. It was a big mistake. Most storeowners had already heard the reports and had acted on the natural inclination to save stock. Smaller stores closed and locked up. And the rest of the stores? You thought you had seen inflation before but this was like from zero to a million in sixty seconds. They turned into near-riot situations I suppose it was just as well that I didn't stop and I went straight home from the bank.

I burst into my apartment exactly one hour after I first heard the news and turned on the TV, which was nothing but frantic news reports. I flipped around the channels. One of the networks was playing videotape from earlier in the morning. A cameraman for the New York NBC affiliate had been wrapping up a fluff story on the importance of adopting animals from the humane society in New Rochelle. He was shooting his reporter with Long Island off in the distance over her right shoulder when a silent, orange mushroom cloud erupted from within the city. He captured the nuking of New York City on tape.

It was absolutely the most terrifying thing I've ever seen.

I tried logging onto the internet but there was no chance as the system was clearly overloading. Next, I tried calling my half-sister, Marissa, in Nebraska. I took half a dozen tries but I got through. She and her husband and kids were all fine, but she was panicked along with the rest of the country. She begged me to come down there but my mind was awash in the enormity of events. I told her I'd get back to her in a few days or maybe a week.

There wasn't much more information in the first hours for us here in the heartland of America. An aerial missile attack was quickly ruled out; it hadn't been a surprise Russian attack or an aggression by a rogue nation. How could this be? In the end, our first instincts were correct. For ten days the country had been on another "Terrorist Alert" warning, which had become routine, 'routine' being synonymous with 'ignorable,' the way city folk ignored car alarms.

After several years we never really expected anything when the government said, "Expect and prepare for something of a catastrophic nature at sometime in the near future." Stocking a six-pack of *Aquafina* in the trunk of my car was about as far as my preparation went. What else is a lone sandpaper salesman to do?

Over previous few years the news had become increasingly riddled with independent acts of terrorism; American, Kuwaiti and French oil tankers and off-shore facilities were attacked by explosives-laden small boats, crowded discos throughout Southeast Asia and Australia

27

bombed, UN peacekeepers or US military men shot while on guard duty in faraway places. Contract workers continued to be kidnapped and beheaded on video. Car bombs exploded outside of American embassies with disquieting regularity, usually killing a handful of indigenous people. The embassy bombings seemed to be more on the symbolic side.

Iran had captivated the world's nuclear attention by constantly rattling its nuclear sabers. They promised to "wipe Israel off the map" and to "punish" anyone who attacked them. Chances of diplomacy would appear and then evaporate. In the end, however, it appeared that Iran had had nothing directly to do with The Attack. I'm sure they were great morale supporters, though.

In America, several chain coffee shops had suffered backpack bombings in the half-year prior and had killed dozens of Americans. The terrorists had tried cyber-attacks – Weapons of Mass Disruption – on major internet nodes called Digital Control Systems. The FBI named the attacks "Mardi-Garden," "Nimda-Shine" and "Moonlight-Maze," amongst other creative monikers. All these acts had the commonality of being linked to al Qaeda. And now, the big finale.

All in all, in addition to the Chunnel in Europe, huge parts of seven major American cities went up in nuclear mushroom clouds that first day. As far as we knew, it might have been only the beginning. Here in the upper Midwest, we didn't even see an explosion, hear a bomb, or feel a ground tremor. More bombs may still be coming and, in fact, probably were, I thought. If the attackers' plans have gone according to schedule, then they have finished with their primary targets. Now they would start on the secondary targets. You just didn't know.

TWO

I spent that first day in my apartment perched on the edge of my couch watching TV and trying to glean any information I could. The president had been stumping for a congressman with dipping poll numbers and was not in D.C. on April first. He and key members of his staff had survived The Attack.

Suddenly there was a message from the Office of the President of the United States. There was just a cheesy placard introduction and then the picture cut to the president who was seated behind a simple desk. He was still being wired for sound by a technician in headphones and then took several seconds to assemble his notes. There was background noise of people talking quietly and equipment being moved around. It was a makeshift studio and there would be no teleprompter. Suddenly it went quiet.

"Are we on?" the president said quietly to someone off camera.

"Go ahead, Mr. President," came the reply from an unseen aide. He looked down, cleared his throat and then looked up into the camera and spoke;

"My fellow Americans, as all of you surely know by now, our beloved country has suffered a devastating nuclear attack. The events of today will go down as the most catastrophic day in world history, probably for as long as humans live and thrive on this Earth – the day of sheer global horror.

"By the powers vested in me, I hereby declare that the United States has existed in a state of national emergency since 9:15 a.m., Eastern Standard Time, of this day. I intend to utilize the following statutes; sections 123, 123a, 527, 2201 subsection 'c', 12006, and 12302 of title 10, United States Code, and sections 331, 359, and 367 of title 14, United States Code. This proclamation immediately shall be published in the Federal Register and disseminated through the Emergency Federal Register and transmitted to the congressional record. A comprehensive list of activated executive orders shall be made public shortly.

"The United States has entered a state of national emergency by reason of nuclear attack on seven American cities. The American cities affected are as follows; Boston, Massachusetts. New York City, New York. Washington, DC. Atlanta, Georgia. St. Louis, Missouri. Los Angeles, California. Seattle, Washington.

"In addition, a nuclear device has detonated in the Chunnel underneath the English Channel. Our friends in Europe will have their hands full for quite some time to come."

The president to another heavy breath and then straightened his shoulders and looked squarely into the camera.

"Under powers guaranteed me in the Constitution of the United States, I am declaring nationwide martial law, effective immediately. Martial law will remain in effect indefinitely from this day forward. Civil Rights are officially suspended as of this minute. Furthermore, I am assuming control of all National Guard troops by emergency suspension of *The Posse Comitatus Act* of 1878. Use of the National Guard is normally a power reserved for states' governors. By suspending Posse Comitatus, the federal government has authority to deploy and command the National Guard within the continental United States as police forces in instance of extreme national emergency. Furthermore, I have issued an immediate service-wide 'stop-loss' order to the Joint Chief-of-Staff, meaning that no service member may leave the military, effective this day forward. The order applies to all branches, including the Coast Guard. Any United States service member failing to report for duty will be dealt with in the harshest of terms.

"The Reserves and National Guard – along with regular police, police reserves and active duty military – are to assume police duties. It does not matter what the main military occupational specialty is of any specific Armed Forces member, all will act as police forces unless specifically ordered otherwise. No civilian will be allowed on the streets from dusk to dawn unless that citizen has explicit and verifiable permission for doing so. Police, along with Reserve and National Guard, will patrol the streets with vigor from this day forward and up until further notice.

"Police and military personnel are ordered to execute swift and harsh justice for the following; cases of looting, theft, assault, breaking and entering, rape and murder. In short, anything known in legal terms as *mala in se*, transgressions that go against fundamental human decency. The suspension of *habeas corpus* allows an agency to hold a person indefinitely and without charge. I strongly urge every citizen to obey the law, observe curfews and to implicitly and precisely follow the orders of any police officer or military member in uniform. Any deviation from these directives and you run the very real risk of being incarcerated or even shot by an agent of the government. The chain-of-command goes all the way up to me and I accept full responsibility. Your local police will be advising citizens further on this subject.

"There is an ongoing danger from massive amounts of radiation generated by today's detonations. Not only are these dangers in the immediate blast areas but, according to my scientific advisors, the radiation hazard will be carried around the globe and result in worldwide peril. Even if you are in a part of the country that did not experience or was not directly affected by the blasts today, there will be elevated radiation levels within days as the contamination circumvents the globe. Experts and teams from FEMA and the Department of Homeland Defense are being dispatched to all corners of the country to brief local authorities on preparing for radioactive fallout. Please listen to your radios and televisions and prepare for contamination. The government will advise you on specifics.

"Prices and wages are to be frozen immediately: I realize scant few citizens will report to work anytime in the foreseeable future. As president, I am ordering citizens employed in the utilities sectors such as communications, power industries and sewage – just to name a few – to report to work. Specific instructions will come down through government channels to your respective utilities and supervisors. If you work in one of these fields specified for mandatory attendance and you do not report to work, you will be detained and charged with one or more statutes outlined under sedition. Again, punishment will be swift and harsh.

"Active duty military forces in the continental United States have been dispatched immediately to guard nuclear facilities, power plants, dams, and other high profile targets. Nuclear Emergency Reaction Teams are searching large American cities in an effort to ensure there will be no more detonations on American soil. However, speaking on behalf of the government of the United States, I can tell you that we simply don't know if any more nuclear bombs are laying in wait, ready for detonation.

"Please listen to radios and watch the television as much as feasible; the federal government will be disseminating information to your local public officials and they, in turn, will tell you what you and your family need to do in order to attain safety and security.

"My fellow Americans, today is the single most horrific day in world history. Maintaining order is now a top priority for everyone. As your president, I am encouraging you in the strongest terms possible to follow the directives of your local police, military and public officials.

"And I ask you to pray for the dead and injured that … surely number … in the millions. May God bless you all … and may God continue to bless America." *Fade to black.*

The president had outlined things to come as best he could, considering that this was his first post-nuclear attack address to the country. Many members of the Senate and the House perished in the D.C. detonation, however. From that day forward the country has been run from some limestone caves in Virginia, a massive underground base designed to house all three branches of government during times like these called Mount Weather. The terror was real, the nightmare was genuine.

I thought about hopping in my car and fleeing but where could I go? I didn't really have much in the way of family, just my half-sister, that was about it. Mom and dad were dead, as were all the grandparents.

There were distant cousins, but so distant that I considered them non-family.

There was a knock on my door. I crossed the room and opened up to find two of my apartment neighbors standing there, John and Brian. They were a couple younger guys from the second floor of the apartment building. They were roommates as well as friends. I had spent many a Friday night in their apartment sipping Budweisers and strumming guitars.

"Dallas! D'you hear what happened?" asked John.

"Of course I did."

"What do ya think?"

"Well," I said, throwing my arms out to the side in a plaintiff gesture, "I'm at a loss, fellas."

"Yeah, that's how we feel," said Brian, I thought somewhat comically given the situation. "Wanna come over and chill at our place? Watch the tube?"

"Sure," I said, though I wasn't sure how much a person could "chill" while under nuclear attack. There wasn't much I was going to get accomplished by myself in my apartment anyway. Might as well share the misery, I figured.

The two were musicians. John was a guitarist and had been giving me lessons on the bass guitar for several months. Brian was a drummer in his early or mid-twenties. Both guys employed themselves as painters and freelance construction laborers as day jobs. They usually got paid under the table and didn't file taxes, which was fine with my libertarian beliefs. They seemed to make just enough money to pay rent and bills, and empty ramen noodle packages were a common sight in their garbage bin. I could tell when they had had a good week because empty pizza delivery boxes signified an indulgence in luxury.

I was grateful not to be alone that day and wound up staying at their place all day and well into the evening. While panic swept the globe, we watched TV and sipped bottled beer. At one point I used the restroom and Brian was making a phone call when I came out.

"So you aren't delivering now?" The response caused him to hold the phone away from his head. "Okay, bye now." He hung up the phone. "That's a no-go on pizzas," he said returning to the sofa.

"Shithead, did you actually think someone was going to bring you a pizza?" John said.

"I didn't know, that's why I called. At least someone answered the phone."

"What'd they say?"

"Well, lessee … it was the owner and he asked me if I was 'fucking crazy' a couple times and then slammed the phone down."

"Do you think Minneapolis could go up?" pondered John aloud as he quickly changed subjects.

"I don't think so," I said. "Minneapolis is a Mecca for foreigners, not the least of which are Muslim."

What the hell did I know? The terrorists might consider foreigners living in America to be traitors, infidels. Minneapolis might have been their Number One Target but the designated cell failed to detonate their weapon. The television showed the nuking of NYC again.

"Bet your life on that?" said Brian.

"Shit," I said. "If Minneapolis gets nuked, I hope the damn thing goes off two feet from my head."

John and Brian both chuckled nervously. Everything seemed like a dream – one big, bad, horrible dream. But it wasn't. Local news channels showed endless lines at gas stations and supermarkets mobbed with consumers intent on hoarding. Owners held guns, sometimes firing into the air. Sometimes you'd see a figure running out of a store with armloads of goods. People were yelling and horns were honking. We continued surfing channels until we found a national bulletin;

*"This is a **Special News Alert**: We would like to encourage the viewing audience to remain calm, but we feel it is our duty to convey the following message out of the Departments of Energy and Homeland Defense: Homeland Defense has no idea if more nuclear attacks are planned or imminent but it appears that major American cities have been targeted for nuclear attacks. If you live in a large metropolis, there is a risk that your city may be attacked. Please remain calm. If you feel you must flee, please follow the instructions of your local police and military."*

"Well, if that don't start mass frenzy, nothing will," John said dryly. And he was right.

Outside of our very building we could hear traffic and horns blaring. On TV, gas station lines went as far as the eye could see. Fistfights broke out between drivers, entire families were packed into minivans and SUV's. Dads were yelling, children were crying, moms were consoling. Police officers and guardsmen were trying to maintain control but the effort was as fruitless as herding cats – the police and military were utterly ignored by a frantic and fleeing populace.

"Mind if I have another beer?" I asked with a sigh.

"Go right ahead, my brother," said Brian. I wondered how they got so much beer so quickly. Turns out that Brian had just got a birthday card the day before The Attack. Grandma had sent him a check for five-hundred dollars.

"I spent a good chunk of that on beer and Doritos," he said. Indeed, the counter top of their kitchen was a sea of bags of all different flavors of Doritos. "I made about three or four trips down Shaggy's," he explained, talking about the liquor store that was one short city block from our apartment building.

"When did you do that?" I asked.

"I heard the bad news about nine-twenty this morning and I was first in line when they opened at ten."

"So the world is ending and all you're thinking about is beer?"

"Hey, I wasn't the only one, you shoulda seen the line. Besides, who's crazy like a fox now?"

"A fool and his money are soon partying," said John.

I *was* thankful to be sitting there drinking a cold beer, I guess. Brian had filled the refrigerator and stacked the remaining haul against the back of their kitchen, out of the way of daylight sun and covered with a white sheet.

We continued surfing TV channels. More and more images were coming in from areas just outside of the blast sites and they were apocalyptic: Herky-jerky handheld cameras showed terrified reporters as they tried to describe the end of all things and not doing very well at it. The reports would show the devastation at one city and then switch to another. All the pictures looked eerily the same.

Images of burned and injured people laying all about screaming or groaning were accompanied by the unnerving background sound of Geiger-counters crackling away at frenetic cadences – and this was miles away from Grounds Zero. Very few emergency personnel were seen. Shock waves and flying debris had destroyed trees and buildings for miles around the detonation sites. Motor vehicles were strewn about like burned and broken toys. The intense heat had started scores of fires all around as well. Gigantic walls of smoke and ash loomed over the landscapes making it look very much as if the Hammer of God had slammed down upon America.

The government kept re-broadcasting warnings that more large American cities were in jeopardy of being bombed. North, south, east and west – the main highway arteries out of town were packed and would remain packed for the first two days after The Attack. The Guard was supposed to enforce the dusk curfew during that time but was just too busy coordinating all the traffic heading out of town. People fled to their cabins, lake homes, hometowns, in-laws' – anywhere but in the city. All over the country, people left large cities in droves. The highways were packed, reminding me of the mass evacuations of southern cities during Katrina and other intensive hurricanes in recent years. For all we knew, the commentators were right and another wave of nuclear blasts was imminent.

I decided not to leave town right there on that first night. I'd always been a loner and, as I said, I didn't have much in the way of family anyway. Combine that with a chronically depressed personality and you've got someone who didn't really care much about little things like 'the end of the world as we know it.' Not as much as a man with a family, at least. And besides, if Minneapolis were going to go up in a cloud, I decided I'd rather die a quick death in the city than get my ass burned running away, then suffering radiation sickness. I tried to think ahead; what was happening? What was likely to happen in the near future?

"Water is still on, right?" I asked.

"Yup," said John.

"I'm gonna take a shower," I said as I got up. "Might be the last one for quite awhile."

"Good thinking, dude," said Brian.

"I'm going home, guys. See you in a bit."

"Bye, Dallas," they said simultaneously.

I had a feeling that things were going to get much worse before they got better. For all we knew, the water would be shut off at any time. I would improve my life by one tiny action at a time, I thought, one moment at a time. Maybe I could squeeze in one last shower before continuing on with my meaningless role in the apocalyptic adventure.

As I walked to my apartment, my back and neck tingled with fear. I spent about an hour under the shower nozzle, trying to let the hot water rinse away the events of the day. I was also ingraining the sensation of taking a shower. For some reason, I semi-seriously thought some lowly slug at the main waterworks would turn some huge crank labeled, "The Main Spigot" and shut off all of the city's water at any time.

Car horns blared all night long and well into the next day. The feeling was overwhelming and I didn't sleep a wink for those first forty hours. There were eleven units in our building, plus a laundry room. Eight of the units were empty of occupancy within 48 hours of The Attack. The apartment residents now consisted of Lee the manager in apartment one, John and Brian on the second floor in apartment #5, a quirky little guy named Ellis in apartment eight, and me on the top floor in apartment ten, back up top on the southwest corner of the building. Everyone else was gone. Two-thirds of our building had fled and I would guess that was an accurate microcosm of the city population itself.

Living from one day to the next was the goal of life now. There were survival tips aired almost immediately on television and the radio. There was a logical order of events that should have been followed when it came to food consumption; meats and dairy products should be consumed first. That didn't matter too much to me because all meat was long gone out of the stores before I could lay my hands on it. After meats, other refrigerated foods should be eaten next, then food from the freezer as it thawed, and then packaged or canned foods.

The good news was that we would have almost the whole city for ourselves. The bad news was, it was in many cases the good people who left the cities and it was the scum at the bottom of the barrel who stuck around for the new world party.

I quit my job right after The Attack. I'm not sure if I actually quit my job now that I think of it. I called in for three days in a row and nobody answered. I had no intention of going back to work, I was mainly interested in getting my last paycheck but the night-ring just kept picking up. I drove uptown but the building was all locked up with heavy chains wrapped around the push/pull bars of the front door. Finally I just left a message on the company answering machine. I never got a response. I never saw any of my former co-workers again and, as far as I know, they all just left town. Even if I had wanted to keep working, I think that recent events had put an end to my sandpaper sales career. To this day, those guys owe me a paycheck

THREE

Al-Jazeera Television showed throngs of joyous crowds in the streets of the Arab world. The images seemed to go on for days. The people were dancing and laughing and jumping up and down. *"The Great Satan is dead!"* they chanted in native tongues. It was alarming that so many people could find so much joy in such a globally shocking event. It was saddening and disturbing. I felt hopeless and I'm quite sure I wasn't alone. The undisputed heavyweight champ was put down on the canvas by the flyweight challenger, and put down *hard*.

The Justice Department's immediate decision to track down and detain or deport Middle Eastern aliens attracted quiet protests. *Very quiet.* If one were too loud or too public, it was within the jurisdiction of the police or central government to lock that person up for "activity detrimental to society." The government had a list of more than 400,000 detainable and deportable immigrants.

Executive Order 11310 granted authority to the Department of Justice "to enforce the plans set out in all other Executive Orders, to institute industrial support, to establish judicial and legislative liaison, to control all aliens, to operate penal and correctional institutions, and to advise and assist the President."

Within 48 hours of The Attack and with the aid of local police departments, the FBI and the INS started rounding up immigrants that so much as looked like Middle Easterners, raiding homes and mosques as they went. According to the Justice Department figures posted on the internet, over 8,200 people had been arrested without charge within a week. Iranians, Iraqis, Somalis, Ethiopians, North Africans, Arabs, American Muslims, and even some Latinos were caught in the dragnet. The number of detainees grew steadily. The stated aim was to prevent the use or detonation of any more WMD.

Mosques all over the country were reduced to ashes and rubble by an enraged citizenry. Businesses with Arab or Muslim owners were, at the very least, vandalized and destroyed in most cases all across the United States. Arabs were beaten and killed. At the same time, the FBI declined to investigate crimes against them; "We're very busy protecting Americans," the director said. The anti-terrorist legislation passed several years earlier had reduced legal protections for immigrants pretty much to zero. Activists who protested too vigorously about the situation were arrested.

The terrorists trained to operate in America spoke very good American English and were instructed to be friendly, pay bills on time, tip well, tell jokes, to wear conservative attire. So *nice* were they that the average American would never suspect a Middle Easterner of being a terrorist as long as he seemed like a pleasant fellow – it would have been politically incorrect. American social behavior was used as a weapon against America.

But now? The government didn't care how affable your personality was or how timely you paid your bills. If you were from that region of the world, life was about to get real tough for you. Fourth-generation

U.S. citizen Middle Easterners were rounded up along with the suspicious newcomers, it simply didn't matter. Political correctness died a quick and merciless death on April 1 as well.

Soon enough the government had a lengthy and ever-growing list of deportable aliens in custody and was forced into the task of deciding which ones were to go first. The federal government hadn't been serious about deportation for years. The majority of delinquents were Hispanic, but all attention was on the Middle Easterners. By focusing resources first on them, the government was merely addressing problems in a logical priority. Like an emergency-room doctor confronting a room full of trauma patients, it had to start somewhere.

And, after all, it wasn't Mexicans who detonated the nukes in America.

<u>FOUR</u>

TWIN CITIES WERE READYING FOR LARGE-SCALE ATTACK BEFORE APRIL 1
By Kirsten Johnson *StarTribune Online Staff Writer*

In preparation for attacks using Weapons of Mass Destruction (WMD), or the "American Hiroshima" as terrorists called it, local emergency management officials created an agency in the Twin Cities called Metropolitan Medical Response System (MMRS) in 2007. As the emergency system evolved, it also transformed from dealing just with natural disasters such as tornadoes to handling manmade disaster to attacks using weapons of mass destruction.

"We've made a helluva lot of progress," said St. Paul Fire Chief Tom Folter at a recent press conference. "We began pushing for such plans after attending a national conference on terrorism in 2005. We were about ready as could be for just about any disaster. Now it's our time to shine."

"We started worrying about really bad things before really bad things happened," said Al Gergen, MMRS co-chairman in the same conference. "The MMRS agencies received almost $4 million over the last few years from federal homeland security appropriations to prepare for a day just like this.

The MMRS, which covered Ramsey and Hennepin counties, was established to coordinate emergency planning among dozens of federal, state and local agencies. Their planning included a tabletop exercise in early 2005 in which agency heads met on short notice and quickly formulated a plan to deal with hundreds of dead or injured victims. The exercise was hailed as a success.

Through a variety of federal sources, local agencies received millions of dollars to develop their plans, buy medicine and upgrade equipment. Not only did the MMRS outfit police and fire personnel with protective suits, but it stockpiled medicine, purchased decontamination equipment and upgraded hospital facilities to deal with mass casualties. Critics assailed the efforts as a waste of resources for something that "probably would never happen."

"Critics," said Gergen, "as they tend to be, were wrong."

One problem area that remained was interagency communications. With each agency using its own communications system, it had been difficult to coordinate actions, deploy personnel and disperse information. A new multimillion-dollar communications system was still at least a year away at the time of the terrorist nuclear attack.

"Overall we were really in pretty good shape, though," Chief Folter said. "The Twin Cities weren't hit on April 1, but we would be remiss not to think of ourselves as a potential target."

We found out a lot of things in those first weeks between the TV, limited newspaper runs and the internet; we found out that Nuclear Emergency Search Teams went into action in the previous 48 hours before that horrible spring morning when credible threats of full-fledged nuclear weapons on U.S. soil were classified as "more than highly probable." We would later read reports off the net that the feds actually interdicted nuclear bombs being smuggled into the cities of Colorado Springs and San Francisco.

Elements of the NEST teams had found and disabled the bombs, but the stories were foggy; the bomb in Colorado was apparently being driven into the city by a semi truck. That was a plausible idea – big cities were ringed with nuclear-detection devices. The terrorists' best bet would be to drive a nuclear bomb in fast, furious and as close as possible to the middle of the target city and then detonate the device once the feds shot out the tires or whatever. Washington D.C. was the exception, having been destroyed by a low-level civilian aircraft. The government knew something was going to happen and had dispatched NEST teams and military Special Ops guys to prevent it, but no one foresaw the scope of damnation that was about to be rained down upon America.

There was news footage released by the government showing victims of the blasts. Triage and treatment centers had been set up around the affected cities, out of range of the worst of the fallout. Hundreds, thousands of school gymnasiums and community centers had become sick wards for the victims of the nuclear blasts – the degrees of injury were wide and varied.

If a person were far enough away it would just look like he fell asleep while sunning and got badly burned. Many people who were a bit closer to a blast were blinded or suffered permanent retinal damage in addition to burns. Thousands and thousands of people were killed and injured by flying debris and collapsing buildings. Burns of all severities were the most common injury. There were those who were closer yet that suffered horrific burns on their bodies, hundreds of thousands of them. Then there were the victims who were still alive but were charred into near blackness. They usually suffered from acute radiation sickness as well and, mercifully, didn't live very long.

Finally, there were the hundreds of thousands, maybe even several million, who evaporated or were just never to be found again. On top of that, add people who survived the initial blast okay but were right in the path of the fallout. Thousands would suffer the effects of radiation, from mild to lethal.

And the cities? The cities that were attacked now lay in charred, largely unrecognizable ruin. They burned and smoldered for weeks like peat moss fires. Just about the only living things inside of thirty-mile rings around Grounds Zero were feds in hazard suits.

I did remember some things from a physics course that I took at the University of Minnesota before switching majors. Detonating a nuclear bomb is no small feat. Simply possessing the fissile materials and a soul full of hatred are not enough. Nuclear weapons are simple and Byzantine at the same time. However, the physics are known to even a sharp high school science student. The key to a nuclear detonation is critical mass. That's why nuclear power plants can't explode; there simply is no mechanism anywhere in the process providing the necessary super-compression of radioactive material. Meltdown, yes – explode, no. Two pieces of sub-critical mass together will only create heat and deadly radiation. But they won't create a nuclear explosion.

After thinking about it, I was surprised that the terrorists actually pulled off eight simultaneous nuclear events. Counting the two nukes that were interdicted, the terrorists had tried to gore us with ten horns all at once. And some people were worried about the possibility of just *one* nuke going off.

The bad thing (one of many bad things) about the nuclear detonations is that, except for the Capital, they were all ground explosions. That meant that dirt, dust and pulverized debris were shot up into the atmosphere as radioactive fallout, which would then descend downwind as a secondary effect of the blasts. A large portion of the deadliest fallout came down within thirty miles or so of the respective blast with fatal levels of radiation. For instance, the prevailing winds over New York City on April 1 deposited the fallout perfectly up along Long Island. The terrorists couldn't have planned that; it was a quirk, a dirty trick from Allah himself. Depending on wind speed and particle sizes, much more radioactivity went on to waft around the country and the world, albeit in smaller doses.

FEMA, the federal agency charged with disaster preparedness, was engaged in a crash effort to prepare for multiple mass destruction attacks on American cities, including the creation of sprawling shantytowns and tent-cities to handle millions of displaced persons. The agency was readying for nuclear, biological and chemical attacks against U.S. cities, including the possibility of multiple attacks with weapons of mass destruction for a couple years before The Attack. This was unknown to the general public at the time.

FEMA had already discreetly notified vendors, contractors and consultants to prepare to handle the logistics of aiding millions of displaced Americans who would flee from urban areas that were attacked and, as the case turned out to be, Americans who fled cities that weren't attacked. Ominously enough, FEMA had urgently ordered major cities to be ready six months before The Attack, as though the powers-that-be knew something really bad was going to happen.

The damage was done: Our greatest cities were gone and millions of Americans had died within a matter of minutes, our doom delivered within a matter of ticks of the clock. At least the same number would suffer the effects of radiation sickness. It was a horrible way to go.

Over the first few weeks, news folks (ones you never heard of, most of the famous news commentators and anchors were dead) and their expert guests had correctly surmised that the The Attack was a well-coordinated and executed operation. After the United States attacked al Qaeda in Afghanistan, many of the higher-educated members dispersed like cockroaches when the light gets flipped on. Some were killed, some were captured, some went on to fight in Iraq, but many disappeared. Also, many had already been trained by al Qaeda and were living in the West, often in America, as sleeper agents, operatives who lived innocuous lives as peaceful citizens until called into action. But how did the group acquire nukes? Pieces of the puzzle were readily found on the internet.

Since the collapse of the Soviet Union in 1991, the uncertain status of nuclear weapons, fissile materials and nuclear scientists in Russia and other former Soviet republics were widely regarded as the most dangerous factors likely to give birth to nuclear terrorism. Despite a concerted effort and assistance from the United States, many of Russia's nuclear facilities were poorly secured, and there was no comprehensive, verifiable system of nuclear materials accountancy. No one even knows for certain how much nuclear weapons material the Soviet Union produced. There were confirmed incidents of Russian-origin fissile materials turning up for sale on the black market.

Former Secretary of Russia's Security Council, General Alexander Lebed, had voiced his concerns about security: After conducting an exhaustive inventory of Russian nuclear weapons in the late 1990's, he found that 84 suitcase nuclear bombs had vanished from the Russian arsenal. Reportedly, at least a few had been obtained by al Qaeda. The danger to the West in general and America specifically was not a hypothetical nightmare; it turned out to be quite real.

But the instruments of destruction didn't only come from outside the country. Massive quantities of fissile material existed around the world, according to **www.itfinallyhappened.net**. Experts warned that sophisticated terrorists could acquire the precious deadly ingredients. Less than 18 pounds of plutonium or 55 pounds of highly enriched uranium would be sufficient to make a nuclear bomb and these materials circulated in civilian nuclear commerce by the ton before The Attack.

Aside from intact bombs purchased off then black market, many of the experts wondered where terrorists could have gotten the necessary materials to construct the weapons. The list of nuclear-related incidents was mind-boggling;

· The Millstone Nuclear Plant couldn't account for two highly radioactive fuel rods – U.S. Nuclear regulatory Commission Press Release.
· Cesium-137 was found in the trunk of a crushed car at a scrapyard in Pittsburgh. The car was last registered to an alien from Saudi Arabia.
· The FBI was called upon to investigate the circumstances surrounding the discovery of a large stash of radioactive materials in the Bronx, New York. Investigators found Cesium, Radium, Strontium-90 and Carbon-14.
· Five dark-featured males were captured on security video stealing radioactive tritium from Arizona State University.
· A Russian-produced fuel assembly with 126 fuel rods containing two-percent enriched uranium went unaccounted for by a US crew in Lynchburg, VA.
· Two Turks were captured by German GSG-9 with 63 pounds of weapons grade uranium intending to sell to the highest bidder.
· An Iraqi and a Saudi were admitted to a Parisian hospital with advanced radiation poisoning and died shortly thereafter.
· Pakistan's top nuclear scientist had sold sensitive equipment and nuclear technology to Iran, Libya and North Korea fueling fears the information could have also fallen into the hands of terrorists.

And those incidents were just the recent incidents, the proverbial tip of the iceberg. Some events were minor and some were serious. For instance, the American public wasn't told that in the years leading to The Attack, 17 men of Middle Eastern descent were admitted to American hospitals severely weak and with bleeding gums. All of them subsequently died of radiation poisoning. The source of the poisoning was never identified.

The trading, shuffling, stealing and moving of nuclear materials bubbled furiously right among Western societies, including the United States, in the years leading up to The Attack. Al Qaeda never hid its interest in acquiring nuclear weapons. U.S. intelligence agencies had long believed that al Qaeda attempted to acquire a nuclear device on the black market, but there had been scant evidence that they had been successful. But even the International Atomic Energy Agency, a staunch promoter of nuclear power, had been urging to improve protection of civilian and military nuclear materials.

It was how the terrorists operated: conduct a major operation and then lay low for a year or two, conduct another attack and then lay low for another couple years. Think big and coordinate grandly, thrust and parry. Al Qaeda sleeper cells had been uncovered in most major American cities, including Minneapolis, and many members had been arrested before The Attack. But they had backup cells, and probably backups to the backups. The terrorists had counted on Americans' short political memories and Americans didn't let them down. American responses to terrorism were laughably stupid and predictable in the eyes of terrorists.

After an incident, America's guard would be 100 percent up, barring and locking the doors long after the horses were well out of the barn. Less than a year later, the public interest in counter-terrorism would ebb and the major political parties were destroying each other over domestic tax-cut issues or the price of medications for the elderly. Our defensive posture would ease. So distracting were the American partisan politics that the internal political machinery of the country was not unlike a man being concerned over an untied shoelace while mindlessly strolling through a minefield.

Within ten days after The Attack, five former U.S. nuclear weapons designers had concluded that, in addition to several suitcase bombs, al Qaeda had developed the ability to design and build workable nuclear bombs from stolen plutonium or highly enriched uranium, with yields in the kiloton range. Critical elements of the bombs were brought here through Mexico, some through our own ports in spite of counter-measures. Maybe one or two of them were constructed here. Despite pre-holocaust claims to the contrary from plutonium-fuel advocates in the nuclear power industry, effective and devastating weapons could be made using reactor-grade plutonium, hundreds of tons of which were processed, stored and circulated around the world in civilian nuclear commerce. Once they had the material, the terrorists had all they needed: desire, means and ability. As the darker-thinking xenophobes always warned about nuclear terrorism, "It's not a matter of 'if,' only a matter of 'when'." That day had arrived.

"This was something I warned about years ago," said Allen Cunningham, Ph.D. He was speaking on a network discussion program that we caught. I remembered seeing him before on cable. He used to be considered kind of a right-wing nut. He was often seen on TV and in public debate forums debating members of the Union of Concerned Scientists, which wasn't a wholly truthful organization: being a scientist or holding a Ph.D. or even a Masters was not a requirement to be a member of the UCS, as Dr. Cunningham loved pointing out. I wish I had seen the whole show. As it was, we clicked in just for the end of the discussion:

"Mathematically speaking, this day was inevitable; like an inch-worm placed in the middle of a large table and slowly but surely making his way to the edge. Sooner or later, he'll get there."

"Yes," said Naomi Slattery, the anti-war activist he was debating. "Mr. Cunningham is doing nothing more than Sunday morning quarterbacking," she rebutted, not familiar with her sports metaphors.

"That would be *Monday* morning quarterbacking," corrected Cunningham. "And I am on record as far back as late 1999 predicting that the United States would be the target of a nuclear terrorist attack."

"Mr. Cunningham seems almost happy that his wild predictions have come true," Slattery said, dismissing Dr. Cunningham and speaking to the commentator.

"Happy? I'm nowhere near happy, Ms. Slattery. I can't count the number of friends, family and associates that I lost in The Attack."

"So what now? Fascists and bigots like you want to launch 'pre-emptive nuclear strikes' and 'surgical bombings' as a reason to exterminate brown-skinned people that you don't like?"

"I'd appreciate you not putting words into my mouth. You and your ilk simply don't see properly."

"See what, you tired old bigot?" sneered Ms. Slattery.

"That the world is no longer comprised of countries struggling against each other: this planet is now in a life-or-death struggle for the very survival of the human race. I'm a mathematician by trade and profession. I believe that everything can be logically explained and, to great extent, predicted," said Cunningham.

"And what's your prediction now, Dr. Cunningham?" asked the moderator.

"Everything will get worse – much worse – before it gets better. We're already victims of a war of apocalyptic proportions. Our country no longer has the ability to deal with disease on a population level, the western United States are in flames, Europe is flooding, the Middle East is awash in war, Pakistan and India, and North and Japan are all on the verge of nuclear conflict, food is becoming scarcer and scarcer, and anarchy reigns supreme in many cities. Sound like anything you've heard of in the Bible? "

"Give me a break! Next he'll say Jesus will cause the Rapture," Slattery barked at the moderator.

"I don't have to say it. You just did," answered Cunningham.

"You're wrong."

"Americans are a benevolent but sometimes stupid lot," Cunningham continued. "We have short memories. After we get through a particularly disastrous event, we wipe our brow and go,

'*Whew! Glad THAT'S over!*' And then our politicians start arguing over piffle such as environmentalism or social spending as evil forces plan our doom."

"Can you cite an example?" said the moderator.

"Certainly. Terrorists tried to topple the World Trade Center in New York in 1993. The building withstood the bomb, was repaired, and everybody merrily went back to work. But the terrorists never stopped thinking about taking down those buildings. It took eight years but they never stopped. When they succeeded, we were all shocked. We shouldn't have been. It was thoroughly predictable."

"What a bunch of *bullshit!*" interjected Slattery. "The planet was in doom when the ozone hole was growing and our fresh water tables were polluted and when Africa was dying of AIDS, all while fat Americans sat back and did nothing."

"Once again," Cunningham said to the moderator, "Ms. Slattery demonstrates an incredible inability to reason and prioritize world events: when she worries about the ozone, it's like a patient expressing concern over a plantar wart as the doctor tells them that they have an advanced case of terminal cancer."

"This country," Slattery interjected, "has consumed a wildly disproportionate share of the world's resources for too long. This country has destroyed the ozone and poisoned the air and the water of the whole planet. We've poisoned and mistreated our Mother Earth, mainly here in the United States. Maybe the chickens have just finally come home to roost."

"Poppycock," said Cunningham. "Your statements, Ms. Slattery, are nothing more than left-wing rantings whose intent is to weaken America. In that regard, yours is a mission that you need no longer pursue. As far as America's role in the world? We fed the world. When natural disaster struck, billions of U.S. dollars flooded to where ever they were needed. Without America, the Stalins and the Hitlers and the Husseins of the world would be running this planet. You should drop to your knees and thank God that you live in a country where your right to voice such profoundly uninformed and irrational opinions is protected."

"Whatever," Slattery said with a roll of her eyes.

"Naomi Slattery and Dr. Allen Cunningham, thank you very much," said the moderator as the screen faded to black. Cunningham didn't realize that he still had a hot microphone and broadcast his personal feelings about Ms. Slattery to the national viewers.

"You, young lady, are one rude little twat," he said in a stately voice.

53

(**Note:** Naomi Slattery was subsequently arrested by the government and charged under statutes of sedition with "patterns of speech and actions detrimental to the United States of America." Some people were a little slow on the uptake; *there really were no more civil rights*.)

Personnel were recalled from most African and Middle Eastern embassies as were American civilians abroad. Some speculated that America was preparing to launch a nuclear strike of her own. Many of the United States military personnel stationed overseas were recalled. If an ally were to be attacked, America would be of little help. The fragile new democracies of Iraq and Afghanistan quickly descended back into feudal warfare as skeleton crews of U.S. forces fell back to airbases within those countries and began a slow drawdown.

America still had most of its military forces, but all of the nation's resources had to be concentrated on rebuilding the country and reigning in an urban populace that was increasingly showing the hallmarks of anarchy. Radical Muslims wanted the U.S. military out of their lands and they accomplished their desires. Certainly a part of the military would be held in reserve to prosecute a renewed war on terrorism. The economy, the cities, the infrastructure, society itself would require years, if not decades, of healing and rebuilding.

Interstate travel had all but ceased after the April Attack and the initial exodus. It was suspected that most of the bombs were sped into target cities via semi right before H-Hour. Every major interstate highway was riddled with atomic checkpoints and military guards after The Attack. As far as the central government knew, any number of bombs didn't make the coordinated detonations but may have still been in existence, their operators diligently working at follow-ups attacks.

Civilian flight traffic dropped to almost nothing after The Attack. After all, the biggest destinations in the country were gone and people had other things on their minds besides vacationing and business trips.

Executive Order 11003 allowed the government to take over all airports and aircraft, including commercial aircraft. Because flight traffic was so restricted, civilians needed a pressing reason to travel; reuniting with family could get you one-way permission. Urgent need of one's skills for a particular job or function in a necessary industry was another. Low-level members of the government often traveled on commercial airliners. Other than that, it was rare to see civilian aircraft flying.

Instead, the skies were scribbled with the giant, arcing contrails of Air Force fighters and electronic surveillance aircraft. NEST teams continued to scour the remaining major cities as best as they could for additional nuclear devices, but now I guess the government was mainly most fearful of a high altitude nuclear blast. There would be no better way to wipe out the communications and communications of North America than to explode a thermonuclear device at a high altitude over the continent.

A high atomic air blast would create a devastating electromagnetic pulse that would scramble and fry most computer chips and transformers. The EMP wave would knock out most electric and electronic devices tied into the power grids. It would also permanently disable any new devices that contain integrated circuits and anything that had an antenna over 30 inches long. That means that your car radio, portable radio, and television would be rendered inoperable, even if the power ever did come back on. Phones, computers, basic electrical services, medical facilities – virtually everything would be affected. Cars with computerized ignitions would be damaged by EMP. Older cars that were made before 1965 would probably remain functional. Needless to say, not too many people owned and operated cars made before 1965.

America stood the very real possibility of being reduced to a society of bicycles, wagons, horses and carts. But then, that is the kind of world that was here in the 1800's. The people then didn't have cars, supermarkets, movies, TV, radio, telephones, modern medicine, airplanes or computers and they survived, right? Humans generally are survivors and life does go on. Another certainty to add to death and taxes. Or maybe not.

Long distance communication was spotty and life itself was already arduous enough. An EMP blast would just about be the death thrust into America's gut. Terrorists couldn't get a missile up into the stratosphere, but they certainly could get an airliner or other high-altitude aircraft up in the sky; the higher the blast, the more widespread the devastation. Air Force pilots were authorized to shoot down commercial airlcraft, if necessary.

As a precaution, civilian aircraft were limited to 6,000 feet cruising altitude for the first few months. At that height, airliners inefficiently sucked JP-5 jet fuel like thirsty dogs lapping water. If a plane broke the ceiling and didn't have a friendly IFF transponder response, it got one radio warning, one shot-across-the-nose warning and then the Air Force pumped a couple air-to-air sparrow missiles into her. That happened only a handful of times with smaller multi-engine transport aircraft, and at least two of them were confirmed mistakes.

Sonic booms – something my foster-dad had told me was a common occurrence in the 50's and early 60's – were now heard on a fairly regular basis, ostensibly as military jets went supersonic while responding to potential threats. Aircraft coming in from overseas were met by Navy or Air Force fighters hundreds of miles out over the sea and escorted all the way to touchdown.

The terrorists had little need to target nuclear power plants and probably would do more damage by not doing so. A bomb on the plant would just blow it to pieces and the material in the plant would only add very little to the radioactive fallout. On the other hand, as a result of the EMP, if a plant were to be left on its own when it loses its computer control, it would more than likely go into a meltdown and release substantial radioactive contamination into the atmosphere.

Welcome to the Third Millennium.

FIVE

The Western markets had quit trading almost completely within two days of The Attack and most financial stocks simply devalued to zero. There was a run on banks as many people, as I did the day of The Attack, closed all of their savings and checking accounts for the security of having cash on hand. The value of 401k's, IRA's and other financial products all but vanished. People stopped paying their bills *en masse*. The economy had recovered from the technology bubble-burst, several high-profile corporate collapses, OPEC production decreases and a deflation/inflation scare. Many people who thought they had secure futures were, financially speaking, like so many lost little sheep. Despite the presidential freezes, price gouging was rampant. The economy started collapsing like the twin towers in New York back on that horrible day. The financial effects were immediate and worldwide.

Days went by and life puttered on for me. I stopped in at some hole-in-the-wall bar, the type of joint that serves beer and greasy burgers whipped up right there behind the bar while you watch. They were out of food but had plenty of beer so I ordered one. There were about ten folks in there, the rough sort judging by their looks. I had just struck up a conversation with the bartender when a scruffy black man in a nasty trench coat walked in shouting and brandishing a shotgun.

"GET DOWN MOTHAFUCKAS!"

People started ducking and hitting the floor. I remained frozen in my chair. If I hit the floor, I'd be right at his feet.

"YOU!" he said to the bartender. "GIMME ALL YO MOTHERFUCKIN CASH!"

"Easy fella," said the bartender. He was an older guy who didn't move very fast.

"MOVE FASTER, MOTHAFUCKA!" yelled the robber as he nervously glanced out the window. The bartender was still struggling with the register and the man became even more agitated. "GODDAMMIT!"

BOOM!

The bartender, whose name I had not even yet gleaned, took the shotgun blast in his left arm and left ribcage. His body flew back about ten feet as if it were a rag-doll – clearly a lethal injury. The shooter turned to me; everything seemed surreal, as though I were watching a movie of myself about to be killed. I just sat there, surprisingly devoid of any emotion whatsoever.

Unknown to the robber, several patrons of the bar were armed. A volley of shots rang out. Whether it was six shots or 20 shots, I don't know. All I know is that I was looking down the business-end of a shotgun one second, and was watching the perp get cut down by gunfire the next.

Some of the customers ran to the aid of the bartender. His name was Red. Three others ran over to the robber and made sure he was dead. He was. One of the men took his shotgun while the other two searched the dead man's body.

Just then two Minneapolis cops burst into the bar with guns drawn. *"FREEZE! WEAPONS DOWN"* said the sergeant. Everybody's put their guns on the floor and hands went into the air. The officer quickly surveyed the scene and then relaxed a little bit.

"What happened in here?" he asked with authority.

"This idiot came in here," said one of the patrons near the dead robber, "tried to rob the place and then blew away Red over there behind the counter."

"How is he?" The cop said as he stepped around to look behind the bar and saw Red's body.

"DOA," said a patron tending to Red.

The officers seemed content that the gunplay was over and they both holstered their weapons. The sergeant looked at the bloody and bullet-riddled corpse of the robber.

"What the hell happened to *him?*" he asked.

The patrons looked wide-eyed at each other for a few seconds before one spoke;

"He slipped on a bar of soap."

I've never been back to that bar.

Aside from the criminals, it seemed that a lot of people in the inner city tended to be the loners or the estranged-from-the-family type. There were, of course, exceptions – some citizens said, "Screw it" and stayed in defiance; some people were stuck in place with nowhere to go because of travel restrictions or because their own hometown had gone up in a mushroom cloud; then there were folks who were stuck in town because of duty, either presidentially-ordered or self-imposed. Though I worried to some extent about the possibility of nuke going off in my hometown, I felt no compelling pull to flee the city and go elsewhere. For me it then became a question of living day-to-day.

The rations of my bachelor apartment the day of The Attack were the usual fare; a box of Pop Tarts, a crusty-topped bottle of catsup, a couple boxes of macaroni and cheese, half a dozen cans of soup, a frozen pizza, some "fire sauce" packets from Taco Bell on the refrigerator door shelf, a 12-pack of Diet Coke and a half gallon of milk. Most of the supermarkets had been cleaned out of everything that could be considered edible, including pet food. I needed to do something to make a living. I needed to survive.

Sometimes shipments came into stores but they didn't last long and prices were extremely high. By a shear stroke of luck, I was one of the first people in line at the back of a semi as it rolled up to a supermarket. They didn't even bother to unload into the store. The truck pulled around to the alley behind the building. I was in a group of about 70 people who followed it like a bunch of ducklings after the mama duck. It reminded me of images I'd seen on the news, images of Third World citizens scampering after U.N. food trucks hoping for anything they could get. I had a sudden sense of knowing. The driver and helper – both armed – got out, locked their doors and moved towards the rear of the vehicle. The driver unholstered his weapon, while the helper simply kept his hand on his Colt.

"Awright, get the fuck back," the driver growled with his pistol raised in the air like some little banana republic dictator. "GET THE FUCK BACK I SAID!" he repeated with a push on the front of the crowd. We complied and took baby steps backward as subtle mumbling hummed from the crowd.

With that he unlocked the trailer and swung the doors open. He hopped inside as the helper stayed on ground level as some sort of punk-ass guard. There would be no unloading of goods into the supermarket – the driver simply moved some boxes toward the rear and began selling. He opened the first cardboard box, reached in and held up some microwave dinners.

"I got microwave dinners here, still frozen. Microwave dinners straight from the warehouse freezer."

"How much for ten?" asked the man next to me.

"Fifty bucks," answered the driver.

"Fifty bucks?" replied the awed customer.

"Take it or leave it, asshole. I GOT MICROWAVE MEALS HERE, WHO WANTS'EM?" the driver barked out like a crude carny hustler.

It was a macabre auction, survival of whoever had a lot of cash in their pocket and was near the front of the line. I wound up paying almost a hundred bucks for 15 microwave meals and ten large frozen pizzas. At that rate, my money would be exhausted within weeks.

I was walking downtown the very next day and saw a government poster that simply read JOBS! in big, red letters. It listed days, times and location to apply for work and I wrote down all the info.

I told John and Brian about it when I got back to the apartment that evening and they were excited about joining me on a job quest downtown. Their Doritos had run out and they were reaching 'situation critical' themselves. The mere possibility of getting a paying job seemed like a miracle to all of us.

We went down to the government center early the next day. We were herded into a room with a bunch of other people hunched over applications. It wasn't so much that the government job givers were interested in education level or references, the applications were simply an expedient way of finding out what people were experienced in.

There was a list of jobs and they all seemed like monkey work; maintenance, morgue assistant, road debris clearing, clerical and data entry – stuff like that. Something caught my eye: Structural Preservation Technician. The job synopsis called for guys experienced in carpentry. John and Brian would be shoo-ins for the job, what with their experience at construction. I thought there was a chance that I could use my nominal carpentry skills to get hired. After all, I did have experience at being a handyman sort of guy.

Back a half-dozen years before the nukes, I had applied to spend a summer working at McMurdo Station in Antarctica (by summer, I mean that it was winter in the Northern Hemisphere). Such are the freedoms of young single men with no families. I was accepted and was flown to the bottom of the world in a C-141 Starlifter cargo jet. Being summer there, the sun was out 24/7. Nonetheless, it was cold, really cold all of the time. Once the temperature hit 35 degrees Fahrenheit and everybody was running around in T-shirts and throwing a football around. It was a veritable heat wave.

We got a little history class during the in-processing. James Clark Ross, who also discovered the Ross Sea and the Ross Ice Shelf, discovered Ross Island in 1841. Ross named McMurdo Sound after Lieutenant Archibald McMurdo, a subordinate officer on the ship *Terror*. McMurdo Station is located on the southern end of Ross Island, an island of volcanic origin approximately 45 miles wide and 45 miles long. Large Emperor and Adelie penguin rookeries and Skua rookeries are the only living things native to the small land mass.

I lived with three other guys in a Jamesway, which is a crappy wood-framed insulated tent structure shaped like a Gomer Pyle

Quonset hut with plywood floor. Sunlight and wind poked through at will like evil little demons and when the Herbies came, I thought the whole damn thing would blow all the way to Australia. (Herbies are unusually strong little windstorms native to the continent. Some of them reach 200 mph.)

There was no night; the sun just went around and around off-kilter up in the sky 24 hours a day, as if some delirious giant were twirling it overhead on a string. Late in my stay, the sun started setting for about an hour a day behind Mt. Discovery. Nonetheless, sleeping patterns remained shattered. I stayed awake for 37 hours once. I did two work shifts and got drunk in-between during one waking. I didn't do it on purpose, my body just didn't feel like going to bed. A lot of people, including myself, were in a semi-zombie state a lot of the time; never quite fully awake and never really able to sleep peacefully. Snow could actually blow through a slit into our Jamesway and pile on the foot of my bunk sometimes. Try sleeping in *that*.

I worked at the Heavy Vehicle Maintenance Facility, or "Heavy Shop." Essentially, I was in the group of workers considered the lowest form of life at the station: I was a GFA. That officially stood for General Field Assistant but we were more commonly referred to as Goofy Fucking Assholes. If there was a shit job to do, we did it; trash removal from the shops, stocking of flammable liquids, stocking the battery room (with its god-awful sulfuric stench), and general shit errands. I also was assigned the detail of picking up liquor rations for my shift. Drinking is a major pastime there at the bottom of the world.

I learned how to drive and operate some big machines down there. I became a downright master at operating a Caterpillar IT28 articulated front-end forklift, which was a huge amount of fun. I also operated a

Caterpillar D8H bulldozer, which was an enormous piece of machinery. Driving these behemoths wasn't actually part of my job description, it just happened as a result of daily life and necessity.

The people there at McMurdo Station tended to be a little on the odd side. At parties, for instance, an uncomfortable number of dudes liked to dress up in drag and dance around. I was supposedly in jest, but some of them really seemed to enjoy it. Also, all the vehicles had been given names there; One of the dump trucks was called *The Madness* and there was a giant jackhammer machine called *Ronald Ray Gun*. There was a utility forklift named *Nefilim*, after a mythical twelfth planet. Another was named *Yoshiwara*, which I think was the name of the drinking district from the Fritz Lang movie, "Metropolis."

Vehicle #169 was a Cat D8H bulldozer named *Beyond Beyond Thunderdome*. That was until the day that I accidentally drove it off the edge of a weak ice pier and into the goddam Antarctic Ocean. After that, the name of vehicle #169 was officially changed to *Das Boot*. And, yes, when we broke through the ice the water instantly froze me to the bone.

Das Boot and I had gone down in 43 feet of colder-than-cold seawater and it was only by shear luck that I popped to the surface. Otherwise I would have become a permanent ice-cube floating around the bottom of the polar sea for all eternity. I was pulled out of the water right away by a couple of U.S. Navy guys. (The bulldozer was later salvaged and it is still working to this day, as far as I know. They even found my cap in the cab of the vehicle.)

They rushed me to Building 85 – Recompression Chamber facility – which is located next to the dispensary and houses a chamber for the treatment of dive-accident patients, carbon dioxide poisoning, gas-gangrene, and others where hyperbaric oxygen therapy is indicated. There was no therapy or building dedicated to treating profound humiliation. The closest thing to that would be about 15 beers at The Acey-Duecy Club. That was the only place I needed to go. I was thereafter known in certain circles as "Der U-169 Kommander." And now I, Dallas Burnette, am a permanent part of Antarctic lore.

The population of McMurdo Station was around 1,000 people during the summer and about 250 during the winter. I applied for a winter-over contract and, predictably, was not taken on.

So that was my history of working in a construction field. Other than the time I spent in Antarctica, my workman skills were limited to simple household maintenance, sheet rock hanging, painting exterior and interior walls, helping acquaintances build decks off the backs of their houses and things like that. That was it. I would have classified my skills as "nominally competent amateur." I was a little nervous as I sat at a desk across from some government minion who was going over my application.

"University grad, eh?"

"Uh, yes." *Maybe I shouldn't have put that down ...*

"And you'd settle for manual labor?"

"Hey," I said with a shrug, "times have changed."

"You can say that again," he snorted without looking up. "What can ya do?"

"I have experience driving bulldozers," I said. Into the Antarctic Ocean, said I not.

"You licensed for big rigs and machinery?"

"No."

"Oh," he said with a little disappointment. "What else?" said the man.

"Well, I know how to swing a hammer and pound a nail."

"Oh, what the hell. That's good enough for me," he said, signing off on the application and slamming my manila file shut. "Take this to Mr. Hudson down at the end of the hall and on the right."

"So I'm hired?"

"Yes," he replied flatly. "Have a nice day. *Next!*"

That was it. I visited the aforementioned Mr. Hudson who handled my obligatory paperwork and told me to report to one of the county workshops the next Tuesday. I walked back out into the lobby and Brian and John were waiting. They had been taken on, too. We celebrated by going to one of the few McDonalds restaurants that were still open and operating and had combo-meals with milkshakes. I had the Number Three with a strawberry shake. I couldn't remember the last time that I'd had a McDonalds shake. I'm sure I must have been a teenager.

We dutifully reported to the assigned location the next Tuesday morning. Our new workplace was a maintenance facility within the long morning shadows of the downtown skyscrapers. It consisted of seven or eight acres filled with orange or dark blue municipal vehicles of all types with the city logo and the words, "City of Lakes" stenciled on the doors. Though we were officially hired by the county, we were attached to a city facility. There was a small two-story brick office building, circa 1930's, connected to a newer maintenance building, circa 1980's, along the east fence. On the north side of the ground was a metal maintenance shed that was big enough to house and service two large dump trucks with a small office on the side. There was a pile of sand here and a pile of black dirt there. Pipes lay in neat piles along one fence line. There were cinder blocks and piles of lumber, haphazardly covered with blue, plastic tarps. A military Humvee with a loaded M-60 machine gun mounted on the gunner's ring sat perfectly parked next to the main building with rolls of razor-wire stacked behind it. The military dudes called the wire "concertina," I found out a bit later.

A couple of dusty civilian extended-cab pickups were parked within the compound, several more on the street right outside, the trucks of the working man. There was a vehicle washing station next to the main building and the facility had its own fuel pumps, gasoline *and* diesel. The complex was ringed with a seven-foot high chain-link fence and topped with concertina.

This labor-and-trucks environment was a whole new world to me. Don't get me wrong, I was happy to have a job but this wasn't really my scene. John, Brian and I crossed the compound to what seemed to be the center of activity, the main maintenance building. Through its yawning garage doors we could see and hear the liveliness of things getting done and we discreetly entered. The radio was blaring out an old REM song as we muddled on through the maintenance bay;

> *It's the end of the world as we know it,*
> *It's the end of the world as we know it,*
> *It's the end of the world as we know it,*
> *And I feel fiiiiiiiiine*

How appropriate. The hard surfaces and size of the structure's interior created a huge natural reverb as the song cheerfully echoed and bounced off the walls. We asked around for the supervisor like nervous teenagers on the first day at a new high school. A gruff, oil-smeared man in his fifties with Popeye forearms was hunched over the engine compartment of a mid-sized maintenance vehicle.

I cleared my throat. "Excuse us," I said politely. The man looked up. "We're looking for the 'Field Crew Supervisor'."

"You the FNG's?" he growled.

"FNG's?" I responded, not knowing what he meant and already feeling stupid.

"*Fucking New Guys*?" he snarled.

"Uh, yeah. That would be us," I answered.

Goofy Fucking Assholes. Fucking New Guys. *Would it never end?*

"Back there," he said, jerking a thumb towards the rear of the bay and putting his head back down into his work. I'm sure that we were out of his consciousness within about three seconds.

We walked to the back of the bay and found him soon enough. His name was Dan Scheerer, Supervisor Dan, Field Crew Coordinator. He was talking into a hand-held radio with his boot up on the back of a pickup truck. Someone had stuck a VISUALIZE WHIRLED PEAS sticker on the bumper.

"Roger, two-four. Put up and secure the concertina and then get back to the Gulag, over."

"*Roger, out,*" came the fuzzy static reply.

Scheerer turned to us. "You the new guys?"

"Yes," we all said simultaneously. He had a commanding presence and I was impressed that he didn't ask us if we were the *fucking* new guys.

"Good. My name's Dan Scheerer," he said extending his hand. "Glad to meet you."

We each gave our names as we shook hands. Scheerer's grip was large and I could feel the calluses on his hands. He was serious and straightforward. Scheerer was a man I guessed to be in his mid-forties and stood about six-foot two, probably about 190 lean pounds. He had a bushy mustache and telephone cable arms – the sign of a guy who worked with his hands all of his life. He wore construction boots, dusty jeans, a green T-shirt and a well-used white hardhat. He also had on a standard worker's luminous orange and yellow safety vest with 'Scheerer' written across the back in thick black magic marker and a rad-counter attached on the upper front right. There was a Navy K-Bar knife and sheath on his right hip, a cell phone on his left hip, and a 9mm Barretta in a shoulder holster clearly visible under the safety vest. He had been an Army Ranger when he was a younger man, I would find out later. He was not the kind of guy I'd ever like to get into a fight with.

I felt a little out of place there in the workshop environment, even with John and Brian along with me. At least they showed up with their own tools and well-used tool belts slung over their shoulders – even if they didn't need them, they looked like they belonged. There I was in my oversized Iowa Hawkeyes sweatshirt, hiking boots and a pair of nice clean jeans that, along with the wearer, hadn't seen a hard day's labor anytime in the recent past. I felt like a damned frat boy. Though I considered myself smarter than my two younger counterparts, I was sure they also knew their way around a work site better than I did.

Scheerer passed us along to one of his subordinates who gave us a tour of the complex. They called the entire maintenance compound The

Gulag, I guess because of the prison-like concertina topping the fence all the way around. I thought we were going to start working that day, but we just got a short tour of the Gulag. All the crews were assigned and out working. After about an hour-and-a-half of showing us around, getting us issued basic equipment and lockers and introducing us to various personnel we happened to run into, the underling had us clean the maintenance bay for about an hour. He cut us loose after that and told us to report in the following morning.

The next morning found us in the briefing room, which was on the second floor of the oldest building. There was a big urn of fresh coffee and, God only knows where they got them, fresh donuts. There were about 30 guys there not including us. The workday began with a roll call and then Scheerer went into his spiel: He gave a briefing on damaged buildings, danger reports on the neighborhoods that the crews would be working in, police activity and shooting and such. Then came the dreaded part:

"Alright, we have some new crewmembers here today ... " (chorus of boos) "... okay, settle down. Three new guys, would you please stand up and tell us a little bit about yourselves?"

We were sitting three-abreast right in the front row. I felt like a complete nerd. Brian went first.

"Uh, hello. My name is Brian Nyboerg; my friends call me 'Cyborg.' I'm 24, I live in Minneapolis and I play the drums. Rock on," he said, sitting down with the index finger and pinky of his right hand extended in the standard rock salute.

John stood up. "Hi, I'm John Thoms, also from Minneapolis. I'm a carpenter— "

"Union or non-union?" an anonymous voice interrupted from somewhere in the middle of the room.

"Uh, freelance … non-union …"

There was a loud chorus of boos. Not even Armageddon itself will shake a union man's loyalty to the union. Incredible.

"Knock it off!" Scheerer growled from the side of the room with his thick, sinewy forearms crossed over his chest. "Go on, Thoms."

"Uh, thanks. Lessee. I'm 29. Uh … play the guitar. That's it." He sat down quickly.

Goofy young men, I thought. Mark Twain said it best: *"A man ain't worth spit 'til he's past thirty."*

Now it was my turn. I stood up. As a former salesman it had been my job to speak to people, so at least I could do this part better than John or Brian. Nonetheless, I thought it best to keep it short and sweet.

"G'mornin! My name is Dallas Burnette, I'm 35 and before April I used to work in the abrasives industry." Hmm. I pulled *that* one out of my ass on the spur of the moment and it sounded pretty darn good, I thought. And it had the added benefit of being true. "I also live in Minneapolis, I have no wife or kids and I look forward to working with all of you." I gave the room a confident nod.

"Excellent," Scheerer said. "By the way, Burnette, your fly is open."

The room burst out in laughter as I looked down and saw that, sure enough, the zipper on my jeans was wide open. Great. I zipped up and sat down.

Scheerer gave the crews a few last minute instructions before wrapping up the morning meeting. I liked the man already: He was tough, but well spoken,; concise and unambiguous. He wasn't prone to macho union silliness or immaturity. He was firm without being an asshole or resorting to yelling. It was obvious that he commanded the respect of everyone and, believe me, some of these guys would be tough hombres to impress. He went on to assign the three of us new guys to different crews. Then everybody milled out of the room and on out to their respectively assigned vehicles and crews.

The job itself involved driving around the county, mostly in the inner city neighborhoods and downtown proper itself, boarding up buildings and businesses that had been abandoned. It was an optimistic pickling of the infrastructure intended for the day when things would get back to normal. We laughed a bit over that one. Things would never be normal, but it seemed like it would be good and relatively easy government work in an economy that had fewer and fewer jobs to offer.

I was assigned to a standard work crew. I was crowded into the cab of a pickup with two other guys with a larger truck following. Being the new guy, I was stuck in the middle. The driver and crew leader was a rough looking, square-jawed guy in his late twenties named Boone. I don't know if that was his first name or his last, he was merely known as Boone. He looked like the hockey player sort.

My other cab mate was a laid back black guy named Aaron Stubbs. Stubbs always referred to himself as "large and in charge." At six feet even and 270 relatively solid pounds, he was, indeed, large. I guessed him to be about in his mid-forties. He had been a defensive lineman for Grambling State University back in the day.

"*Mothafuck* … ain't nothin but bullshit work," Stubbs complained as we convoyed to our first job site.

"You ain't makin shit any better by complaining about it," Boone said as he spit chaw juice into an empty Mountain Dew bottle.

"If I want any shit outta you, Boone, I'll squeeze yo head!" Stubbs said and laughed to himself.

"Kiss my ass, Stubbs."

Christ, I felt like I was in junior high again. Thankfully, Stubbs tried to curb their friendly argument.

"Yo, I needs to be kickin it in the crib wit my woman. Instead?" he said as he looked out the window and then shook his head.

"*Mothafuckin terrorists* ..." his voice trailed off.

"Whatever," Boone said. "What about you ... *Burnette, is it*? What are you doing working here?"

"Me? I needed a job," I chortled.

"*I hear dat* ..." Stubbs mumbled.

"What did you do before all this bomb stuff happened?" Boone asked. Spit.

"I had a desk job. Sold sandpaper over the phone."

"No shit, really?"

"Yeah. Wasn't too bad. I had a decent number of accounts, pretty easy sales after you work that kind of sales job, ya know, accounts and repeat business? I was pulling in low-forties there up at the end."

"Jus sittin at a desk?" Stubbs asked, his voice a full octave higher than normal.

"Yup."

"*Daaaammnn* ... now *that's* a job!"

We arrived at the first job site. Boone screeched the truck to a halt in front of the building and double-checked that it was the correct address against the work order. It was a small, one-story auxiliary social security building on the outer edge of downtown that had been abandoned in the interest of government contraction.

There were water crews that went around the city turning off the mains and collecting all the fresh water that they could from deserted structures. One huge radioactive rainfall could turn drinking water into a precious commodity, so the water crews harvested as much clean water as they could. Fresh water could be found in hot water heaters and toilet tanks. Their schedule was parallel to ours and they usually were in a given structure a day or two before we were.

But we arrived at the same time as the water guys on this particular day, so we sat around in the sun for about an hour-and-a-half. Can't say the guys on the water crew were working awfully hard or awfully fast. Finally, they finished their tasks. They poured the water that they harvested from the building into a tanker truck and treated with a mild de-contaminant. The haul would later be added to the general reserves.

Then we went to work. First, we did a walk-through to make sure that no one was hiding in the structure. We were pretty sure the place was free of squatters since the water crew had just spent over an hour in the structure. The building tenants were supposed to clear the place of possessions and valuables. Anything left over was fair game. We found a boom box in almost brand new condition and a nice captain's chair behind a desk and put them in the back of the pickup. Other than that, there was nothing but nasty used office furniture and the usual empty-building debris.

Then we went around locking windows from the inside and measuring them from the outside. Most commercial windows came in standard sizes but we had an abundance of lumber and power tools ready to compensate for any odd sizes and shapes.

When the final exit was ready to be secured, we were required, by protocol, to give a standard warning through a bullhorn three times throughout the structure:

"THIS IS THE HENNEPIN COUNTY STRUCTURAL PRESERVATION TEAM TO ALL PERSONS WITHIN THIS STRUCTURE AT (give formal address of building). IN THREE MINUTES, WE WILL RELEASE A HAZARDOUS ANIT-PESTICIDE WITHIN THE STRUCTURE AND WILL BOARD UP AND SECURE THE (describe exit with street name and cardinal direction). PLEASE EXIT THE BUILDING NOW."

We gave another warning at two minutes and the final at one minute. The last thing we did inside most secured buildings was to set off what we called a "roach bomb" – it was actually much more toxic than the bombs that the Orkin man used to set off in your house. Our bug bombs not only killed all the bugs, but it also would kill cats, dogs and rats. If there were a homeless person hiding in a secured structure, he'd probably die in there. Then we put up warning posters and fluorescent orange tape over all boarded access points. That way, cops and guardsmen could readily see if a structure had been invaded.

We finished and went on to one more job and then out to a warehouse and lumberyard complex to load up the trucks with a whole bunch of building supplies. All we had to do was unload the trucks back at the Gulag and then that was it for the day. It was just an extra little duty, and then we were done with work and walking out the gates of the compound by quarter after four.

SIX

It felt great to be working. I almost felt like a normal guy living in normal times as I strolled out the gates of the Gulag at the end of that first full day of work. John and Brian were still out on crew so I got in my car and started driving toward home. But I didn't feel like sitting alone in my apartment. I wanted to feel like I could ease back into something resembling normal behavior. I yearned for a simple kind of life.

The Kaiserhof was a rustic, old dark and corner tavern less than a mile south of downtown. It wasn't far from my apartment and I had actually seen it many times from the outside but never actually patronized the place. However, with its thick stone walls and heavily stained-glass windows, it beckoned to me as a safe haven.

I stopped my car in front that day at about 5:15 in the afternoon. The place had a German theme and the decor was provincial European. But the folks there were just a bit on the suspicious side that first time there. My eyes had to adjust from the bright sunlight to rustic darkness as I entered. There was a guy guarding the door who roughly frisked me when I came in. His name was Carl. Satisfied that I was Kaiserhof-worthy, he nodded me inside.

I made my way towards the back to the dim, wooden bar room. The bar area was dark and cozy and smelled of cigarettes, yeast and beer-saturated wood. Instead of a barback mirror, there was a series of gaudy stained-glass partitions behind the bar. You could see one of the two dining rooms through the stained glass, but very opaquely. Beer mugs and wine glasses dangled from overhead racks. A tall man of more than about six foot one would have a difficult time maneuvering back there.

The bartender was a short, thick, paunchy guy of about fifty. His longish gray mustache was yellowed in the middle by cigarette smoke and he had a workman's arms with a Navy tattoo on his left forearm. He approached me and spoke. "You look new. This your first time here?" he asked gruffly. The man had a .357 plainly in view on his belt and I thought that simple answers would be the best.

"Yes," I said.

"You from around here," he asked, not friendly and with a hint of suspicion in his demeanor. I suddenly felt like I was going through a roadside interrogation from an ACLU-hating cop. *Jeez, I just wanted a beer.*

"Yes, I actually grew up in South Minneapolis. I just live a few blocks away," I said, pointing in the direction of my apartment building, as if that would matter. "I've just never stopped in before."

"What do you do for work?"

"I work for the county. I board up buildings," I said with pride, as though I'd been doing it for years.

"That a full-time job?"

"You *betcha*," I answered in my best Minnesota cliché with a hearty nod.

"Hhmm," he said looking me up and down before deciding I was all right. "Okay, here's the deal: My name is Jack and I'm the manager-by-default here. You can keep coming back if you'd like, you seem like the decent sort. Don't fight in here or bring in undesirables. Don't do anything but drink and socialize, and everything should be all right," the de facto manager told me. "Screw up just *once* in here and that's it. No more drinks or food." Those seemed like easy rules to follow. And with that he took my order. "Now, what would you like?"

"A Pilsner Urquell," I selected after quickly perusing the different brands of beers. Jack nodded and walked away. I looked around the bar. Though it was broad daylight outside, the Kaiserhof had an intimate, dark feel about it. The exterior stained-glass windows let in only subdued light from the outside and there were no lights lit up on the inside. The bar, stools and booths were all made of heavy dark wood; German sturdiness and simplicity at its best. There were six other people in there, five men and one woman. There was one other employee, a younger guy also packing a blaster. He cleaned and shuttled in and out through the swinging doors of the kitchen. Jack came back with a foamy German beer.

"If you want to eat here, we no longer have a full menu. We do usually have a big vat of soup going every day and, depending on the day, we can whip up some bratwursts or sandwiches. Last week the owner had about fifty filet mignons dumped on him that we had to eat quick. Too bad you didn't stop in a week ago."

"Thanks. I'm not hungry right now."

"What's your name again?" he said offering a hand.

"Dallas Burnette," I told him.

"I'll start you a tab," he said, presuming I'd be there for more than one beer. He was right. "Just holler if you want anything."

"Thank you, Jack," I said. I preferred to sit there and sip German beer and get lost in my own thoughts. On the wall parallel to the row of barstools was a series of windows overlooking a garden area. I decided to go sit out there.

The Kaiserhof had a gorgeous enclosed courtyard right outside the bar. It was an alcove with high stone walls on three sides, the east and south barriers being the exterior walls of adjacent businesses, and a six-foot wrought iron fence on the street side. The garden was about 40 feet wide and a hundred feet deep. There was a canvas canopy that could cover the whole yard that was set up on a pulley system – it took at least two strong guys to unfurl the damn thing. There was a sculpture, a babbling fountain and the garden was otherwise comfortably filled with wrought-iron tables and chairs. I sat down at one of the tables and continued to look around.

The courtyard was lush with greenery and partially covered with an overhead valance that held a thick system of clingy vines. Most of the walls were also overgrown with clingy vines, too. There were small, spidery trees planted on the restaurant side of the iron fence and vinery on the fence itself, so it was hard to see into the courtyard unless you were deliberately trying to do so. It was a warm, breezy day and the yard was extremely peaceful.

"Do you mind if I sit here?" an unfamiliar male voice startled me out of my thoughts.

"Uh ... sure. Go ahead." I said, a little bewildered.

"I don't usually ask to sit with a strangers," the man said as he pulled out a chair and sat down. "My name is Ken. Ken Leland."

"Dallas Burnette," I said, shaking his hand.

"You're sure you don't mind?" he said. He put his drink down. A gin or vodka tonic, I thought it might be.

"No. This is actually my first time here myself. Always happy to meet new folks."

"So what do you do here in Minneapolis?" he said leaning back in his chair and diving straight into small talk.

"I work for the county. Monkey work," I said with a sip of my beer. "How 'bout you?"

"Me? I owned a catering service. It was small but I made a pretty decent living."

"Really?" I said, slightly impressed. But I had a little trouble picturing this guy making sure the cocktail weenies were the right temperature and that the florals were arranged just so.

"So how come you didn't leave town?" I asked.

"Well, I'm divorced. The ex got remarried and lives in Phoenix with the kids and the new hubby. Been there for a couple years now."

"Kids, huh?"

"Yes," he said, excitely pulling a picture out of his wallet and leaning over. "My daughter, Lauren, is seven and Jason there is five," he said, clearly proud of his children.

"Cute kids. You must miss them," I said eyeing the picture and nodding.

"I sure do. I thought about going down there after, ya know, the bombs. I had a lot of trouble trying to get booked on an airliner. I'm not really up to driving across the country by myself, so I guess I'm stuck here for now."

"What are you going to do to live?" I asked.

"I don't know," he said with a sip of his drink. "I honestly don't know. I wasn't very liquid and, as you might guess, my present portfolio couldn't finance a pack of cigarettes." He sighed, shook his head and then sipped his drink. I sort of felt sorry for the guy. I'd known him for mere minutes but could already tell he was a good man. Ken Leland looked to be in his mid-thirties, about my age. He struck me as the kind of guy who probably played high school football and then kept in okay condition by joining a health club in his mid-twenties, or maybe he was a weekend jogger. He was a plain looking guy with the beginning of some extra pounds around the middle but looked in pretty good shape otherwise.

"*Hmm* ..." I pondered.

"What?"

"Well," I started hesitantly, "would you ever consider some manual labor?" I didn't know how a former business owner would feel about working with his hands.

"Hell *yeah*!" came his enthusiastic response. "You're damn right. You know a place that's hiring?"

"Yeah, there's no guarantees here, mind you, but I actually think I could get you in down at the shop where I work," I responded. I hoped I wasn't over-extending my ability to make good on a claim.

"And what is it you do again?"

"We just drive around with work orders and board places up. I used to be a professional guy, so it's not like I'm Mr. Toolbox or anything like that. It's pretty easy work, to tell ya the truth."

"And it pays?"

"Sure. Fifteen bucks an hour."

I know that didn't sound like much. But despite the fact that a bag of groceries could run a person well over a hundred dollars sometimes, it was offset by the fact that most landlords and mortgage companies weren't exactly pounding down people's doors demanding rent payments. The Hennepin County Sheriff's Department sure as hell wasn't handing out eviction notices as far as we knew.

"Huh," Ken pondered. "That sounds pretty good. Say, uh … this is a bit embarrassing but … what was your name again?"

"Dallas," I said with a laugh. "Don't worry about it, I forget people's names all the time," I lied.

"Well, Dallas, I'm glad I stopped in," my new friend Ken Leland said with raised low-ball. We clinked our glasses together and drank.

"Glad I could help out."

We continued talking for several hours. Sports (World Series gone by), politics (To nuke or not to nuke? And whom?), and life in general. It was good to talk to someone other than John or Brian. One can only discuss rock music orchestration theory so many times before it becomes pretty darn pedantic. When the bar tab came, we divvied it fifty-fifty, even though Ken was drinking pricier drinks.

I approached Scheerer early the next day down at the Gulag to inquire about taking Ken Leland on. I found him in the bay talking maintenance with a couple of mechanics and writing on a clipboard.

"Yo, Dan?"

"Yeah," he said without looking up, "what do ya want, Burnette?"

"Just wondering if you need any more bodies."

"You bet, we just lost two guys, Alder and ..." he snapped his fingers trying to remember, "... Mathiasen. They split town or something."

"Punks."

"Why? Do you know somebody?"

"Yes. I just met a guy at the bar yesterday. His name is Ken Leland. Used to be a small-business owner, says he knows how to work with tools, in his mid-thirties, seems like a decent guy."

"Sounds good. Send him on down and I'll hire him on the spot. When can he start?" Scheerer said while writing on the clipboard.

"I guess whenever you want."

"Make it ASAP," he said as he turned and headed to the office.

I brought Ken Leland to work with me the very next morning. True to his word, Scheerer talked with him for about five minutes and then shook his hand and sent him back to the office to get his paperwork together so he could get paid. Leland was out on crew that morning and grateful to be there. I wasn't on his crew but I heard from the other guys that he was actually quite knowledgeable about general contracting and he made a good impression. Leland bought me a couple beers down at the Kaiserhof that afternoon to show his appreciation.

The internet was the main tool used in gaining current and useful information. There was a little trouble getting online sometimes, but the government was leaning the major directories and search engines to keep up things fully and running. I think they used that "swift and harsh punishment" threat again. I don't know about anybody else, but that warning was starting to loose its *oompf* with me.

Things were peaceful in the city in those first weeks. Everyone was in shock and I think that there was a general feeling of bonding through sharing of common hardship. A few people and families started to trickle back into the cities. And, of course, we tried to catch TV when the power was on.

The central government had taken over the power industries under presidential order. Much of the national power-grid had been damaged so there was a lot of power being re-routed around the country. The feds were busy trying to restore the infrastructure around the blast areas and I guess that they needed more power on some days than they did on others. Regular household electricity came in spurts that the power companies called rolling blackouts. They seemed to have no rhyme or reason; sometimes they happened for days in a row, other times we could go a week with uninterrupted power. Hospitals obviously had their own generators as did other key facilities and installations.

I was hanging out in John and Brian's apartment, drinking beers and watching "Seinfeld" reruns one day after work. The entertainment industry wasn't cranking out product anymore so re-broadcasts were all that was on the tube aside from news and government stuff. The show was suddenly interrupted by a FOX News Special Report. We all looked wide-eyed at each other. What new horror was about to be relayed to us?

"This is a FOX News Special Report. The BBC has received a new videotaped threat from al Qaeda. Without further ado, here's the tape received by BBC Television:"

The picture cut to a grainy video of an al Qaeda operative. The spokesperson on the tape was an erudite young man of Middle Eastern descent who spoke in nearly flawless American English. The terrorist held up the previous day's front page of the *Frankfurter Zeitung* during his statement, so the recent taping of the threat was guaranteed. It wasn't a rehash of a tape made several months or a year prior.

"The nuclear attacks of April were merely the first wave of strikes against the American Empire. There are not less than 15 more nuclear weapons under al Qaeda control within the borders of the continental United States, ready for detonation. America will feel the wrath of Allah, and she will tremble with a level of terror she never thought possible. Praise be to Allah." *Fade out.*

"Well, that's just fucking peachy," John said.

The recording had very recently been hand delivered to a BBC Television producer and was soon aired worldwide. The timing was perfect as far as the terrorists were concerned; it came at a time when American refugees were just starting to filter back to the outer suburbs of various big cities around the nation. There was no doubt that repopulating metro centers was better for overall society, and the latest threat chased a large number of people back to their rural hideouts and made the remaining citizens of major cities edgy and nervous, to say the least. The goal of terrorism continued: Terror.

Was the threat real or was it a psychological warfare tactic? It either case, it had its intended effect. Chaos was guaranteed to continue to reign supreme throughout America. Because I worked for the government, I knew that major cities were being scoured by NEST teams almost 'round the clock. Cities were ringed with so many layers of detours, roadblocks and choke points that it would be all but impossible to bring a weapon into an urban area now. I knew that the latest video threat was more than likely just a ploy. But to the amateur risk-analysis of the common person, the possibility of being fried in another round of nuclear strikes was horrifying right down to the bottom of the very soul. Metropolitan citizens would remain in hiding and the inner cities would remain the Wild, Wild West.

I was sitting on my favorite corner bar stool at the Kaiserhof engaged in one of my favorite activities – staring straight ahead and thoroughly enjoying romping around inside my own brain while slowly working on a beer. I understand that to the casual observer it may look like I'm depressed, lonely or possibly even mentally challenged. These can actually become almost meditative sessions where the world almost disappears as my eye focuses on a picture or a smoldering cigarette butt … anything. Someone giving me a hard elbow-to-elbow nudge suddenly jolted me out of my trance.

"Hey! I said, 'It looks like you lost your favorite puppy dog'."

"Excuse me?" I said, snapping back into reality.

"You're kinda lost in your own world, aren't ya?" said the man, a jovial bloke in his late forties.

"That's kind of the point."

"My name is Derek Juravek. How ya doin?"

"Dallas," I responded with a nod. I wasn't really in a talkative mood and was rather enjoying my quiet time alone, but he persisted.

"Just down here having a drink?"

"That's about it," I said, trying not to be unfriendly while trying not to encourage any further conversation.

"Yeah, me too. So what did you do before all the nukes?"

It was useless. The man was obviously searching for some light conversation and I couldn't quite bring myself to telling him that I preferred to be left alone.

"Salesman," I said. "I sold sandpaper."

"Really? How unique."

"Why? What did you do?" I said, finally engaging him in conversation.

"I used to own several hardware stores. 'Juravek Hardware,' maybe you heard of them?"

I knew that his last name sounded familiar. Small world. "Yes. In fact, I tried opening an account with your chain once. Your purchasing manager for the chain, I forget his name ..."

"Bob Kasano?"

"Bob Kasano," I nodded. "That's the guy. He was very rude to me on the phone. I think he actually hung up on me while we were talking."

"Yeah, you gotta understand, in his position Bob was getting about two dozen sales calls a day, everyday."

"Nonetheless, I thought he was a rude bastard. What's the jerk doing nowadays?"

"Bob? I sent Bob on a business trip last spring. He was in Atlanta on April first."

"Oh," I said, suddenly sheepish.

"Yup. His hotel was very much within the blast area of the Atlanta nuke. Haven't heard from him since, pretty sure he's a crispy critter."

"Jeez, I'm sorry."

"Fuggedabowdit," Derek said with a slug of his pilsner and a wave of his hand.

"So how are your hardware stores?"

"Empty. Looted. Burned. Out of business. Any combination of the above."

I shook my head in incredulity. "You seem to be rolling with things quite well."

"Not really any other choice, is there?" Derek said.

He was right, there was no choice. We were all in the shit together. Derek seemed like a good guy and I was glad to have made his acquaintance. And so it went; one by one, I started building a network of friendship and acquaints at the Kaiserhof. Periodic callings turned into regular visits and regular visits turned into daily stops. It became a home away from home and a place where I knew that I could trust the guy next to me. I brought buddies from the Gulag down every now and then. They even let us run weekly tabs there. It was an exclusive little club of decent and hard working people. I liked it there.

SEVEN

One of the general tendencies of human behavior is that people will try to get away with whatever they think that they can get away with. Someone once said that "character is what you do when nobody is looking." If that were true, I fear, the majority of humanity would go down in the cosmic ledger-books as a bunch of nose-digging, fart-ripping, belly button lint-picking, masturbating slobs. The truth, I once heard a pastor say, is that less-than-perfect behavior is often the manifestation of a wandering mind.

I remember reading stories of "fragging" in Vietnam, when it was rumored that, in isolated cases, soldiers would shoot a superior out in the field where the incident could ostensibly be interpreted as a battlefield fatality. In a brutal environment, people can do things they otherwise couldn't do.

My mind wandered … I thought of all the personal enemies I'd kill if I knew that I could get away with it. There were actually only two or three folks I would kill in my wildest and darkest fantasies if I could. But, if I could kill only one person and one person only, it would have to be …

Erik Johnson.

Erik Johnson was an arrogant little prick. He was the manager of a sales and distribution firm that I worked at after I had gotten back from Antarctica. With his sardonic, nasally voice and perpetual smart-ass smirk, he was easy to dislike. He claimed that he had a law degree but was such an out-and-out bullshitter, God only knows if he did. Either way, I didn't like lawyers then and I don't like lawyers now. As far as I'm concerned, lawyers just feed off of human misery and discontent. If there weren't conflict and misery between people, lawyers couldn't live. Living like that has got to be bad for the soul at some point.

Smug and rude, Johnson was one of those people who thinks he's got an IQ about 35 or 40 points higher than it really is. I don't know if there's a more detestable set of qualities in a human than arrogance coupled with a hyper-inflated sense of intelligence. He was the main reason I quit that particular company. I told him what I thought of him. He didn't take it well.

After I left, he blatantly lied and accused me of taking sales files from the office and left several threatening voicemails on my phone. I mean threatening as in the old playground caveat, "You better hope you see me before I see you," or "I'd be looking over my back if I were you." He was immature and childish. I couldn't believe a 39-year-old man would speak in such terms.

Normally, such threats could be ignored, but I also knew that Erik was a sleaze who was into cocaine and that he carried a loaded 9mm pistol in his leather shoulder bag. Since he had respect for nothing and no one, it was within the realm of possibilities that he could inflict harm upon me. God only knows what the paranoia-inflicting effects of drugs can lead a person to do. I moved on with my life.

After leaving his firm, I got a job working as a furnace and air conditioning salesman and was doing quite well. I enjoyed the job and my fellow workers, and was starting to average $4,000 a month in commissions. I was very happy. But, after my three month probationary review, I was released. No reasons were given and, because Minnesota was an "at will" employment state, no reasons were required to be given. I was perplexed.

It was several months later when I found out what happened. I bumped into one of the other salesmen in a restaurant, Harvey Martin. Harvey was one of those guys at a company who knows all the gossip. We rapported for a bit and then I turned the conversation to the situation of my dismissal. He reluctantly, and with great discomfort, told me that a former manager of mine had contacted the folks at the new job and told them that I had been fired from my previous position for "corporate espionage." And the name of the person who called in?

Erik Johnson.

The little bastard made up a lie and cost me a damn good job for no other reason than childish spite. I had no idea how he found out where I was working but he did, and he took it upon himself to ruin my new career. So, anyway, I had always thought since that moment on that if I could kill someone and get away with it, he would be the one. I knew where the arrogant piece-of-shit lived. Johnson lived in a rambler in Columbia Heights, a suburb located several miles north of downtown. He threw a football party there once while I was still working for him, so I knew exactly where the house was. Murdering him should have remained just a dark little fantasy, never to be acted upon.

Fast-forward to post April Attack: It was the end of a work day, we happened to be driving down that very street where shit-fer-brains lived and I'll be damned if I didn't see that evil little bastard putzing around in his yard. I actually had to do a double-take.

So ya didn't leave town, huh, you little asshole?

Now I'm a peaceful guy, but I decided right then and there that I would kill Erik Johnson if the opportunity ever presented itself. The decision was as carefree as deciding to go for a bike ride on a sunny Sunday afternoon.

The smells of engine oil and diesel exhaust wafted up into the briefing room of the Gulag and mixed with the aroma of coffee that had been sitting on the burner too long. The elements came together to create the distinct and unmistakable odor of a male workplace. Every now and then, once a week or so, we all had to sit down and get classes on various things like first aid, emergency protocol, post disaster survival tips, decontamination … you name it. Sometimes we'd get government types coming in and giving a presentation. It was usually interesting and always helpful. This week, however, we had no guest speaker and it was Scheerer's turn to give a class on hunting animals for food. Free-range cuisine, he called it.

"Listen up ladies! This week's lecture is on hunting."

Most of the guys perked up a bit. At least this might be interesting and entertaining for a half-hour or so. Scheerer began reading, casually injecting his own thoughts here and there.

"Hunting: The surviving animals will be competing with you and your family for food. Hunting could supply meat for your diet but probably won't be a main source unless you're really out in the wilds. Sooner or later, I'm sure that some of you, maybe all of us, will find yourself in more rural settings, reuniting with family or what have you.

But, as many of you also know, many animals are getting more and more courageous about lurking into urban areas." He looked down and continued reading.

"Lessee … 'A vegetarian diet will not cut it. Meat will be essential for healthy survival. Ideally, you'll have a diet mix of somewhere around 15 percent protein, 52 percent carbohydrates, and 33 percent fat'."

"Who made that up?" asked Boone.

"I dunno …" Scheerer said with some disinterest, "some FDA idiots."

"Is there any way you can get sick from radiation by eating animals?" Brian asked.

"Good question," Scheerer said, turning the pages of his outline. He began reading again.

"'When animals ingest radioactive contamination, it is stored in certain locations in their bodies. Post-nuclear war survivors need to learn how to avoid eating parts of the animal that will be collecting the radioactive materials. If you avoid the parts with high concentrations of contamination, you will be able to remain healthy while still being able to take advantage of the available meat. Parts to avoid; thyroid glands, kidneys, liver, and meat next to the bones as well as the marrow in the bones. Avoid eating these and eat only muscle meat. Another important precaution is to thoroughly cook the meat so that ALL bacteria are killed in the meat; since radiation lowers resistance to disease, the animal may have higher than normal concentrations of bacteria in it and you will be less able to fight off such bacteria. Bury the parts in an area where they can not contaminate your water or crops'." He put down his notes.

"Lovely," came a sarcastic comment from the other side of the room.

"You can also contract West Nile virus by eating infected animals."

"Any other good news?" I asked dryly.

"Yes. If life ain't rotten enough for ya yet, here's one more thing to deal with: Bovine Spongiform Encephalopathy, otherwise known as BSE. Who knows what that is?"

My hand went up. "Mad cow disease?"

"Roger that. Good one, Burnette."

"Hey man, even a blind squirrel finds a nut every now and then," said John.

"Shut up and listen … BSE, or mad cow disease, has spread to the North American deer population. To date, there have been a couple dozen documented cases of the disease in domestic cows, and those were reported out in New England. But deer in about a dozen states, including Minnesota, Wisconsin and Canada do carry a form of the disease. But, in deer it's called chronic wasting disease."

"What does the disease do?" one of the young guys asked from the back.

"It's a neurological disease. It affects the brain. The clinical disease usually lasts for several weeks and it is fatal. If you eat an animal with this disease, you will become sick and you will die. Parts of your brain will get eaten away and will leave hollow little pockets. Essentially, it turns your brain into Swiss cheese. By all accounts, it's a rotten way to go. I know that some of you are deer hunters. I know I was. I guess the moral of this story is, consume venison at your own risk."

With that he wrapped up. After class we were given pretty easy tasks and told we could go home, or wherever, at two in the afternoon. The day was hot and sultry and we were glad to be given such light duty. I was with a crew of eight guys and all we had to do was walk around downtown with lawn bags and pick up litter – very easy. It allowed me to think.

How could I kill Erik Johnson?

I was working side by side with Aaron Stubbs that day. Aaron was a pleasant enough man but he had a quiet toughness about him. He sometimes regaled me with tales of football glory from his Grambling days. He didn't work fast, but he worked steadily and diligently as he hummed quietly to himself. We were working our way down a city sidewalk and I decided to strike up a conversation.

"Hot out, eh?"

"It's not the heat, it's the muggadidity."

I didn't know if he was being clever or if he really thought that 'muggadidity' was a word.

"Stubbs," I said.

"Yes?"

"If you had to kill someone that you really hated, how would you do it?"

"Death-by-baseball," he replied instantly. He didn't even have to think. The answer to my hypothetical question came out of his mouth so quickly, it was as though it were at the top of his consciousness.

"What in the hell is 'death-by-baseball'," I asked, truly curious.

"Well, you kidnap the mothafucka, take him to the middle of the woods," he replied matter-of-factly. "Tie his ass to a tree and throw baseballs at him til he dies."

"This is an original idea?" I asked with furrowed brow.

"Sho'iz."

"What if you get tired and he's still alive? Can you bring in a reliever?" I was joking but Stubbs didn't miss a beat.

"I 'spose. You could do play-by-play while you throwin at the mothafucka, too. Ya know, like '*Oh-oh, that one got away ... looks like another beanball, Bob*'," he said in a cheesy baseball announcer's voice. "Why, Dallas? How would you do it?"

"Well," I paused for thoughtful reflection before I continued, "depending on how much you hate a guy, I guess it'd be fun to strangle someone, ya know, watch the life ooze out of their eyes?"

"Yeah, dat'd be fun but dat would prob'ly involve a fight befo' hand, right?"

"Yeah, probably."

"Mothafucka might get the besta *you* and strangle *your* ass."

"Yeah," I said with a nod of agreement.

Though it would have been delicious to strangle Erik Johnson with my own two bare hands and watch the life drain from his eyes, I thought that close-order combat might indeed be too risky. Stubbs was right. What if he was able to reach his gun or what if he had a knife on him? Or, God forbid, what if the little bitch defeated me in a fistfight? Though highly unlikely, that would just be too much. Besides, if we battled and I didn't kill him he would be a witness for any further action and there would undoubtedly be scads of evidence against me; shreds of clothing, hair, skin under the nails, blood stains, eyewitnesses. This was not a good time to be sentenced to incarceration or to tangle with the law. No, if I were going to kill the man, it would have to be remote and quick.

Just musing here, mind you.

EIGHT

Many medical, fire and rescue personnel had immediately gone to the outlying areas of the attacked cities to render whatever aid they could. The cities and towns outside of the nuclear blast and fallout templates were overwhelmed with the sick, the dying and the dead. Turns out that a fair number of citizens from unaffected parts of the country didn't go into hiding afterall, but traveled to these places to help in anyway that they could.

The police and military that were left in Minneapolis and St. Paul had their hands full with traffic control and looting at first, predictable group misbehavior. Then the baser elements of human conduct raised their heads. The fifth police precinct had a huge handmade sign erected right outside their building:

OUR MISSION:
Help the Saints,
Save the Sinners,
Punish the Satans;
Make all contribute to society.

We started hearing of broad daylight street muggings, then business robberies. Business owners got roughed up at first, but in short order they were just blown right out of their shoes on an increasingly regular basis. And if the bad guys didn't beat you up, the cops or National Guard might.

In late May, I spent a little too much time at the Kaiserhof one night. Feeling more than a little on the buzzed side, I walked out of the heavy oak front doors and stepped out into the late dusk evening. Army Hummers and police cruisers patrolled the nighttime streets just looking for people to skirmish with. I only had four blocks to cover in order to get home. I shuffled along at something between a fast walk and a jog. I turned the corner and saw my apartment building. I just had one block to go. But it was dark.

"FREEZE!" blared the trooper's voice over a hand-held megaphone as a spotlight suddenly glared on me. It was a National Guard Humvee crewed by recently activated troops. In this situation, you'd rather be stopped by an experienced beat-cop. The cops tended to be a little bit older and a little bit more on the common-sense side of things.

"Get your hands in the air," said a young black sergeant emerging from the passenger seat with an M-16A2 rifle pointing at me. There was another trooper manning the machine-gun cupola on top of the vehicle and he was pointing an M-60 at me. It was all a bit of overkill for dealing with a slightly drunken bloke walking home while it was still technically dusk out. My hands went into the air.

"Turn around!" he barked.

I spun around.

"On your knees!"

I dropped to my knees. I heard his boots running towards me and felt the searing pain of his knee digging into my back. He slammed my torso to the ground and mashed my face into the earth. My shoulders and head landed in the three-foot grassy boulevard between the sidewalk and street.

"What are you doing out here? Looking to jack someone? Casing a building to loot?"

"No," I said breathlessly and somewhat in pain. "I live right here on this block," I said, gesturing as best I could toward the apartment house. "I'm just a little bit late coming home."

"Can you prove that?" he said angrily.

I nodded.

"Listen up and do as I say: I'm going to get off you," he said. "There's a machine gun mounted on the Hummer pointed at you and my driver has a .45 pointed at your head. Do you understand?"

I nodded.

"Do you have any weapons on your person that I should know about?

"No," I replied. With that he took his knee out of my back and gave me a quick, one-handed frisking. Then he got all the way off and backed up about seven feet.

"Slowly turn over and assume a sitting position on the ground," he ordered. I complied as he trained his weapon on me.

"Now, do you have ID with your current address on it?"

I nodded.

"Slowly reach for your ID with one hand and toss it on the ground in front of you." Painfully, I leaned on my left butt cheek and pulled out my wallet from the right, rear pocket. I removed my driver's license and frisbeed it several feet in front of me, meanwhile having three live weapons trained on me. I kept my hands in the air. The sergeant, whose name was Washington according to his BDU tunic, picked up my ID and confirmed that I lived on the block. He nodded confirmation to his comrades and gently tossed my license back to me.

"Put your ID away, sir, and then stand up," he ordered. Once on my feet, he continued.

"Don't let me catch you out again after dark. Next time I won't be so nice."

"You're a little overzealous, aren't you?"

"I can still take you to jail, fool. You wanna go to jail?" he threatened.

"I just want to go home," I said shyly.

"Than *get* … next time I'm going to slap you around like a red-headed stepchild. I don't care if I catch you sitting on your front steps sippin a Colt .45."

With that, the soldiers got back into the Hummer and drove off. I continued on home.

"Motherfucking guardsmen," I said upon entering John and Brian's apartment. They could tell that I'd just been roughed up and Brian wordlessly went to fetch me a beer. He handed it to me and I held the bottle to my forehead for a second, then I told them the whole story. They commiserated with me and then John chimed in with a tale of his own. His story, like mine, all started with a few beers. I suppose many stories of woe start out the same way.

"This happened back five years ago or so. I was kinda drunk down at Liquor Lewey's Bar … I hardly ever go there. It's a tough bar but they got real good food. Anyway, the kitchen is about to close so I'm flashing my cash, ya know, trying to get the bartender's attention so I can order something to go. This broad starts coming on to me like I'm going to buy some sex from her and, I'm like, 'No way.' We trade some insults. Next thing I know she's starting to make a scene. I say 'screw it' and decide to leave.

"No sooner do I get outside and this broad and about 20 people are after me and the broad is saying. *'That's him, that's the mothafucka who took my money!'* So I get assaulted by this huge group of people. I get knocked to the ground and the bouncer sits on my back and tries to break my arm, he keeps twisting it at the elbow."

"Goddam," I said.

"Fuckin-A. I was in torturous pain, dude. They knocked me into the pavement and I was bleeding from somewhere on the top of my head. At some point, someone reached into my pocket and took 50 dollars cash and my cash card. 'That's the motherfuckin money he took from me!' This bitch screams and the crowd goes nuts. I was beaten and robbed."

"Jesus Christ!"

"Yeah. When the cops got there, they had to call the paramedics. I was being treated and couldn't hear the witness statements being taken. Apparently, they got some bullshit story from the 'witnesses.' The paramedics finished and the cops put me in the squad. We started driving toward downtown. I just wanted to go home and I go, 'Hey, why doncha just take me down to the river and beat me up? I won't tell anybody.' I was serious."

Brian and I laughed. Back in the day, the Minneapolis police had a reputation, true or untrue, of taking suspects down to the river flats and pounding the crap out of them. Some exposure of the alleged practice by some alleged nosy reporters quietly put an end to the alleged surreptitious beatings. Allegedly.

"No, listen, it gets better," continued John. "The cop riding shotgun goes, 'Aw, we're not supposed to do that anymore.'"

Brian and I laughed some more.

"But the fun was just starting. I get taken down to the county jail, that nasty place in the bowels of the old clock tower in downtown Minneapolis. I get in-processed and get into my bay at about two in the frickin morning and tried to go to sleep. Fuckin roll of toilet paper for a pillow."

"Yeah?"

"This deputy comes in the next morning to distribute the nasty breakfast food and I ask how long I was going to be held. The fucker laughs and says, 'You're on 72-hour hold, get comfortable 'cause you're not going anywhere for awhile.'"

"That's three days!" I said.

"No shit, Sherlock," John shot back. "We couldn't even use a phone so, for all intents and purposes, I was going to disappear from the face of the fucking planet for a few days. There was no way I was gonna stay in that hole for three days, man. My family, friends, employer and girlfriend would have no idea where I was. I had to get out. It wasn't even in question."

"Brian couldn't spring you, man?" I asked.

"No, dude," said Brian, exhaling a puff of cigarette smoke. "I was all out of dynamite and my helicopter was down for repairs." We laughed again.

"Fuck you guys. Anyway listen," John took a swig of beer and continued. "Cops seem to like me if I get a chance to talk to them so I decide to ask for an interview with a detective and just agree to everything, I decide I'll be pleasant and charming the whole time. I wouldn't contradict anything they said and would, thereby, get in their good graces. Right? I figured I'd get charged with a petty misdemeanor, at most."

"Sounds like a bad plan," I said.

"Listen to this; less than half an hour later, I was led to an interview room with a plain-clothes female detective. We started out with friendly small talk that actually went on for quite awhile. I knew what she was doing. I just played the affable doofus."

"Shouldn't have been too hard," Brian smirked.

"Actually, it wasn't. This female cop says, 'So, I understand you want to talk about last night?' I said, 'Well, actually, I'd like to get out of here. Do you think I'll get out of here today?' and she says, 'Well … that depends on how things go, I guess.'

"Showtime – that was my cue. She said we could 'just talk' about what happened but she had to tape-record the conversation. That was fine with me as long as I could be out on the street. She walked me through this whole fucking story that the bar crowd had told the patrol cops and I just agreed with everything."

"Not smart, guy. Cops never 'just talk'," I said.

"I know, but I thought that if I contradicted anything she said, she'd have to 'investigate' further, and that would leave me in the fuckin slammer for three days. So, anyway, we finish the interview and I say, 'Do you think I could get out of here soon?' and she goes, 'Oh … sure. You've been pretty cooperative. I just have to make out the paperwork. You should be on the street within the hour.' So I figure I'm done. She didn't mention one word about charges or court dates.

"About two minutes later she came back and says, 'You know what? I forgot to read you your Miranda rights on tape. We'll have to do the interview all over,' and I go, 'No! I'll stand by everything I said. You don't have to worry,' and she goes, 'Nope. We have to re-do the interview. Can't let you go before we do that.'

"Then what?" I asked, somewhat intrigued.

"What nuthin, it was a fucking brilliant interrogation tactic: She gets all cozy and friendly and says that you just want to 'talk.' Promises to let me go if I cooperate. She doesn't read the Miranda rights because, you see, once a police officer starts reading *You have the right to remain silent* ... the first thing any normal person does is to say, 'Whoa! What am I being charged with?' and then the cop is in a hostile interview situation, right? So she gets me on tape agreeing to everything, gets me all excited about getting out of the fucking pokey, and then comes back claiming that she 'forgot' the Miranda reading and the interview has to be redone. She knows I've already already spilled my guts and I'm probably not going to change my story, right?"

"So what did you do, wiseguy?" asked Brian.

"What could I do? They wouldn't let my ass outta jail if I changed my story at this point. She unwraps the cellophane off of a new mini-tape and put it in the recorder, which I thought was odd."

"Why didn't she just tape over the previous interview?" I wondered aloud.

"That's exactly what I was thinking. Where the first interview was this long, meandering chat where I agreed with everything she said and just did this big *mea culpa*, in the second interview I pretty much responded in one-word answers. The first taping was about ten minutes. The second taping was, literally, no longer than about 40 seconds."

"But you walked out of the pokey, right?"

"Yeah, that day I did. But six weeks later, I get a felony summons from the State of Minnesota. Assholes said lifting valuables off of a person's body, as opposed to taking something off a bar, is a felony. I had unknowingly confessed to a felony. Like I said before, that deceitful bitch never mentioned anything about charges or crimes. We just had a 'friendly talk,' you see. Sometimes I tend to outsmart myself. My just-agree-with-everything-the-cop-says' strategy blew up in my face."

"So what'd you do?"

"I fuckin lawyered-up. I told her the full story and she did some casework. Turns out that, if it were true that the officer had conducted two interviews and 'forgotten' the Miranda warning the first time around, there was a good chance we could get the whole thing thrown out. All I needed was an honest cop to tell the truth."

I could already tell where this story was going: "So then what?"

"That bitch cop totally denied that there were two tapes. And she said she remembered me and the interview quite vividly. My attorney played the tape back for me; the damn cops had spliced the two interviews into one, so now it sounds like I'm read my Miranda rights and then I go ahead and give this big, gushy confession. I was going to fight all the way, but my attorney advised me that since there was a 'confession' on tape, it would be hard to convince a jury of my innocence. I was livid, fucking livid. I made a big stink in front of the prosecutor out in the hallway. Luckily, she finally said she'd drop everything down to a misdemeanor and a slap on the wrist.

"So the bad guys got my money, the cops got a felony arrest and confession, the prosecutor got a conviction … and me? I got my ass kicked, my money stolen and a theft on my criminal record."

"That's fucked up," Brian sympathized.

"Hey," John said as he leaned back and swigged some more beer. "That's just how shit gets done in the big city."

And that was the *peacetime* police in action.

The moral of the story? Government, left to its own devices, naturally turns tyrannical. I wondered about the scope of our enemies; Terrorists were obviously our enemies. Robbers or people who beat you up on the street were our enemies. But, to a certain extent, it was as though people in the government were sometimes our enemies as well.

A large and quietly growing number of people indicated their fear about the fact that we were living in a police state and under martial law. The omni-presence of U.S. military personnel or para-military police forces haunted street corners and alleys. Enter armed law enforcers, exit constitutional rights. *It is the foreign element that commits our crimes. There is no native criminal class except the government.* I'd like to take credit for that thought, but I think it was another Mark Twain chestnut.

There were daily instances where one could argue that the country now epitomized tyranny by government: We didn't have rights in the eyes of the government, we only had privileges; the privilege to walk around during the daylight hours only, the privilege to try to survive by any scrounging means possible. And, to assure that we obeyed the privileges given us, the government used armed force.

Most important, though, is what would happen if you refused to comply. Any person refusing to comply could be forced to at the point of a gun, or several guns. The "offender" would have loaded, cocked, and ready-to-fire weapons pointed at his head. He could be forcibly removed from his car or tackled on the sidewalk and thrown face down in the dirt or blacktop of the shoulder of the road. He could be cuffed and hauled off to jail like a rabid stray to the pound and treated just as poorly.

Essentially, the point of firearms had replaced our system of justice. And, it was going to get worse, not better, with the expanded authority of law enforcers. If law enforcers wanted to kill you or kick the shit out of you and seize all your property, all they had to do is say you acted or looked like a terrorist or a looter and it appeared you were going to react violently. And God help you if you even *looked* like a dark-haired foreigner.

I spoke to my sister on the phone. The small Nebraska township where they lived had circled their wagons and formed in a community with two nearby small farming towns. Everything was fine, according to Marissa, and the kind of urban violence that I saw everyday was almost unheard of. Farming continued in the heartland, more hampered by the lack of rain than by world events. She even told me that Lincoln remained relatively populated and life was chugging along, "struggling but chugging." Apparently, people there felt like the risk of a nuclear detonation was all but impossible. I guess I couldn't fault them.

I lived in a major city that the FBI had identified as a major host to al Qaeda terrorist cells before The Attack and I continued living there. Is that insane or what? It seemed on odd thing to me, a major city in nearby Nebraska with most of its population intact and struggling to live normally. It felt like we were mice living in an abandoned mansion. But not all was in order in Nebraska.

"I'm not sure how comfortable I feel, Dallas," Marissa said with a sadness in her voice that came right through the phone line.

"I thought you said you were safe there."

"Me and the kids are fine. It's just that ..."

"What?" I said trying to pry the words from her mouth. "What's bothering you?"

"There are men here, good men, family men ... who kill people."

"What do you mean?" I asked sternly.

She responded in halting language that was hard for her to get out; "Right after the attack, a group of local ranchers and farmers ... went around and killed as many Middle Easterners as they could find ... I mean, even people who weren't Muslim but just looked like they might be, ya know ... like a Hindi from India."

"What do you mean kill? Like— "

"Just like it sounds; they pull people out of cars and houses and shoot them."

"Did the police or anybody intervene?"

"You don't get it – it *was* the police. And all the other pillars of the community; churchmen, fathers, leaders."

"Damn," I said in an understatement.

"Yeah, and Blacks or Chicanos aren't safe either. If you're black and someone doesn't know you, you're liable to get beat up bad."

"Are you talking Americans who are black?"

"African Americans, yes. Jeez, if you're black and from Africa, you'd probably get shot."

"I had no idea it was like that out there," I said somewhat astonished.

109

I'd hoped that maybe she was exaggerating a bit. I thought that we cosmopolitan city dwellers were the only ones exposed to the true grit and gruesome realities of our new world. I understood the anger toward Middle Easterners and, God knows I felt it myself, but the summary murder of anyone who looked Islamic disturbed me in ways I couldn't put into words. Detain them, jail them ... hell, put them in a concentration camp, but don't just kill them.

I mean, at least I had a *personal reason* for wanting to kill Erik Johnson.

NINE

I particularly enjoyed working with Henri (pronounced: *On-ree'*) Lebenze on my crew. Lebenze was a French national who got stuck in America after The Attack. The only people being deported now and for the foreseeable future were persons from recognized terrorist states and terrorist sympathizers. We joked with Henri that France should have been near the top of the list. He thought it was funny. At least he chuckled and said he did.

Being a common civilian and booking a seat on an international flight after April was like being hit by lightning twice – not very likely. So here Henri was, stranded in America and in need of a job. Though his command of English was strong, he still spoke with somewhat of a pronounced accent. When someone speaks in a heavy foreign accent, it is quite natural to expect a limited vocabulary, so when Henri cracked a joke or delivered a well-turned humorous comment in conjunction with a topic at hand, it only added to the merriment.

"Henri," I said one day while out on crew.

"Oui?"

"What in the hell are you doing here?" I didn't mean to be rude, his presence was just darned peculiar.

"Merde, zat iz a *storee'*, let me tell you," he started, leaning on his rake. "I come to America looking for romance. I find a *byoo-tee-fool*

American woman on *ze* internet, *oui?* I come here, to Illinois and proceed to *sharm* and romance her in *ze* way *zat* only I can."

"But, of course," I said.

"*Oui.* So I finally get her to agree to *ze* marriage, *non?* We go to *ze* INS *offeez* in Chicago. *Zere* we are interrogated about *ze* true nature of our love."

"And?" I said with anticipation.

"*Zay* said I was full of *bool*-shit! *Zay* tell me *zis* right to my *visage* … uh, face. It *wuz,* how you say? *Outrageous*'!" he said with thick French incredulity.

"You really loved her, huh?"

"Of course not! I was looking for *ze* Green Card. No matter, I *zought* *zat* my performance was flaw*less*'."

"Then what?"

"*Zay* booted my ass out of *ze* country! What *ze* fuck do you *sink?* A few days later, America is attacked, and I am stuck in Minneapolis on *ze* deportation flight layover. I can stay in *ze incarceration*', *zay* tell me after a few weeks, or I can go to work for *ze* state. I choose *ze* work."

"What did you do back in Lyon?

"I teach *Fransh* to *ze* Japanese businessmen."

And that was Lebenze's story. He liked me because I had a French last name. I told him how the French explorers and American Indians had more than a working business relationship and that many Indians had some French ancestry in their blood. Chippewa Indians in Minnesota even say 'bhoo-zhoo' for hello, a take-off on 'bonjour.' He liked that.

I brought co-workers down to the Kaiserhof every now and then. Henri enjoyed the European flavor and said that Germany was "close enough" to France, so he liked it there. Anytime Henri met a female his tagline would come out sooner or later. It didn't matter if she were young or old, slender or heavy. At some point he would lean in with his deep and affected voice and utter, *"you know, you have ze most byoo-tee-fool ice."* The comment always fetched nothing less than a blush. He was a colorful character.

The federal government had seized control of most of the hotels in downtown Minneapolis. The nicer ones were reserved for the out of town feds and lower level government workers were allowed to live in the other ones. Scheerer had boarded up his own house in the suburb of Richfield and lived in the Marriot. Stubbs lived there, too. Lebenze lived there but had to share a room with some odd guy from Luxembourg who had a desk job for the county. They told me that I was eligible for a room there but I declined; I lived mere minutes from downtown.

Working for the county, our days were busy. When we were on straight boarding up detail, we had a crew of six men and a clipboard full of work orders. We had two trucks, a extended-cab pick-up and a bigger truck filled with materials. There were three of us in each cab and we drove from job to job, clearing buildings and securing them as best we could.

Then, of course, there were days when other duties called. There was garbage detail, poster detail, garrison detail, you name it. Our list of responsibilities seemed to grow by the week. We were never quite sure what we'd be doing when we reported to work on any given day.

Scheerer's personal supervisor's truck was named *Duck Tape Six* – and, no, I don't mean duct tape. The moniker was stenciled on the upper-left of the rear gate. It was a small allowance of frivolity from an otherwise serious guy. I told the guys about my time in Antarctica and about how we had a tendency to name all the vehicles down there. Sure enough, names started popping up stenciled on the noses and tailgates of the Gulag's vehicles. Since Scheerer already had *Duck Tape Six* emblazoned on his truck, he couldn't really say anything about the new practice.

I also told the guys about my trip to the bottom of the polar ocean in the bulldozer named *Das Boot* and how I almost became a permanent ice-cube. Scheerer quickly refuted that claim.

"That would be impossible," he said casually.

"Oh?" I said with a degree of curiosity.

"Humans are calcium-rich organisms and ocean water is calcium-poor. You would have eventually dissolved like an aspirin in water."

Christ, that was a fate even worse than the ice-cube theory.

TEN

"Burnette, you're on detail with me today," Scheerer said one morning at the end of briefing. That was fine with me because a day with the boss meant easy duty. It was my turn to ride shotgun as we picked up supplies that we needed around the hootch, as well as just general supervisory duties. "Management-By-Driving-Around," he called it. Scheerer always took the opportunity to motor around town and look at recent jobs, making sure that squatters weren't breaking into our freshly-pickled buildings. We were in his orange supervisor truck in which he had installed a rifle-rack and deer rifle with scope. We zigzagged around the streets of Nordeast Minneapolis. It was the Polish section of town, ergo 'Nord' instead of 'North.'

Scheerer was the topic of many a conversation around the Gulag and out on sites. He had a wife and two kids that he had shipped off to North Dakota to live in a small town while he stayed back. Hell, if it were me? I'd be chillin' and grillin' with my kids and wife up in the country, away from all this bullshit. But not Scheerer. I was curious.

"Why do you stay here, Dan?" I asked as we drove along. "You've got a family."

"Well," he said taking a sip of coffee from his travel mug. "My family is alright. It's real peaceful where they're at and there's family and good people all around."

"Don't you miss them?"

"Sure I do," he said. "But people gotta have something to come back to. Don't you think?"

"C'mon, you gotta feel helpless about this whole situation sometimes."

"Look," Scheerer said. He took a big sigh and slowly let it out before finishing his sentence. "There's a simple law of human nature that says it's inherently more difficult to do the right thing."

"Is that right?" I said with a hint of sarcasm.

"*Was mich nicht umbringt, macht mich stärker.*"

"Say again?" I said.

"That which does not kill me makes me stronger.' It's Friedrich Nietzsche."

"Is that what society has boiled down to? We're living by the words of Friederich Nietzsche?" I said through an ironic chuckle.

"It's a whole new ballgame," he said as he casually sipped his coffee. It sure as shit was, I thought. I decided to change subjects to something a little lighter.

"*Ah feel like Ah'm in Tax-ass,*" I said with my best Texas drawl and nodding toward the weapon in the rifle rack.

"Peace through strength," Scheerer said with a wry smirk and a wink as he sipped his coffee again. We continued driving through Nordeast Minneapolis, the Polish part of town. On the other side of the Mississippi was North Minneapolis, long renowned as the black part of town, the mean streets. The long running local joke was that the span over the Mississippi connecting the two divergent parts of the city was the longest bridge in the world: It connected Poland to Africa.

116

As we turned and started heading towards downtown proper, we saw a black minister on a street corner. He was standing on a milk crate and yelling prophecies:

"KNOWLEDGE HAS SURPASSED THE SOUL," he shouted with a bible held over his head. *"THE WELL OF SOULS IS EMPTY AND THE TIME IS NIGH. GOD SHALL JUDGE A NATION BY HOW THAT NATION TREATED ISREAL. THE TIME IS NIGH."*

"Do you believe in God?" Scheerer asked after we passed the street corner minister.

"Well, I guess I'm what you'd call agnostic."

"You know what they say about agnostics, right?"

"What's that?" I asked.

"An agnostic is an atheist who's hedging his bets."

"Yes," I laughed. "I don't believe in the eternal lake of fire but I'm scared of it anyway."

We were driving through the industrial area near Broadway and Washington when Scheerer suddenly slammed on the brakes.

"Jeez! What'd ya do *that* for?" I implored, somewhat confused as I peeled myself off of the dashboard. He backed the truck up about 20 feet slammed on the brakes again and then threw the truck into park.

"Watch out," he said, frantically grabbing his rifle off the rack and bonking me in the back of the head with the barrel in the process.

"Ouch!" I said, grabbing my head.

Scheerer swung the door of the truck open and stepped out. He took up shooting position using the open door as a stable platform.

What in the hell is he doing?

"FREEZE! COUNTY DEPUTY!" he bellowed. I looked about 150 yards down the railroad tracks and saw a man struggling with a young woman. She was clearly in distress and the perp had his forearm around her throat from behind. It appeared as though he was trying to drag her into a warehouse.

"God, help me!" the woman squealed.

"I SAID *FREEZE*, MISTER," Scheerer yelled again.

The man kept on.

"Shit!" Scheerer whispered as he took a breath and leaned into the scope. How could he hope to hit anything with accuracy? The two were still struggling and they were almost to the warehouse door, after that it would be out of our hands.

We had been given strict orders that we were not to act as police or vigilantes, only to respond to actions readily before us and assist uniformed peacekeepers when applicable – ABSOLUTELY NOTHING MORE THAN THAT. A couple of county workers from a different department had chased some bad guys back in May and wound up walking into an ambush. They were killed and their bodies looted.

The perp and the victim were close to the door. Scheerer looked relaxed. They were almost inside … another three feet. I didn't think that Scheerer was going to fire – he was utterly motionless, a statue.

BLAM!

The crack of the .308 made me jump. Damn, that was loud. The off-white warehouse wall behind the two struggling people became instantly splattered with what I thought was an obscenely gigantic cone of blood spray.

In the movies, people who get shot always take awhile to fall down. In the movies, people stand there for ten dramatic seconds "in shock" while they absorb the fact that they've been shot, and then they fall over. But this was real life. Both people instantly fell to the ground like a couple of dropped bowling balls. *Scheerer killed both of them,* I thought. I just watched death first-hand.

But there was movement. From afar we could tell that the woman was wrestling the dead man's arm from around her neck and struggling to get to her feet. Once upright, she turned and gave the corpse a healthy kick in the torso, just for good measure.

"You okay over there?" Scheerer yelled.

"I'm fine. Thanks you guys," she said as casual as could be with a giant wave of her arm.

"You need a ride or anything?"

"No, I'm okay!"

She brushed off her clothing and ran her hands through her hair. Whoever she was, she was one tough little chick. Scheerer clicked the rifle back to "safe" and placed it back in the rack. We drove down the tracks to where the man lay and got out of the truck. I'd never seen the dead body of someone who had just been shot before.

The round from Scheerer's rifle had entered the man's upper right chest and blown out the back. His mouth was loosely ajar and his eyes were half-open and slightly crossed, clearly devoid of life. Scheerer sat back in the cab of the truck with one foot on the ground as he picked up his cell and hit a speed-dial number.

"Yeah, this is Scheerer. County 1024. Request dead body pickup on Second Street, one block North of Broadway. Yeah, that's right, right off Washington. Victim is a male, dark features and red windbreaker with a gunshot wound to the upper torso. He's near the warehouse right off the railroad tracks … alright, out here," and with that, he casually hung up. He swung his other leg into the pickup and closed the door.

Then he took a breath and shook his head just a bit. "I hate doing that," he said in a near whisper as he eyed the corpse. He turned to the woman; "You're sure you're okay?"

"Yes, thanks again, guys."

From a distance, any woman is a damsel in distress, but up close this gal was what I would guess to have been a crackwhore even before The Attack.

"You ain't so damn tough now, are you, Rodney?" she yelled at the dead body. She simply spun around and resumed walking.

"Shit," I said, "and I thought today was gonna be an easy day."

"The only easy day is yesterday," Scheerer said.

Scheerer was clearly disturbed but did his best not to express it. He took another few moments to compose himself, took a deep sigh, and then put the truck in gear and continued driving.

Body removal had become an exercise in impersonal, detached garbage disposal. Civil defense had posted the body removal phone number everywhere: It was casually known as the Dead Body Hotline. Expedient corpse removal was necessary to prevent the spread of disease, not to mention getting rid of that nasty-ass smell of a rotting summer corpse. You could never be sure what kind of vehicle would show up after you placed the call; sometimes it was an ambulance, sometimes a hearse, sometimes an orange dump truck. The latter seemed to be reserved for multiple body pick-ups and shitty neighborhoods. Sometimes they zipped the deceased up in body bags and sometimes they just did the "one-two-three" heave into the vehicle.

When society breaks down, life turns cheap.

It was nasty business. It wasn't unusual for our crews to find dead bodies in and around the buildings we worked on every once in a while. Once we entered a structure and found three stinking bodies absolutely boiling with maggots, eyeballs eaten out and swirling with larval movement. I felt sorry for the poor bastards stuck on body removal.

They brought the bodies to the old armory downtown. It had been converted into a mass-processing center for the dead unless specifically designated for an operating funeral home. Corpses were quickly searched for ID. If there was no identification, the bodies were weighed, measured, X-rayed for dental characteristics, had front/side/oblique photos taken of the head no matter how decomposed or traumatized, and had hair and fluid samples taken. It was all categorized and filed and bodies burned immediately thereafter. Women, children, men, white, black, wealthy or street thug – it simply didn't matter. We, American humans, had become so much trash, our bodies an inconvenience to be dealt with quickly if not robotically. That was the fate that awaited the corpse of the man that Scheerer shot.

Later that day, I came home and parked in the back of my building. I noticed that one of the ground floor apartment windows had been broken out. It was a unit belonging to one of the residents who had fled the city. I yelled inside but there was no response. After hopping through the window, I got a chance to look around. Someone had been squatting in the apartment. There was a dirty sleeping bag laid out in the bedroom and signs of food consumption, crumbs and wrappers. Whoever slept here was out and about. He wasn't there the next morning when I left for work either.

The next day, I convinced Scheerer to stop at the apartment as our first stop of the day. We looked quasi-official with our hardhats and orange vests as we ducked into the unit through the unsecured window. Sure enough, upon entering the bedroom we found a scummy-looking dude who appeared to be in his mid-twenties. Skinny, with a pointy nose and longish, greasy hair, he clearly needed a shower. The smell of funk and hopelessness wafting from him was enough to make you feel as if your own life was about to go down the tubes just by standing near him.

"All right, buddy, move on outta here," I said.

"Aw, man, I ain't hurtin nothin. Can't you let me stay here?" He was lucid and alert and I was glad that he wasn't whacked on drugs or alcohol.

"Negative," I said, trying to sound as authoritative as possible. "The structure is being secured. Grab your belongings and hit the road." I didn't want him to know that I actually lived there.

"*Motherfuck*," he muttered under his breath as he quickly rolled up his sleeping bag. We escorted him to the window and one of the other guys on the crew offered a hand and helped him, Scheerer and I followed.

"What the hell am I supposed to do now?" he asked, turning to us.

"That's not our problem," I said. "Go on now, get moving on down the street."

The man's head dropped and he slowly turned around and headed down the alley.

"Hold on there, Sparky," Scheerer said suddenly.

The man stopped and looked back.

"You got something to eat today?" asked Scheerer.

"No, not really."

Scheerer poked his torso into the cab of his pickup and came out with a Mountain Dew and an unopened medium bag of Cheetos. He walked over and handed them to the squatter.

"Oh, man, *thank you!*" he said to Scheerer, truly grateful.

"That's alright," Scheerer said gently. "You get on outta here now, okay?"

"Yessir!" said the squatter. He turned and shuffled out of the parking lot and down the alley, his mood noticeably buoyed.

"Well, that was darn neighborly," I said after the homeless dude was out of sight. Scheerer could have just let the guy wander on down the alley.

"We just took the guy's home. So, listen, you want to board up this unit or what?"

"Yeah."

Right then, Lee the manager came walking out of the back door.

"What's going on, Dallas?"

"Lee, this is my supervisor, Dan Scheerer," I said introducing the two.

"How's it going?" Scheerer said as the two men shook hands.

"Okay, still on this side of the dirt," Lee said.

Scheerer nodded in a knowing understanding. "Listen, we were going to board up the one unit here," said Scheerer as he glanced at his wristwatch. "We could go ahead and board up all the basement apartments if you'd like," he offered Lee. I was surprised.

Lee was dumbstruck, too. "Uh, yeah. That'd be great!"

It *would* be great; the ground floor of our building was half-sunken, so the windows were quite accessible to squatters – obviously – and other intruders. We went to work and had boarded up and secured the windows of all three apartment units and the laundry room within two hours. Then we anchored concertina razor-wire to the outside wall near the back door and ran it around and stopping at the front door, then repeated the process around the other side. The only access points to our building now were the front and the back doors. If another person tried to break and enter, they'd get pretty scratched up by the concertina and the damage to our boarding would be evident. We had our own little fortress and felt quite secure in the building after that.

Later that night, I thought about Scheerer. Probably the toughest man in the Gulag, he never swore or drank much, not that I can recall anyway. But I saw him grease a man with a deer rifle one day and feed a vagabond the next. When I asked him to board up my apartment building, I figured for sure he'd say no. He agreed without hesitating a second. Was he atoning for killing the guy on the railroad tracks? I had to think about that.

ELEVEN

We had a young National Guard Sgt. E-5 named Fred Zampoli detached to us as some sort of low-level military liaison. Fred was originally from *Noo Yark*. He had come to Minnesota for alcohol treatment a few years back and never left. He got a transfer from the New York Guard to the Minnesota Guard. Fred was authorized to sign out materials from us for military use. In return, we were to go through him if we had any need for anything that might involve the military. We had no idea what they meant by that, at least I didn't.

We also worked loosely in tandem with some guys from the Department of Energy sometimes. Federal government guys set up and monitored radiation detectors all over the metropolitan area. Sometimes they traveled with our crews for safety and navigation. They were usually out-of-towners so they didn't know the city very well. It was an economical use of time and effort for them to hook up with us lowly local worker types.

The feds had discreetly set up NBC detectors on cell phone towers all over the country in the two years prior to The Attack. Why cell phone towers? Because they tended to best track the general population's living and movement patterns. It wasn't long before they registered higher-than-normal readings.

Decontamination would be a major undertaking, especially if radiation readings reached dangerous levels. Radiological defense manuals, published by the government, suggested hosing down or sweeping driveways and sidewalks, plowing and scraping radiation from the garden areas, vacuuming carpets and washing clothing in a washing machine. Our radiation problem wasn't really all that bad. Yes, it was higher than normal but not at a level that could cause health problems. But the on-going latent threat did wear on the mind.

Because of the latent threat of contamination, however, we had to take potassium iodide, chemical name KI, which is much more familiar to most people than they might first suspect.

"It's the ingredient added to your table salt to make it iodized salt," as one of the feds, Phil Kleinhoffer, told us.

Potassium Iodide is approximately 76.5 percent iodine. The government distributed enough doses for the population. Being in the city and working for the county, we were among the first to receive tablets. But with so many citizens scattered all throughout rural America, there was a concern that not everybody would get the appropriate dosages.

The U.S. Food and Drug Administration said that KI was "safe and effective for use in radiological emergencies" back in the seventies during the Cold War and approved its over-the-counter sale. In late 2004, the FDA said that KI was a safe and effective means by which to prevent radioiodine uptake by the thyroid gland, under certain specified conditions of use, and thereby substantially reduce the risk of thyroid cancer in the event of a nuclear or radiation emergency. So we had *that* going for us.

Kleinhoffer told us some stories after work one day while we were all hanging out in the yard sipping on beers. Phil Kleinhoffer was another nuclear Ph.D. guy, but seemed to have a little more personality than some of the others.

It was a warm summer's eve as the long shadows of tall buildings crept through the Gulag and the sun cast orangish-red light on everything else. Dr. Kleinhoffer sat perched on the hood of a Hummer, Budweiser in hand. There were about a dozen of us gathered around him like disciples, hanging on his every word.

"Back in '66, the Chinese blew off this big nuke and it resulted in a fallout cloud that covered most of the United States," Kleinhoffer said.

"No way," said Bernie Olsen, a grumpy old dispatcher. "I don't remember anything like that."

"Anyway, this one Chinese explosion produced about 15 million curies of iodine."

"What does that mean?" Brian asked.

"Well, put it this way; fallout from the approximately 300 kiloton Chinese test explosion caused milk from cows that fed on pastures near Oak Ridge, Tennessee, to be contaminated."

"You're shitting us … "

"No, I'm not. It wasn't contaminated to dangerous levels but the point is that just *one* bomb on the other side of the planet had contaminated milk of cows in the United States. That blew our minds. Now, we've had *seven* atomic events in our own country, plus the one in Europe, just to add the radiation factor to the jet stream for good measure."

The guys and I were riveted to Kleinhoffer's every word. A couple more guys would come up every few minutes and start to quietly listen. Kleinhoffer was holding court.

"What's it like to get radiation sickness?" Boone asked.

"Well, the first symptoms of radiation sickness would be nausea, vomiting, headache, dizziness and a general feeling of illness. Exposure to radiation is measured in rads. Very few people receiving acute doses of less than a hundred rad would get sick, even briefly. But, under post-attack conditions of stress and deprivation, some people who were exposed to acute radiation doses of a hundred to two-hundred rad could die of infectious diseases because of their reduced resistance."

"Will you get sick if you're exposed to more than that?" someone asked from the back.

"Sure, but for the most part, the human body usually can repair almost all radiation damage if the daily doses aren't too large. The majority of folks with acute doses of less than about 350 rad can recover without medical treatment."

"What about bad cases?" Boone followed up.

"In the final phase of a bad case of exposure the victims of fatal radiation sickness will usually suffer from reduced resistance to infections along with diarrhea, loss of hair in clumps and small hemorrhages of the skin, mouth and intestinal tract. Diarrhea from common causes are easy to confuse with radiation sickness, but hemorrhages and the loss of large clumps of hair are pretty good signs of serious radiation exposure."

Damn.

"The final phase usually lasts for one to two months," Kleinhoffer continued. "For thousands of other folks, the large radiation doses that they received from the nuclear attacks are sure to result in serious long-term cases of death from cancer. That's probably what's gonna happen to the people who were in close proximity to the blasts."

"Where'd the terrorists get the bombs?" someone asked.

"Anyone hear of MS-13?"

A couple people mumbled affirmative.

"MS-13 is an organized crime gang that helped the terrorists smuggle people and technology across the border of Mexico. We knew about that, we figured they were bringing in suitcase nukes. We knew al Qaeda had this 'American Hiroshima' scenario in mind."

"But?" I asked.

"Those weren't suitcase nukes that went off around the county. Freakin suitcase nukes are firecrackers compared to the kilotonage that went off on April first."

"So how could the terrorists get so much useable nuclear material?" I asked.

"There were rumors that the Soviet Special Forces – *Spetznatz* – pre-positioned some hefty nukes on U.S. soil during the Cold War. Word was that al Qaeda was paying big bucks to former Spetznatz and Soviet technicians to disclose where those bombs were."

"Would they still be usable?"

"As they were? After that many years? No. Even an idle nuclear bomb needs upkeep. The nuclear triggers decay very quickly, especially the tritium ones. Which makes me wonder if the terrorists built one or more of the bombs from scratch, too. It'd be a pain in the ass, but it can be done."

"Where would they get the materials?"

"Well," Kleinhoffer said thoughtfully and sipped his Bud before continuing. "I'm just guessing, but one way would be theobacillus ferrooxidans," he said.

That's the problem with super-intelligent people: They don't realize that their speech patterns are often about ten feet over the heads of us normal folks.

"Thero … *what?*" Boone queried on behalf of us all with squinted eyes.

"*Theobacillus ferrooxidans.* One way to refine impure materials is with a certain bacteria called theobacillus ferrooxidans. It oxidizes metal sulfides. Essentially, it eats bad dirt and rocks and leaves behind good ores and metals."

"So the terrorists could get ahold of any shitty leftover radioactive material and turn it into useable … *uh …*"

"Fissile material? Yes, pretty much. It's very time consuming, though. I'm talking years, and it's inefficient to refine that way, but it allows poor-grade ores to produce high-grade uranium that would otherwise be unavailable. They could make a gun-style nuke with it."

"*Zat iz* un-fucking-believable," Lebenze offered.

"You got that right. The process is a poor man's refinery. It provides materials needed to produce a weapon of mass destruction. We had a loose idea how much weapons grade material was out on the market and, trust me, we didn't think the terrorist world had enough for ten nukes."

"Guess you were wrong, *oui?*" Lebenze said, trying not to be disrespectful.

"They got the material from somewhere, that's all I'm saying," Kleinhoffer said with a humble shake of his head. "And, yes, we were wrong."

"How'd they know how to build the bombs? Off the internet or something?" asked Zampoli.

"That's a good question: First off, these are highly intelligent people we're dealing with here, not some Third-world dunces blowing off shit-bombs at the side of the road. For a nuclear detonation to occur, nuclear triggers make multiple events happen within nano-seconds and compress sub-critical pieces together in just the right configuration. It's really tough. They want to loosen neutrons which will then, in turn, bump other neutrons, called 'doubling' or 'Alpha,' and thus creating the nuclear chain reaction."

"Aahhh ..." several guys said at once as though they suddenly and thoroughly understood nuclear physics.

"The elements have to be brought together in a specific form, and then a compression of the entire mass of stellar proportions must take place very quickly after that. That's usually done with conventional high explosives. The conventional charges *must* all go off at the exact same nano-second to create the density and configuration necessary for an atomic doubling."

"What happens if they don't go off at the same time?" Zampoli asked.

"You'll get a dud or a fizzle. An uneven triggering explosive force will instantly misshape the carefully shaped core area. That would prevent the weapon from reaching critical mass. That's why sometimes a nuclear weapon can 'explode' with no subsequent nuclear event."

"Are you shitting us?"

"Again, I'm not. Once the rocket portion of a nuclear missile exploded in its silo out in Nevada. The damned warhead landed two miles away but there was no nuclear explosion."

"How can that be?" Boone posed the question that we were all contemplating.

"The necessarily huge levels of compression at just the right moment were not achieved. Nowhere close. In other cases, a bomb designed to detonate at a yield of 20 kilotons may only go off as two kilotons. A multi-step series of events must occur in chronological order within a couple nano-seconds, a nano-second being one-billionth of one second, in order for a full-capacity nuclear event to occur."

"Merde ..." Lebenze uttered.

"Unless ..." the Ph.D. mused.

"Unless what?" Boone asked.

"There's also a method for creating critical mass called 'gun style,' I mentioned that a minute ago. You just shoot a piece of fissile material into another piece – literally through a gun barrel – and if you do it right, it will cause a nuclear detonation. I could build one with a high school science class if I had the materials."

"Yo, Dr. Kleinhoffer?" said Stubbs.

"Yeah."

"Is it true the feds think that the terrorists might get ahold of airliners and explode a nuke up in the air?"

"It's true that we – 'we' being the federal government – had a fear that aircraft with nuclear weapons might be used as aerial weapons. I'm not really in that particular loop, but I think that they're going to ease up on altitude restrictions pretty soon."

"What would be so bad about an explosion in the air? It's better than a ground blast, isn't it?"

"You mean because of the radiation generated by a ground blast and all the fallout?"

"Yeah."

"Well, aside from the lack of excessive radioactive fallout, nuclear airblasts are pretty vicious animals," Kleinhoffer said.

"How so?" asked Boone.

"There are three main effects from a nuke going off; blast wave, light radiation and radioactivity. A surface blast is obscured and diffused by buildings and ground clutter. A lot of the blast energy bounces right off the earth and just goes straight up into the sky. Very inefficient. But it's a different animal when it's up in the air. A nuke has unfettered blast and light-radiation effect when it goes off up in the sky. A large percentage of the energy creates a destructive blast wave and causes a lot more damage. Then you also got a lot more light radiation."

"What's that?" said Zampoli.

"That's the burning caused by the brilliance of the explosion itself. On a clear day, people exposed to a blast at a distance of 15 to 20 miles would be blistered, and from 20 to 25 miles they would get a nasty and very painful sunburn. Any closer and it's lethal radiation or getting fried to death. For sheer destruction, a nuclear weapon should be detonated at an altitude around 2,000 feet for maximum effect."

"What if it were a cloudy day?"

"All the better. They would want to detonate right below any overcast so that light-radiation could reflect off the bottoms of the clouds and create a double-burn effect."

133

"How's that?" Zampoli followed-up.

"For a split second before they evaporated, the bottoms of the clouds would act just like a mirror. You'd get *twice* the light-radiation burn if a nuke were detonated right underneath the cloud ceiling."

"Dat's fucked up," Stubbs crudely said with a shake of his head. Everyone mumbled in agreement.

"I'll tell you guys one more little tidbit of bad news as long as we're on the subject. You all know we interdicted two nukes on American soil, right?"

"Yeah," came a collective answer.

"So do you think the terrorists went seven-for-seven on their remaining nukes?"

"What are you getting at?" asked Boone.

"What I'm saying is that statistically speaking, if they were successful in detonating seven nukes, that means anywhere from three to, oh say, another six or seven bombs didn't go off."

The group went almost silent. Finally Scheerer spoke up.

"You mean, more cities were supposed to go up?"

"It's a certainty. You just don't realize the maintenance, the preparation, the delicate series of events that needs to take place to detonate a nuke. There's no flippin way those ass-clowns detonated seven out of seven nuclear bombs, no way. There had – or should I say *has* – to be more nukes on our soil."

"Wouldn't our gamma detectors find'em?" I asked.

"Well, that's what we're doing now."

The group continued asking questions and the Ph.D. kept answering. Kleinhoffer was a hit with the guys in the Gulag. What started as a bunch of dudes relaxing after a hard day's work turned into an impromptu tutorial from Professor Kleinhoffer. He entertained and educated us for two full hours that evening with facts and stories about nuclear weapons and technology. Everyone down to a man was mesmerized and I felt like I'd learned more in those two hours than I had in the last ten years of my life.

TWELVE

Water conservation had become a high priority, so we couldn't wash away our radiation problems by going around hosing everything down. The feds' cleansing goal was summed up in the acronym ALARA: As Low As Reasonably Achievable. The county had the foresight the year before to order hand pumps through Amish catalogs that would pump from as deep as 200 feet. Real estate and architectural firms were obligated under federal law to provide engineers and architects to lay the plans for emergency infrastructure needs.

We had a different guy from the feds detached to our county who was in charge of measuring radiation, a nerdy guy with no personality whatsoever. He was very interested in seeing if the natural rainfall contained any radiation. The odd thing was that sometimes it did, sometimes it didn't. As a result, it was a standard operating procedure to seek shelter immediately when the rains came. It was a relatively dry summer so we relished the few thunderous downpours that we had.

Mother Nature does sometimes clean herself. When the clean rains came, the heavy precipitation rinsed down the roofs of houses and the sides of buildings. It cleansed the leaves of trees and the bushes and the grass. It washed our cars and trucks and then flowed like little rivers into the sewage systems and then into the Mississippi River.

Rain, sweet rain. (As long as it was free of too much radiation.)

Procuring the basic staples of life was disappointing and problematic because trucking and shipping of goods had become spotty. On a larger scale, international trade and shipping trickled and then stopped completely within days of April first. As far as we knew, trains had largely stopped running. Many semi trucks were used for relocating. Some truckers trying to move commercial goods got hijacked and killed, their loads pillaged.

Executive Order10998 allowed the government to take over all food resources and farms. Executive Order 10990 allowed the government to take over all modes of transportation and control of highways and seaports. However, with seven cities smoldering in radioactive ruin, it was understandable that the central government might take the position that us folks in cities that weren't attacked would have to, in large part, fend for ourselves. There was a national priority of events that had to be addressed in sequence and we in Minneapolis weren't anywhere near the top of that list.

Back in Minneapolis, gas stations and businesses started clubs. You could only shop or get goods if the proprietors knew you. Corner grocery stores often had armed guards, a trusted employee or the owner's son. My haunt, the Kaiserhof, stopped letting new folks come in. There was a select group of 35 people, including me, who could patronize the place.

Bottled water and canned foods had become nearly non-existent in the market place within the first month after The Attack. Some organizations had purchased and stored military food rations as emergency food supplies in the event of severe weather, ice storms, blizzards or other emergency situations. The county had pallets and pallets of MRE's (Meals Ready to Eat), which are the battlefield meals for the armed forces. They were edible but they were what they were – prepackaged food for soldiers in combat. The guys started to call them "Meals Rejected by Ethiopia." MRE's came in tough little plastic pouches and could be warmed in many ways. You could microwave them obviously, or cook them as if they were conventional food. We would sometimes put them in a pan of warm water for five to ten minutes.

But we were out in the field all the time so we had to come up with other methods. The newer MRE's came along with their own little chemical heaters but you didn't always get one. It didn't take long to discover that we could lay the dark heat-collecting pouch in direct sunlight, allowing it to warm, a trick one of the guys learned when he fought in Iraq. He also told us that in the colder months we could put an unopened pouch inside our shirts, allowing body temperature to warm the food inside – clever stuff. That might very well come in handy in the coming winter. Although the pouches were reasonably sturdy and durable containers, they could be damaged if too high of a temperature were applied. One of the young guys tried to warm up a pouch of food over an open flame and incinerated his meal.

As it turns out, a friend of the Scheerer family was the comptroller for the major MRE manufacturer to the Department of Defense and had been talking to him about letting the county buy a truckload of MRE entrees, not the whole package. The main meal entrees, usually meat and eight ounces each, came 72 pouches to a case and are the main course of the full MRE meal.

Negotiations on price and quantity were completed in the first week of June and Scheerer got approval on the finances from the county. The food pouches were manufactured in Texas. I-35W went straight from Minneapolis all the way down to the Lone Star state, so the guy drew up a distribution route that brought shipments straight north, all based on his friendship with Scheerer.

The first MRE cases arrived in the second week. A second truckload arrived June 14 and we now had about 2,000 total cases of the different menus. They were all new, recent manufacture, with nothing older than the previous summer's production. That was unusual because MRE's offered for sale to the public are, more often than not, surplus or a stock rotation many years old. These were the primary main meal entree, not the more expensive full meal pack with the side dishes, crackers, napkins, spoons, etc. The entree menu flavors came in a nice variety; country captain chicken, beef enchilada, meat loaf, beef with mushroom, Jamaican pork chop, turkey breast and more. The variety was nice. It was very easy to appreciate the simple pleasures in life.

Because of slightly elevated ambient radiation readings, by protocol we had to act as if a full-scale nuclear war had taken place. It was kind of a pain in the ass. Before opening canned or packaged food, the package had to be wiped or washed. Fruits and vegetables harvested from fallout zones in the first month post-attack needed to be decontaminated before consuming. Decontamination could be accomplished by simply washing exposed parts, removing outer leaves and peeling. Soft foods such as strawberries and raspberries were not to be eaten. If contaminated, they would have absorbed radiation through and through.

However, a deficiency of vitamin C could cause symptoms of scurvy within four to six weeks. A good expedient way to get this vitamin is to eat sprouted seeds or beans or citrus fruits. Or vitamin C tablets, of course. I thought of the old stories of pirate-era sailors eating limes and oranges in order to prevent scurvy and rickets. We'd be okay, though. As a county employee, we got food and soft drinks whenever we went on duty.

Services and facilities died slow deaths as some of their stewards fled to rural areas. By presidential order, the absent workers could have been incarcerated or even shot, but who was going to hunt them down? For government workers and peacekeepers, there simply weren't enough hours in the day to do even half of what needed to be done.

Some cell phone services stopped working – mine, for instance. A lot of the county guys had the cell phones with the walkie-talkie feature. The walkie-talkie seemed to sometimes work even if the cell function didn't. Garbage and debris littered every street, alley and boulevard. We sometimes had to go on garbage detail but there was no keeping up with the litter blowing into every nook and cranny of the urban landscape. I developed a whole new respect for the friendly neighborhood garbage collector now that he was gone.

Public parks and private lawns became overgrown with weeds and unkempt shrubbery. Critters of all sorts roamed around with increasing bravery. Raccoons are nocturnal animals, so one that was walking around in the daylight was probably insane from rabies. Every now and then we'd see one lumbering around the streets – big suckers.

And the water? Sometimes the water came out of the tap just fine, other times it would come out green or brown, smelly and undrinkable. Sometimes it wouldn't come out at all. Obviously, things were not business-as-usual down at the water treatment plant. If you were smart, you bottled as much water as you could on the days when the water was good.

Landline telephones were more stable than the other utilities but they could still go out for a day here and there. Life was difficult when compared to living with the everyday luxuries that people had simply taken for granted before The Attack.

Overall, nearly half – or perhaps more than half – of the fatalities nationwide were directly attributable to causes other than the bombs. What were the causes of post-attack mortality? According to government reports on the TV, the main thing was exposure. It was a sweltering summer and the sick, the weak and the elderly perished on a regular basis because of frequent power loss – no air conditioning. There was also a shortage of emergency medical care. People died from complications that had resulted from things like moderately bad car accidents or acute maladies like appendicitis.

In addition, there were the plague-like infestations such as SARS, West Nile virus, Asian bird flu, encephalitis, influenza, typhoid, malnutrition, hantavirus pulmonary syndrome, lyme disease and dysentery. While not always fatal in and of themselves, they had an antagonizing effect on the human spirit, particularly in the elderly and the severely wounded, a condition that doctors called "failure to thrive."

Proper management of toilet facilities during times of emergency would have a greater effect on health than any other single element of sanitation. The federal government went out of its way to communicate these things to us. Bacterial infections such as typhoid and dysentery could be just as devastating as the bombs that caused the emergency situation. Dysentery is simply defined as diarrhea containing blood. Although several organisms can cause dysentery, shigellas are the most important. Shigella dysenteriae type 1, or *Sd1*, which is also known as the Shiga bacillus. The modes of transmission tended to be person-to-person contact or contaminated water and food. Once they showed signs of the malady, many thought they had radiation poisoning, which only served to add to the mayhem and discontent.

In addition to bloody diarrhea, the illness caused by Sd1 often included abdominal cramps, fever and rectal pain. Less frequent complications of infection with Sd1 included sepsis, seizures, kidney failure and the haemolytic uraemic syndrome. Approximately five to 15 percent of Sd1 cases tended to be fatal; it was therefore of the utmost importance to take care of human waste. We couldn't count on ongoing toilet usage and, besides, sometimes the water worked and sometimes not. Excessive toilet flushing was frowned upon. We were given field-expedient instructions on how to deal with human waste.

The means of disease-related mortality could be looked upon as being more of the natural: It resulted naturally from the breakdown of the infrastructure that society depended on for day-to-day existence. The luxuries of modern life, it could be argued, had made people weak over generations. I found life to be difficult and wondered how pioneer people or pilgrims or Indians – pick your group from history – managed to live and flourish. Now a person practically had to plan the next bowel movement like they used to plan a weekend camping trip.

THIRTEEN

There was lawlessness. The effects of anarchy could not be ignored. As if the general plight weren't challenging enough, there were elements of society that relished mayhem. There were those who thrived on a life with no rules and no expectations, living merely existentially, following the most basic impulses of their reptilian brains with no compassion or empathy for other humans. We'd already seen examples of the behavior during the infamous riots of America's past. There are people who will destroy their own neighborhoods because, they say, they are oppressed. Me, I've never figured out that logic.

There was a palpable and steady increase in violent crimes against people. There were simply people in society who regressed to an almost animalistic way of living, seemingly surviving only moment-to-moment, hour-to-hour. We had heard of horrific stories of innocent people being killed and their bodies being stripped of every stitch of clothing and property.

Sometimes people killed for robbery and sometimes they killed for "score settling." If someone felt wronged by another in the past, the times were ripe to exact revenge. Hell, I was a pretty normal guy and even I was seriously considering murdering my old boss, Erik Johnson. Why? 'Cause I just might be able to pull it off. And I felt like it.

Within about ten weeks, violent street crime had directly or indirectly touched everybody. Our department had the newly-inherited duty of going around putting up posters that warned of harsh penalties for unruly behavior, but in the end it didn't seem to matter.

Some of the self-proclaimed meek thought that The Attack was their cue to start "inheriting the Earth." The news showed footage and interviews of white supremacist groups and radical African-Americans in other parts of the country who were arming to the teeth because they thought that some idiotic long-awaited "race war" was now upon us. Religious nuts were outnumbered only by different theories of the apocalypse.

Women wore whistles around their necks. The prudent person just assumed that the stranger on the street was armed and intent on causing harm. Conversely, it was not uncommon for the police or the military to blow civilians away before a situation could escalate. Shoot first and ask questions later. Simple city driving was hazardous as well. Fender benders or road-rage incidents sometimes escalated quickly into shoot-outs or outright murders if one of the principles was unarmed.

The Violent Crime Control Act of 1991 provided additional powers to the President of the United States, allowing the suspension of the constitution and constitutional rights of Americans during a crisis, which he'd already done. The act also provided for the construction of detention camps and the feds were laying the groundwork for doing just that. City and county jails released almost everybody except the most violent offenders – they were making space for a whole new crop of vicious perpetrators surely to come. The freshly sprung low-level criminals found themselves on government work detail. They were warned that if they went AWOL, the guard was authorized to summarily execute them. I don't know if that was really true or not.

The loss of cops and military personnel to death and desertion become problematic in the city. Unattacked cities like Minneapolis were allotted skeleton crews of police and military resources; God knows they were desperately needed in other parts of the country far worse than we needed them. As an employee of the government, one of the county commissioners told us that some of us were to be deputized. People were picked based on age, education, temperament and recommendations of superiors. Scheerer had submitted Boone, Stubbs and me to be armed deputies.

We were just laborers, but there we were down at city hall getting sworn in as peace officers. Guys like us weren't expected to respond to calls of public duress, but rather we were supposed to react to incidents that we personally witnessed and/or assist uniformed peacekeepers. Failure to assist would be dealt with harshly, a warning issued to us over and over.

A police officer named Marty Klevens came over from the Fifth Minneapolis Precinct and gave us a series of very nominal classes in protocol and restraining subjects. There wasn't a lot spoken about Miranda rights or constitutional due-process. I wasn't planning on apprehending anyone, but I did get a 9mm with shoulder holster and an "after dark permit." The permit alone was worth the deputyship. I'd been hassled more than once by over-zealous cops or guardsman if I got caught out at dusk. With the after dark permit, I just flashed my credentials and ID and the harassment stopped. We had to come in that Saturday with some deputy candidates from other departments for an eight-hour class on shooting, gun safety and a rules-of-engagement briefing.

It was about 7:00 on a Tuesday morning. Scheerer called us deputized workers into a side office and gave us some standing orders: "Now that you cowboys are armed, you have an extra little duty: Shoot raccoons and dogs with distemper. If you see a raccoon during the day, shoot it. Raccoons are nocturnal which means if you see one during the day, he is probably deranged from the effects of rabies. Understand? Also, if you see a dog and even think he might have rabies, shoot it. Got it?"

Yes, we all mumbled.

"Watch your backgrounds. We don't want to accidentally shoot some citizen and start a damn riot or anything."

After that, we went out for the morning roll call and were given duty assignments and the safety-intelligence briefing, tips for the day, hot spot parts of town, latest violent blotter-report incidents, stuff like that.

FOURTEEN

I met a girl at the Kaiserhof.

It was about six o'clock on a Friday night after a particularly stressful week of labor and five of us, including Lebenze, had gone down for some libations. I was intent on inebriation that particular evening at the Kaiserhof. *Why the hell not?* I figured.

The first Pilsner had gone down like water, as had the second. About two sips into my third I noticed a decent buzz hitting. A couple guys filtered out after a drink or two, a couple guys got wrapped up in conversation with another group at the bar and soon I found myself all alone. Being a lone wolf at heart, that was fine with me.

I continued quaffing. My head started swimming, ever so pleasantly. People conversed, told stories, chuckled and drank all around. No one bothered me and I kept to myself, honing my life-long practice of being alone in a roomful of people. The din was hypnotic as I lost myself in thought while the beers went down.

I casually glanced out the window separating the bar from the courtyard as I was starting my fourth Urquell and that's when I saw her. She was just standing there all alone. She had dark hair, dark brown eyes and a firm build. She wore comfortable jeans, suede shoes and an untucked short-sleeve shirt that matched her socks. Nothing fancy but enough to show that she still cared about her appearance. She

147

wore no makeup; her features were naturally beautiful enough. Who was she? What in the hell was she doing in this bar? In this neighborhood? In this *city*? I thought they had cut off letting new people come in, and I'd never seen her before.

Single young women in town were quite rare. I was cocksure that this woman must have had a companion. Certainly she was waiting on someone who was using the restroom or getting a couple more drinks from the bar inside. But as the minutes ticked by, subtleties of her body language led me to believe that, indeed, the woman was there all by herself. I decided to approach her before Lebenze could spot her and lay his '*byoo-tee-fool ice*' line on her. I decided to approach her.

Don't act like a nerd. Be different. Be interesting. Don't act too interested. Talk slow ... move slow ... act like you don't care if she talks to you or not ... that will make her attracted to you.

I walked up to her and fired away with the first thing that came to my mind.

"So, d'you come here often?" *Oh crap, could I have possibly been any less imaginative that that?*

"Just hanging out. How 'bout yourself?" she said. She seemed friendly enough.

"Same thing. By the way, my name is Dallas," I said as I stretched out my hand. She shook it. I casually leaned against one of the four-by-four posts that supported the overhead trellises. I thought there was a pretty good chance I might be looking cool.

"I'm Sarah," she said.

"Huh ... ya know, I come here pretty often but I've never seen you before."

"Everybody's gotta be somewhere. I'm here," she said, somewhat pragmatically.

We engaged in the regular small talk and within minutes learned that she was 28-years-old and had been working as an editorial assistant or proofreader for some downtown publishing company before The Attack. She had been a third-stringer for the women's basketball team at Mankato State when she was in college and the athletic training still showed. I wanted to keep talking to her.

"Can I get you something from the bar?" I asked her as I finished my beer.

"Sure," she finished off the bottle of beer she was working on. "One of these," she said holding up the empty bottle.

"You got it," I said and headed toward the bar. *"Ah'll be bock,"* I said in my stupid Arnold Schwarzenegger-voice. She laughed.

I was a little on the woozy side but I got two more beverages and headed back out. The whole re-supply mission had taken just a few minutes. I returned to my wooden post for a good, and increasingly-necessary, lean. Sarah was still there, alone and uncourted by any other potential suitors. I handed her the drink.

"Here you go," I said as I handed her a beer.

"So what is it that you do, Mr. Dallas?"

"No, Dallas is my first name," I corrected. "I work for the government, full-time job."

It was an ambiguously true statement: 'Working for the government' can be anything from being a super-spy to a lowly street sweeper, and I was pretty close to the street sweeper end of the spectrum.

"You actually work and earn money?" she said incredulously. I don't know if she was more surprised than impressed.

"Yes. Would you like to sit?" I said gesturing to an empty wrought-iron table.

"I'd love to," she said.

It was nice talking to a real girl. So many of the females left in the city were homeless crones or hardcore 'hood sistahs. There were scant few young women who weren't selling their bodies for twenty dollars, especially hanging out by themselves. I was sorry that I had started out the evening by slamming so many beers so quickly. Romance had not been high on my list of day-to-day priorities since April and I was quite thrilled to be engaged in verbal intercourse with such a pretty and single young woman. I wanted to act as though I had my wits about me.

"So tell me about yourself," I asked.

"Little ole' me? Well, I live near Uptown and ... that's about it. I live," she said with a shrug.

"Oh. So, you don't work, huh?" I said.

"Not really."

"Oh, well that could be a problem."

"Really?" she asked, a bit perplexed. "Why is that?"

"Well, how could you support us?" I asked with a serious tone. "If we get married, I would want to be a stay-at-home husband. Ya know, keep an eye on the TV and the fridge ... stuff like that."

Sarah laughed, a quiet but sincere little chuckle. "Seriously, daddy has money, so I don't really need to work," she said with humility.

"Ah. So what are you doing here?" I asked, truly amazed that she would be patronizing my humble hangout. "I'm not trying to be nosy, it's just strange that— "

"No, don't worry about it. I just came here for something to do, it's no big deal. I own a house nearby. I had heard about this place, that it was real nice and quiet. I've got nothing else to do. It's so wild around town, ya know?"

Yes, I did know.

"No boyfriend? No hubby?" I innocently queried as I lifted beer to mouth.

"No."

Yessss! No boyfriend! Outwardly I had no reaction. In my mind I pumped my fist in jubilation.

"How 'bout your family?"

"My family? My Dad lives in Texas with his new wife who could pass for my slightly older sister. And my Mom? She's trying to pickle her liver with white wine, probably as we speak. She lives out in Minnetonka but she's drunk anytime I try to call her."

I suddenly felt uncomfortable. Sarah obviously wasn't totally averse to drinking. She was drinking herself, but here I was drunk. Not stumbling, not bumbling, but I was well on my way and here she was complaining about her drunken mother out in the western suburbs.

"What about you, Dallas? What's your story?"

"Me?" I was glad that she changed the subject. "I'm 35, single, no kids, no wife, full-time job?"

"You describe yourself like a singles ad. I was waiting for you to say that you like long walks in the rain or some crap like that."

I laughed. A sense of humor, very good.

"Oh, yes," I chimed in, "*I enjoy nuclear decontamination and I know how to make ten different entrees out of the common Tabby cat,*" I said facetiously.

151

Sarah covered her mouth as she tried to contain her laughter. Whether she thought my silly joke was funny or not, she knew that a man feels greatly at ease if a woman laughs at his stupid jokes. I liked that.

My love life had been somewhat unremarkable up until The Attack. After spending my high school years as a shy and dateless young man, I entered college and started turning my life around, romantically speaking.

My first two years at the U were a blur of keg parties, pizza and pretty young coeds who were always all too willing to have sex. I have almost no memory of doing my coursework, but I chugged through those first few years with a respectable 3.25 GPA.

Then I had a couple long-term girlfriends over the last three years – my four-year degree took me just under six years. My love-slash-sex life after the U tended to consist of casual dating punctuated by the occasional three-month relationship here and the one-night screwing of a waitress there. Then there was the "Season of Celibacy," as I called my time in Antarctica.

Upon my return, it was back to casual relationships. I'd made it all the way into my thirties and never even came close to so much as getting engaged. Now I couldn't remember the last time I even seriously thought about a *relationship*.

But I'll tell you this: I liked this girl. I decided to slow down my rate of alcohol consumption. I didn't want to screw things up with some drunken gaffe.

FIFTEEN

I watched TV when I could, usually at John and Brian's house. It was *All Government, All the Time*; Executive Order 10995 allowed the government to seize and control the communications media, and seize they did. Tele-governance.

Ignoring southern coastal cities was a stroke of brilliance – or a lucky happenstance – on the terrorists' part. The season's hurricanes ravaged Miami, Savannah, Tampa/St. Pete and Corpus Christi: All cities lay in ruin with absolutely no federal aid to ease the pain of another round of disaster.

The western United States was ablaze and had been for weeks. Forest fires raged unchecked through California, Colorado, Arizona, New Mexico, Wyoming and Oregon. Asian bird flu snaked its way through society at a steady pace leaving a certain percentage of fatalities in its wake. West Nile virus had made its way to the upper Midwest and was now a genuine health-care crisis, especially since mosquito control was a non-existent priority for the government earlier in the summer. Nursing professionals were siphoned away from eldercare hospices and the old folks perished like flies. CDC and many health professionals from all over the country were busy helping survivors of the initial blasts, who knew when we would ever see them again?

Adding to that was a new, natural threat churning from within America itself. According to the USGS, there was increased hydrothermal and earthquake activity at the Norris Geyser Basin in Yellowstone Park, which suddenly took a huge step towards a worst-case scenario volcanic blast. It was conceivable that a disastrous eruption could cover the central United States in six inches of ash all the way to Chicago. Simply put, anyone living within six-hundred miles of Yellowstone National Park could find themselves sitting in the throes of a modern day Pompeii. As if fretting over nuclear blasts weren't enough, now the Earth itself was threatening to regurgitate all over us with suffocating ash. Worst-case scenario, that is.

Volcanic and nuclear blasts aside, we still had to grind the daily grist of maintaining a city: Garbage was an enemy that grew stronger and more menacing with each passing week. Aside from being unsightly, rubbish would sour, decompose and breed bacteria in addition to its normal characteristics of attracting insects and small animals. Garbage had to be carefully stored and handled if odor and insect nuisances were to be prevented. The head of county sanitation came to the Gulag to give a class on garbage along with a fed.

"Um, excuse me, my name is Bill Olsen from the county. The information that I'm about to share has come from CDC officials. We are joined today by Mike Berlander from the Centers for Disease Control," he gestured to a fed sitting at the side of the room. A single person applauded for a second or two.

"One of the ones that wasn't fried in The Attack?" came a sarcastic comment from the back, in reference to the nuking of Atlanta. I couldn't tell whose voice it was.

"Yes, one of the ones from an auxiliary location. As you can see, Mr. Berlander is in quite good health. Anyway," he began reading, "'Garbage should never be dumped on the ground because it will attract rats, skunks and other scavengers. If collection by authorities is not possible garbage may be buried in a hole deep enough to cover it with at least 18 to 24 inches of dirt, which will prevent insect breeding and discourage animals from digging it up.'"

Fascinating. *Yawn ...*

The guy had all the classroom presentation skills of a nervous fourth-grader. He kept his head down almost the whole time and read from laminated sheets.

"'Trash and rubbish may be burned in open yard areas or left at dumps established by local authorities. Cans should be flattened and bottles should be broken to reduce their bulk. The main intent, however, remains rodent control.'"

Well, hell, we were already promoting yard burning to help diminish the mosquito population and I'm sure it had the secondary effect of making life horrible for rodents trying to lurk around in there. Did this guy never get out and see the huge trash mounds constantly smoldering in Loring Park on the southern edge of downtown?

He continued: "'The rodents can carry hantavirus pulmonary syndrome, or HPS.'" The parade just never ended; disease was on the brink of launching an all-out war on humanity.

"What does *eet* do?" asked Lebenze.

"Uh," he flipped through some pages of notes. "It looks like the disease eventually causes the lungs to fill up with fluid if you get a bad case and it goes unchecked; you'll drown in your own body fluids while on dry land. All hantaviruses known to cause HPS are carried by the New World rats and mice, family ... *Muridae*, subfamily ... *Sigmo* ...*dontinae*," he squinted as he eeked out the words. Olsen had difficulty pronouncing the cladistic names. He was already starting to lose us.

"Each virus has a single, uh, primary rodent host. Other small mammals can be infected as well, hmm but are much less ... likely to transmit the virus ... to other animals ... or, ya know, humans."

"Let me say a few things," the CDC guy Berlander said, cutting Olson off.

"Be my guest," Olsen gladly sighed as he moved toward a seat. The fed took his place in front of the group and began speaking.

"Hi, guys, Mike Berlander, CDC. Let me give you a quick overview: Most diseases were cured or well on their way to a cure by the mid-1970's, man and science had won over nature, or so it seemed. Then a bunch of previously unknown diseases emerged; Legionnaires' disease, herpes, lyme disease, AIDS, mad cow disease, chronic wasting disease, salmonella, the ebola virus, SARS, morgellons, Asian bird flu and a host of many others. And if that weren't bad enough, old diseases like yellow fever, malaria and dengue fever reappeared and then spread to new areas. We had been lulled into a sense of complacency by our wonderful sciences, so dealing with pestilence was a new thing for everybody. Some microbes, like the ones that cause tuberculosis, malaria and food poisoning, had become dangerously drug resistant."

"You mean like because of over-prescription of anti-biotics?" Boone asked.

"Yes, very good. That was one way that certain diseases and infections have become resistant. Health authorities have also identified a half-dozen factors that could affect the distribution and emergence of infectious diseases. They included human factors like population growth, migration, war, sexual behavior, intravenous drug use, overcrowding and international travel and commerce. Then there were technological and industrial factors like food processing, livestock handling and organ transplants; microbial changes like the development of antibiotic resistance. Then after The Attack there were breakdowns in public health measures such as sanitation, vaccination and insect control. I'm sure you guys know about that stuff."

We all nodded in agreement. Berlander was cool and comfortable speaking to us and, like a lot of the other feds, was interesting and informative when he spoke.

"See guys, the mass immigration of humans to rural America after The Attack means that some species of critters, in turn, are forced into more urban settings. To a small extent, there was a swapping of environments between people and certain animals. As urban refugees quickly develop the wilderness and rural areas, and animals' specialized habitats are destroyed or taken over by humans, opportunistic creatures like rats and crows are forced to adopt a more commanding presence in the urban bioscape.

"They're what we call generalists or opportunists; animals that thrive near developed areas tend to be hardy species that can eat almost anything and live almost anywhere. If, like crows, they also happen to be capable of carrying a disease and spreading it through mosquitoes to people, they become important factors in the accelerated outbreak of disease."

The man knew his stuff. Berlander fielded questions for about twenty minutes and then wrapped up. When he was done, most of us had a whole new respect for sanitation and varmint control.

I stopped by Sarah's house later in the week at about 7:30 on a Thursday evening. I had walked her home from the Kaiserhof the evening that I had met her. She lived only a few blocks west of the bar, whereas I lived just four blocks to the north. We were practically neighbors as it turned out. All the houses in this part of town tended to have been built pre-1920s and Sarah's was no different. It was a modest two-story Queen Anne style house. The yard was a little better maintained than most of the neighboring yards but it was starting to look a little bit on the run-down side. The electricity had been out that day since mid-morning so I knocked. After several seconds, I heard her voice.

"*Who is it?*" she said in a friendly, yet cautious voice from the other side other the door.

"Dallas. From the bar? Ya know, Dallas?"

"*Yeah, what would you like?*" She said a little harshly through the door. This wasn't a good sign. I thought we had gotten along smashingly down at the bar and figured she'd be happy to see a friendly face. Now she wouldn't even open the door to talk to me. I was suddenly uncomfortable and felt a bit like a stalker.

"Well, I just finished work and I thought you might like to hang out a bit or something. I could come back if you're busy or … if you already have company."

"No, I'm home alone," She said as she cracked the door, still secured by a chain. "That's why I have to be so careful. You understand, right?"

"Of course I do." Of course I did.

"So what's in the bag?" she said with a coy smile and a nod to the sack in my right hand.

"This? Oh, I thought we might cook something but the electricity is out."

"Guess what?" She slammed the door and I heard the chain being undone before she swung it back open wide.

"What?" I said.

"I got a gas stove here."

She grabbed me by the arm and yanked me inside. Her mood had noticeably improved. She shut the door and re-locked it before turning back to me. This was the first time I'd seen her when it wasn't night or I didn't have a couple drinks in me and I wasn't disappointed. She was wearing nice denim shorts and a short sleeve floral print shirt, which was unbuttoned in a casual, yet not overtly seductive way. Her hair was up in a loose bun and she wore no makeup. She was stunningly beautiful in her simplicity.

"So. Wha'cha got in there?" she asked, eyeing the sack in my hand.

"Well," I said stepping over to the dining room table, "I've got a box of Minute Rice," I said pulling the box out the way Santa would pull out a gift in front of a child. "And I have several meal entrees courtesy of the United States Army." I pulled out two MRE beef and teriyaki pouches and two Jamaican pork chop pouches. I also had some soy sauce and a couple sticks of butter.

"*Oh my God!*" she squealed while clapping.

"Got a kitchen?" I said jokingly.

"*This way, my dear sir,*" she said in a feigned English accent and then giggled. "Oh, man, you have no idea what a godsend this is. I haven't been able to find any food for sale for days now. I am, like, down to wiener-water soup."

I laughed a bit. "Do you have any condiments?" I asked as a put the bag on the counter a looked around for pans.

"Condiments I have in abundance," she said as she swung open a cupboard, revealing rows of spices and flavorings. "And here, she said disappearing into a small pantry and quickly reappearing with a full plastic bottle. "Fresh, clean water for boiling the rice."

"You are perfect," I said with a smile. "Get me some pans?"

She gladly obliged and fetched a Teflon frying pan, a saucepan and a measuring cup. I put in the requisite amount of water to make half the box plus just a little extra. I'd need the extra hot water to re-hydrate the MRE meat entrees.

"You're not a vegetarian or anything, are you?" I asked.

"Naw, I tried it once. Wasn't for me."

"That's good," I responded. "Besides, think about what life would be like if we didn't eat hamburgers and wear leather shoes and stuff."

"What, what do you mean?"

"We'd be up to our eyebrows in friggin cows, man."

Sarah laughed. It was a short but hearty laugh.

"Yeah, they'd be like squirrels. You'd be at the bus stop and there'd be a cow standing there. They'd be everywhere. They'd be on your lawn, hangin out in front of the coffee shop."

"Oh!" Sarah suddenly said. "You know what would be perfect?"

I slapped my head. "Yes! I have a big bottle of *Sebastiani Zinfandel* in the car." I moved toward the door.

"No, that's not what I was going to say," she said as I stopped in my tracks. "I was going to say it would be perfect to have some nice music playing. But there's no electricity."

"Oh, so I shouldn't get the wine?"

"Yes, you goof," she said with a playful slap on my arm, "go get the wine."

I fetched the bottle and came back inside and locked the door behind me. Once in the kitchen she handed me a corkscrew and I opened the bottle and let it breathe. By then it was time to drain the water from the teriyaki beef. I told her to save the pork and rest of the rice for another time.

I had some butter, a dash of garlic salt, some soy sauce and brown sugar on low heat going in a saucepan. I chopped the beef into bite-sized pieces and let them sauté. The rice was ready a few minutes later so I tossed that in with the beef along with some more garlic salt and a healthy sprinkling of soy sauce and stirred it all up.

"We can let that simmer on low for awhile. Want a glass of wine?"

"I'd love one," she said demurely.

I poured a glass for each of us and then started to admire the first floor of the house. The decor was a cross between Victorian and hippie-light. The windows were covered with heavy paper all around the first floor for security, except for some stained-glass work up high over the dining room hutch and the main living room window, which was enough to let some ambient and delicate evening light in.

The floors in every room were made of beautiful hardwood and were tastefully adorned with oriental rugs in the main rooms; dining room, living room, and den. The furniture tended toward the conservative side, even with a few antiques thrown in, only to be offset by a few lava lamps and the pleasant aroma of nag champa incense. There was a book-marked copy of *The Little Prince* on the coffee table.

"So what about you? Do you own this house?" I asked.

"As a matter of fact, I do. But it's not because I'm some super-responsible person or anything like that. Want to sit?" she asked as she gestured to the love seat.

"Sure," I said. We sat together and she kicked off her sandals and tucked her feet up under her legs. I noticed that she had a little yellow rose tattooed on her ankle.

"So where's the weirdest place you've ever been?" she said initiating some comfortable small talk.

"Bottom of the ocean at the South Pole." I didn't even have to think about that one.

"Really?" she asked, truly astonished. "I usually have people beat on that question with my trip to the Blue Lagoon in Iceland. So what, were you in a submarine with the Navy or something?"

"Nope. I was in jeans, boots and a parka."

"At the bottom of the ocean? I don't get it."

"You heard me right. It was a construction mishap and I wound up at the bottom of the ocean in the cab of a bulldozer while wearing nothing more than work clothes."

"Wow, I think you'd definitely win just about any 'weirdest-place-you've-ever-been' contests," she said.

"So, anyway, how'd you get the house?"

"Daddy," she replied, with a sarcastic toast of her wine glass up into the air. "Dad thought I should follow in his footsteps and be this business tycoon sort of person, or something. He gave me this property for me to manage. It's a five-bedroom frickin house! I used to have three roomies."

"Where are they now?"

"All gone, back to Nowheresville. Sutherland, Iowa, or whatever hovel they came from. I wasn't much of a property manager. Two of the girls were living here for free."

"How so?" I asked curiously.

"They just got behind on their rent last year and me, being the nice person that I am, barely said a word about it. They just stopped paying altogether after awhile."

"That's no good."

"Whatever," Sarah said with a sigh. "It wasn't really my choice to be a property manager. I have a degree in English. I was mostly interested in publishing."

"Like being a writer or an editor?" I said with a casual sip of my wine.

"Maybe being an editor in the future, but for the immediate future I just wanted to work quietly behind the scenes as a proofreader. I thought that'd be a good start on a career. I don't really want to be a writer. As for the property, I guess I placate myself by saying that I helped those two out. The deed is free and clear in my name. I just have to pay for property taxes. I mean, who doesn't want free rent, right?" she shrugged.

"Sure, I guess," I responded.

We made small talk for another six or seven minutes before I remembered the food cooking.

"I think dinner might be ready. Want to eat?"

"Oh god yes!" she said.

Sarah went and got place settings from the cupboards as I transferred my stir-fry into a large ceramic bowl and found a big spoon for serving. She was still working on setting things up.

"Candles?" she asked.

"Absolutely," I said. The weather was a definitely on the warm side but the candles wouldn't produce too much heat and with the windows covered there would be a need for a little bit of light. Besides, this was one of those times where the mood factor outweighed the logic factor. I grabbed the bottle of wine and we sat down together at the table.

We toasted as we settled in for dinner and had comfortable conversation throughout. And my little Minute Rice and MRE stir-fry dish was actually quite savory. Afterwards we retired back to the loveseat with our wine.

"So I get the feeling that you know more about me than I know about you," I remarked. "Tell me about yourself."

"Well, what do you want to know? I'm 28 and single. What else?"

"Every been married?"

"No. Proposed to, but not married."

"You obviously turned them down, huh?"

"Yeah, it just didn't feel right. One of the guys, Jeff, went on to make a couple million dollars in some technology company," she said with a shrug.

"Do you regret turning him down?"

"The ironic part is that I dumped him because I thought he'd never amount to anything. And I didn't like his politics."

"So you do regret it?" I persisted.

"What am I supposed to say? I'm a liberal who wishes I could've married this conservative young millionaire? It's in the past. I've broken hearts and had mine broken, I've made my share of mistakes. It's all part of the process."

"So, is there anyone now?" I asked.

"Now? If I had someone, he'd be in a heap-load of trouble for leaving me alone in this house at a time like this! No, Dallas, I don't have anyone. I haven't been with a man in eight months. Is that the answer you wanted to hear?"

"Truthfully?"

"Truthfully."

"Yes," I said. "That's exactly what I wanted to hear, Sarah." She smiled and looked away. I decided to change subjects.

"So you're a political liberal?" I asked.

"Well, I *was* a liberal. But since April, jeez, are there even Democrats or Republicans anymore? I can guarantee you that 'abortion rights' or 'saving the rainforest' aren't on my top-ten list of things to think about when I roll out of bed in the morning. For me, 'Clean Water Action' means filling my bottles on days when the drinking water is good."

"I see ..." I chuckled in quiet agreement.

"I was one of those people out there marching against the war in Iraq. Now they say that the bomb that exploded in the Chunnel came from Iraq." Sarah took a deep sigh. "Now I'm not so sure the protesters were right."

"I'm sure your intentions were the best."

She nodded. "So. How about yourself? And don't say some crapola that you *think* I want to hear, say what you really think. I hate it when guys are obsequious."

"No ass-kissing, I'll tell you. *Ahem* … I've always been pro-military and I believe in conservative economics in a peacetime world. I always thought that most cops were nothing less than a badass gang on the streets and I strongly believed in due process and defendents' rights – and the death penalty. I have voted for both major parties."

"Man, you're all over the board!" Sarah exclaimed.

"I like to think that I'm an independent thinker."

"Ahh," she said as she sipped her wine. "I think you've definitely achieved that elusive 'independent thinker' status."

"Yeah."

I laughed. Sarah didn't try to engage me in argument or take umbrage at things she disagreed with; she merely appreciated my beliefs for being my own. My heart was one more step closer to hers for that. We were halfway done with the bottle and I could feel its effects just beginning to start on my head. It was about ten o'clock in the evening and it was all but dark outside. Crickets were chirping and I recognized the occasional whine of Hummer engines as they drove through the neighborhood.

"I have to tell you something," she said.

"Okay," I responded.

"Okay. Under normal circumstances this would be the part of the evening where I would tell you that I had a nice time and you were welcome to call me anytime."

"But?"

"But now," she said with a small bit of hesitation, "now I'm hoping that you'll stay for the night," she said as she wrapped her arms around my neck. "And you would thrill me to no end if you knew why I want you here."

I smiled a knowing smile. "Hmm," I said, looking up to the ceiling in fake contemplation. "Let me guess ... you like me."

"Uh-huh," she said with a nod and a smile.

"You'd like to keep seeing me."

"Yes. Keep going," she confirmed with a smile.

"But it's scary in this house all alone and you don't mean that you want me here for sex. For now, you'd like a friendly spirit in the house so the night isn't so long and lonely and frightening."

"Oh my god! A guy who has a clue! I'm very impressed," she said as she snuggled a bit closer. "You're not mad are you?"

"Why would I be mad?"

"You don't think I'm a cocktease or anything?"

"Hardly," I said shaking my head. "I'm in my mid-thirties, not my late teens. I can control the ole' hormones for a night or two," I winked.

"I know, but I just don't want you to think that I'm leading you on or playing with you."

I understood. "You know," I said in a moment of courage, "you have a very pleasant face. I'd like to kiss you." I gave her my best cocked-head puppy dog look.

She leaned back and smiled. "I find you a very pleasant man, Mr. Burnette." She hesitated several seconds before leaning forward and kissing me full on the mouth. Her lips were soft, yet firm ... and perfectly wet. Did I want to make love to her? Of course I did, I'm a man.

I felt like telling her that being with a government worker, even a lowly worker-slug like me, had its perks. I would always have food, a job, a weapon and friends to back me up. But I didn't feel like putting that in front of her. Certainly she could bethink these things for herself. I wanted her to be with me for me. But I also didn't want to screw this thing up. How could I be so lucky? Single, young attractive women simply were not to be found in the city, yet here I was sitting on the couch with a girl I found to be almost perfect. Here in the middle of a saddening worldwide Armageddon, could it be that I finally found *the one*?

Don't put the cart before the horse, studboy ...

We slept in the same bed that night, me in my clothes and her in a T-shirt and sweatpants.

The electricity was on by morning and we had coffee together. Soon it was time for me to go to work. Sarah walked me to the door, put her arms around my neck and gave me a peck on the lips.

"Have a good day at work, honey," she said mockingly as though we were a married couple.

"I think I should stop over after work today," I said.

"I think that would be lovely idea," she responded with feminine charm.

I kissed her. "Be safe today, okay?"

"Yeah, yeah," she replied.

"I mean it."

"I know you do, Dallas. I will be careful today."

"Okay, sweetie," I said. "Bye-bye."

"Later, 'gator."

I walked out her front door to a beautiful summer's morning. Birds were chirping and the sun was shining. I could usually tell early on if it was going to be a hot day, but today felt like it was going to be just a pleasant summer day. I hopped in my car and went to work.

I was all but walking on air that day at work. We had our normal morning meeting with coffee and bagels. I grabbed three leftover ones as we left for our assignments and put them in a bag. We had a normal workday, boarded up a couple buildings and completed a few extra details. I didn't give a hoot what we were doing – my mind was swimming in joy that whole day thinking about Sarah.

I returned to her house that evening after work with a box of food. I had MRE entrees, snack chips, rice and a six-pack of Coke. To my surprise, Sarah had also procured quite a haul of food – she finally found someone with food to sell and, God knows, she had the money to buy it. I wound up spending the entire weekend at her house.

I awoke Monday at 5:30 in the morning to the sound of thunder. That meant rain, and rain meant potential radioactive contamination. I quietly got up, went downstairs and called the Gulag – there was always someone there.

"County refit, good morning," the dispatcher said answering the phone.

"Yeah, this is Burnette. What's going on with the rain?"

"Rain is expected to last all morning going into the afternoon. We are advising all workers to stay indoors and avoid contact with precipitation. Feds are out monitoring right now, checking radiation levels."

"Okay, just make sure you mark me down that I called in."

"You got it. 'Burnette called in'," she said as though she were writing it down.

"Thank you. Goodbye." I quietly hung up the phone and went back up to bed. Sarah was sleepily stretching as I lay back down.

"Who were you talking to?" she said through a yawn.

"Work. Guess who's got the day off?"

"You? Why?" she asked slightly surprised.

Just then there was a moderate thunderclap. I gestured to the window. Rain pattered down outside.

"Radioactive rain, baby. I am under strict orders to stay inside this house," I said as I sidled up to Sarah and put my arms around her. "I am supposed to stay in this very house and make love to you all day."

"You are, huh?" she smirked, still with sleepiness on her face. She stretched a morning stretch with her arms over her head and a little groan of pleasure.

"Uh-huh," I muttered as I nestled in and kissed her neck. "Orders straight from the government."

"Well … I'd hate to be charged with sedition," she said as she put a loving arm around me and lifted her head back giving me complete access to her neck as my hand ran over the feminine contours of her flat tummy and curvy hips. I kissed her ear and then planted my mouth on hers. She yanked at my T-shirt. "Get out of these clothes and make love to me."

I obliged.

We stayed in bed most of the morning as it rained steadily outside. After making love three times, we finally decided to get up and make something to eat. I took the paper off some of the windows, not only so we could see outside, but also to let in some light. There were no vehicles or pedestrians outside, just the patter of large heavy raindrops pelting the streets and sidewalks for endless hours, sounding like juicy steaks sizzling on an open grill.

We were bumming around the main floor. Sarah was wearing only a robe. The electricity was out again so she lit a few candles and incense. I had the battery-operated boom box that I'd found in one of our preservation projects and I put in an old Coldplay disc.

"Hey, lover," Sarah said as she plopped on the couch. "Fucking is just about a good a way as any to pass the time as anything else, doncha think?" she purred as she spread her legs.

My mouth dropped. I couldn't believe my demure little brainiac had said something so vulgar and was acting so slutty. It turned me on.

I reported to work on Tuesday morning. According to the feds, the previous day's rain contained negligible amounts of radiation and only in certain areas, mostly in the far western metro region. That meant that not only was Monday's rain a much-needed cleansing for the buildings and streets, it was a free day off work. We went out on a five-man crew in two pickups with Boone as leader, Stubbs, two younger black guys, Gregory Griffin and Tony Isaacs, and me.

We worked all morning on two small jobs and took a lunch break at noon in an empty parking lot. We sat on the open tailgates of the trucks and ate our food. My mind was on my blossoming relationship with Sarah and I was saying very little. But Griffin and Isaacs were very talkative. One might say overly talkative. Idle conversation turned to banter, and banter led to more blabbery mouths. It didn't take long for patience to be tested.

"Yo, man, I don't blame the terrorists," said Griffin. "Po-leece be pullin brothers over jus cuz they be lookin Mideastern and shit, harrassin them and throwin they ass in jail. Why wouldn't they want to bomb our asses?"

"What?" said Boone in disbelief. "Because someone's civil rights might have been violated, America deserved to be nuked?"

"Ya'll white boys don't know what it's like to be a brown-skinned man in America. What goes around, comes around, that's all I'm saying," said Griffin.

I was trying to stay out of a conversation that was clearly headed straight for racial politics, Stubbs was keeping his lip as well. Boone couldn't contain himself, however.

"Hey, Griffin, move back to Africa if you think it's so fucking tough living in America."

"Yeah, that's original," said Isaacs sarcastically. "Anytime a white boy start losing an argument with a black man, first thing out yo' mouth is '*move back to Africa.*' I am a proud to be an African-American, bitch. I'm an American, but my roots be in Africa."

"You got dat right bra," Gregory said with a subtle low-five hand slap. "Yo, ask this older brotha," he said nodding toward Stubbs.

"What you want, man?" Stubbs grumbled in his baritone voice, clearly not wanting to join the debate.

"You stand up for your ancestors, right, Stubbs?"

"Wha'choo talkin about?" Stubbs said with increased annoyance.

"Where are your ancestors from, *dat's* what I'm talkin about, brotha."

"My ancestors be from Chicago," said Stubbs.

"No, no," retorted Isaacs. "Before *that.*"

"Before that, my ancestors was from Louisiana," responded Stubbs.

"What about you African roots, *that's* what we talkin 'bout," said Gregory.

"I'm gonna learn you younger brothas a thinga' two," said Stubbs, now standing up with all of his 270 pounds, hands on his hips, clearly annoyed and ready to deliver his words. "I ain't never been to Africa, I don't speak no African, I don't want to visit the damn place, I got nothin to do with Africa. You ask me where my ancestors be from, I'll tell you Chicago, you ask me where they be from before dat, I'll tell you Louisiana. I'm a goddam American."

The two younger men looked at each other before Isaacs spoke.

"Whoa! *Chill*, Uncle Tom!" chuckled Isaacs.

"Don't you *dare* call me 'Uncle Tom' negro!" Stubbs rejoined with an elevated and angered inflection in his voice as he stepped closer to the younger men. The smiles dropped off of their faces and their eyes widened.

"I'll knock that mothafuckin grapefruit-head right off those skinny-ass shoulders of yo's!" Stubbs bellowed. "Ya'll mothafuckas best learn somethin: Ain't no mo civil rights or political-correctness or nice white liberals filing class-action lawsuits on yo' African-ass behalf. *We livin in martial law!* You mothafuckas keep saying, *'America deserved to be nuked, America deserved to be nuked,'* you keep saying dat shit and one of these National Guard crackers gonna pop a .223 round in your black ass fo'sedition."

The two younger men were rendered mute, as were Boone and I.

"And if they don't," Stubbs boomed, "*I WILL!*"

After several tense seconds everyone sat back in his original place and we finished our lunch break in near silence. The rest of the workday was quiet and uneasy, but we finished our work orders and were out of the Gulag before five.

Sarah asked me if I wanted to go to a poetry reading that evening during dinner that night. I would have gone to a public autopsy as long as it was with Sarah, so off we went. We got in the car and drove towards Uptown. There was a basement coffee joint on Hennepin Avenue called *The Word*. We entered under a neon sign and went down the stairs.

It was a dark place that smelled of incense, clove and Irish crème. There were little round tables and chairs on the main floor. The walls of the place were lined with upholstered benches with throw pillows here and there, and there was a coffee bar against the back wall, all oriented to a little ten-by-ten stage. There was a Jackson Pollack splatter painting on the far wall. I don't know if it was an original or a knock-off.

The stage was made of finished maple and was elevated about two feet off the floor. On it stood a microphone on a stand and a single wooden bar stool. Red and yellow lamps, recessed into the ceiling so that you couldn't really see the lighting fixtures themselves, warmly lighted the stage.

There were about 20 or so people there, quietly chatting and laughing, their faces illuminated by flickering candles on their tables. A slender and tallish older man with a gray ponytail named Gary Matherly greeted Sarah almost immediately. Gary was a hippie, a geriatric specimen from the sixties.

"How are you, my darling Sarah? It's been too long!" he said with a gentle embrace.

"Well, you know current events and all."

"But, of course. And who is this young man?" he said turning his attention to me.

"Gary, this is my friend Dallas," she said as she introduced me.

"Good to meet you, young man," he said with a handshake.

"Dallas, this is Gary Matherly."

"Good to meet you," I nodded.

He turned back to Sarah. "So, are you reading tonight?"

"I thought I might get up and try something. I had this edgy thing ready to go before, you know, April first. I thought I might try it out tonight."

"Wonderful," the older man said. "You be good to this one," he said to me. "This one is the keeper you were always looking for, trust me."

I smiled and nodded in gentle agreement. Sarah rolled here eyes and shook her head a bit in embarrassment.

"Gotta run in back, make yourselves at home," Gary said as he kissed Sarah on the forehead and walked away.

"He was a nice guy," I said as soon as he was out of earshot.

"He owns the place," Sarah said.

"Really?" I said, a little astonished.

"He published some books, collections of short stories and poems back in the late eighties and made a buck or two. Actually a million or two. After that, he always jokes he was living the liberal's nightmare."

"Which is?"

"How do you whine about the upper class when you're part of it?"

"Sounds like one of those problems that you'd *like* to have."

We found a nice table off to the side of the stage. I got us a couple of coffees and we waited for the night to start. The emcee for the evening was a local poet named James Bando. Apparently the poetry readings barely missed a beat after the April bombings. This was Sarah's first night back, however. Bando talked for a bit, thanked people for coming out to hear poetry, reminded everyone that donations were welcome and then read three short poems of his own. After that, he introduced the first open mic participant of the night. When that person was done, he introduced another. After four people had read their pieces, he looked at Sarah.

"And now, we're going to hear from someone we haven't seen since before April Nukes Day, Sarah P." *Polite applause.*

Sarah got up and made her way to the stage. Bando offered her a gentlemanly hand up onto the stage. I thought it was courteous that he didn't disclose a woman's last name into a public microphone, even though it seemed like a loose-knit group of friendly acquaintances. Sarah smiled and waited a few seconds as the applause quieted. Her poem went like this:

My First Time
By SK Pennington

Like magic, growing from disinterested, pliant flesh it
Rose to become a steaming steel pipe,
Drooling anticipatory pre-cum
From its red-hot tip
A pussyholic on a bender, a throbbing one-eyed warrior
Looking for conquest
'Twas an evil fellow, attached to the groin of a seemingly
Normal male, its singular goal? An act of vulgarity and
Delirious pleasure
Turgid and unrelenting, it served its master only as a
Cherry-busting, thrusting pole of spunk-gushing
Selfish indifference.
Now, covered in blood, it lay flaccid and satisfied,
glistening, limpid

As its master was snatched by Morphius into delta-wave
slumber
Within seconds of his final and most palpable blast
If it could, I'm sure it would have lit up a ciggy
I never came

With that the poem ended. There was applause. I was speechless. Eyes from every corner of the room leered my way, or so I thought. A bearded young patron from a nearby table leaned over my shoulder.

"Dude, was she talking about you?"

"Jesus Christ, I don't think so," I said. I felt self-conscious as though all eyes were casting suspicious darts at me. Sarah folded her sheet of paper in half and delicately stepped from the stage and came back to the table.

"Well, what did you think?" she said quietly as she sat down.

"Everyone thinks you were talking about me."

"Oh, quit being so paranoid. They know it's art. So? What did you think?"

"I'm not sure if I know how to critique this kind of, um, art."

"C'mon, I'm not asking you to write a review for the New York Times. Didn't it make you feel something or visualize something?"

"Yeah, I was a little jealous of the guy who got the first shot at you. Who the hell was that?"

"It doesn't matter. What else did you feel?"

I was a little uncomfortable, to say the least. Not knowing what the theme of her piece was going to be, I was taken aback by its content and again by the fact that she'd taken such vulgarity and turned it into, well, poetry.

"That was quite the creative piece," I said.

She smiled and leaned back. "It's an acquired thing, I know it's not appreciated by everyone."

Now I'm a fairly intelligent guy and can converse with many people on many topics, but poetry ain't one of 'em. For starters, I believe that poetry should rhyme. No, not 'roses are red and violets are blue.' I guess I appreciate people who play guitars and sing on a stage as more of a dedicated medium, but that's just me.

We watched several more poets and then milled about for a bit afterward. I was glad to meet some of Sarah's circle. Aside from the fact that I wasn't overly-impressed with the art form, I was pleased to have come there.

I had all but stopped living at the apartment building. I spent every waking moment with Sarah that I wasn't at work. This was something that didn't go unnoticed by John and Brian. I had told them all about Sarah and then introduced them when we all bumped into each other at the Kaiserhof. I wound up working a crew with both of them the day after that and it didn't take long for the topic to come up.

"Yo, Dallas," said Brian as we exited our vehicles at the day's work site. "So are you not living at the apartment or what?"

"I guess I still have the apartment. Lee hasn't thrown my stuff out, has he?"

"Hell no, it's just that you're never around."

"You know I'm pretty much living with Sarah, right? I just don't really have much need to hang out around the apartment."

"Somebody's whipped," John teased.

"Hey, man," I said as I was unloading some boards, "the girl lives all alone in a big house and, yeah, I like her very much. If you want to called it whipped, that's fine with me."

"We're just messin with ya, bro. I'm happy for you. Finding a single good-looking chick like Sarah? Shit, man, I'm actually jealous. You musta done something right."

"Thank you, man," I said, thankful for his maturity.

We started to build a life for ourselves in Sarah's house. Between the two of us, we always had food on hand. I had made alliances with the few other residents on the block and we agreed to look out for each other. We had neighbors over for dinners and sometimes went to their houses in return. No one ever bothered us, though. Sarah would often go out by herself during the day and was only mildly hit up for money by the occasional panhandler.

We came up with a contingency plan: If we were separated and were out of contact with each other, we would try to find a working computer and email each other. We wouldn't have to count on the luck of reaching each other at a certain phone number. We could leave our communications out there in cyberspace for the other to retrieve at the earliest possible convenience.

Another deal was struck: We could listen to the news in the morning, but that evenings were reserved for cooking, drinking and music – no bad news or talk of terrorism. Sometimes we'd go down to the Kaiserhof in the evening and hang out with friends out in the garden. More than once we danced in the living room or we sat on the front steps with neighbors sipping iced tea or a beer.

We spoke of the big things and the little things: I wondered aloud how she, such a lovely and awesome woman, could be single. She told me that her focus on relationships after college was finding a "successful man," a man who could take care of all their financial needs for all the years to come. But, she said, her heart needed a loving male who could be passionate, someone not be afraid to jump in with both feet; a man who would be thoughtful and creative at home in the evening while slaying the financial world during the day. By age 28, experience had taught her that the two qualities were "mutually exclusive," as she put it, and that she needed to decide on one or the other. "Money is money, but a life without love is a life not worth living." Yeah, yeah, it sounds like a bad line from a bad movie, but she said it was what she felt.

Then the bombs came.

I dwelled on her words: Was it some sort of backhanded compliment? That she was 'settling' for a worker schmoe like me? I would never have been – and certainly now was never going to be – a tycoon like her father. But I was educated, articulate and a little bit creative. I worked hard and had a full-time job. Okay, I had no appreciation for coffeehouse poetry and felt I was the better man for it, but aside from that we clicked fantastically. But the insecurities gnawed at me. Was I good enough for her?

I watched her working in the back yard one evening. Her hair was pulled up in a sexy messy bun. The early evening sunlight shone through her yellow sundress and I could see her clean flowered cotton panties and the lacey bra that restrained her firm breasts. She was, to me, physically perfect. Yet, for all her beauty, I loved her for her wit and intelligence. I loved her for making the bad parts of the world go away. As I thought about it, I didn't know what I did to deserve Sarah, but I was happy to have her. She made me yearn to be a better man. I wanted to spend the rest of my life with her.

Worries melted when I was with Sarah. People with advanced degrees and security clearances and positions larger than ones I'd ever have would take care of the big things. Me, I needed to keep pounding nails for the county and to continue making a home with Sarah. My world was making sense.

At least a dozen times we had John and Brian over with their guitars and bongos. Sometimes we had some guys over from the Gulag. A few of Sarah's poetry friends would usually join us and we would sit in the back yard as food sizzled on the Webber. People would hand off instruments and knock out acoustic versions of any and all songs; Patsy Cline, Beatles, AC/DC, Journey, Johnny Cash, U2, Willie Nelson, Smashing Pumpkins … anything that came to mind, you name it. Henri Lebenze turned out to be quite a guitarist and could figure out almost any song on the fly. *"Just tell me ze key,"* he'd say. I felt like we were building a sense of community; musicianship, friendship, singing, wine, beer, food and love.

Those were good and memorable times.

SIXTEEN

"This went fast," I said to Sarah one day as we lounged in the living room. I was truly relaxed was feeling completely at home with her at the moment I said that.

"What? What do you mean?" she asked.

"This relationship, doncha think?"

"I think circumstances helped a bit," she said.

"You don't think you could love me in a peaceful world? A different timeline?"

"Sure I could. I just think that what we have is more a case of time and place."

"Of course it is," I said, "every relationship is a question of time and place. It's hard to fall in love with someone if you're never at the same place at the same time."

"What we have is more like a 'locationship'," she said. "If you think about it, we would never have met if it weren't for the terrorists."

"You can't say that, we only live seven blocks away from each other," I retorted.

"Baby, I'm not trying to say what we have isn't nice, just that there are delicate threads of circumstance, impossibly thin membranes of chance that are never broken. Sometimes the greatest love stories never happen and sometimes ones that should never have been sowed, flower and blossom into something meaningful."

I was confused. Was she being poetically philosophical or trying to start an argument? In relationships, the one who dumps first is the one who always has the power thereafter: Was she going for the pre-emptive dump? My little Sarah going for the power-grab? Or had she found another guy while I was out working? I was flailing back on my heels in my mind while hoping that I looked calm and collected on the outside.

She continued. "I mean, do you know how often I go out alone? *Never!* The night you met me was sheer chance. I was going out of my mind hanging out in this house all alone. I went there out of loneliness and boredom. I'm a coffeehouse poetry fan with my heart in the arts and publishing and you're this salesman, free-market quasi-conservative. We just never would have met under normal circumstances. We are different."

"We are mutually complimentary."

"Yes, and different, too."

"Differences are *good*," I offered.

"And I, for one, think that poets are brilliant and I think that public poetry reading is pure art. You think that, when it comes to poetry as a performance medium, we're a bunch of simpletons."

"I never said that, sweetheart." *The chick's reading my mind!*

"Could you see yourself in a long-term relationship with someone like me?" she asked as she cocked her head.

"Do you love me?" I asked, unsure of the answer to come.

"Of course, I do," she said without hesitation. She got up and put an arm around me. "I'm just thinking out loud, don't put too much on anything I'm saying right now, okay? I'm not trying to start a fight."

"Okay."

"Truth is, Dallas, I don't know what I'd do without you," she said as she laid her head on my shoulder.

I was coming back to a sense of ease. An impulse struck me at that instant and I acted on it without thinking:

"Marry me."

Sarah's head popped up off my shoulder and she looked wide-eyed at me. "What did you just say? It sounded like you just said 'marry me'."

"I did. Marry me."

"This is a little quick, isn't it?" She chortled a bit.

"Life is short … and I love you." It was a simple and direct declaration.

Now I'm not a naive man and I know how things work: The first two months of a relationship, any relationship, are always dreamy, filled with hope and optimism. The sex is always exciting and it's hard to imagine how this you could have been so lucky to find this other available and attractive person all for yourself. I felt all those things and more. Yet, I was careful not to put Sarah on too high a pedestal. There's only one thing a person can do from a pedestal, and that's fall.

It takes time, I always tried to tell myself. You need to see the other person's rough spots and annoying habits. Does this person unnecessarily slip in factoids about past lovers that prick the heart like tiny stickpins? You need to have a couple knockdown, drag-out arguments and see how the recovery goes. Does this person hold grudges? Does this person accept or offer apologies like a mature adult?

Was it fast, my offer of marriage? Sure it was fast, but why wait? To give bad luck a fair chance to rear its head? To see if something better might come along? Meeting a girl and asking her to marry so quickly would have been insanity to me before. Now it made all the sense in the world. We were certainly within that two-month window, but I had yet to find serious fault with Sarah. Okay, maybe that poem in the coffeehouse was a tad weird, but hardly a deal-breaker.

The mating sequence does take time under normal circumstances, but these were extraordinary times: There was no more competing with unseen co-workers, dating service matches, coffeehouse Lotharios or internet suitors. I imagined these were more like pioneer days when you had to latch onto a mate and hold on for dear life. And, trust me, I could have done a lot worse than Sarah. I humbly presumed that she could do worse than me.

Maybe that's what she was thinking, too, because she said 'yes.'

We were married ten days later in a downtown basilica – a strong and majestic church that had been built in the 1800's and had gone untouched by modern society's wrecking balls. The minister was elated to be doing some normal church business and even provided an organist who worked for free. I had a late night at the Kaiserhof the night before. Nothing outrageous mind you, and then I slept at my own apartment.

I woke up to a sunny and warm day. I spent Saturday morning shining my shoes until they looked like black mirrors and then went and got my hair cut. I was due for a trim anyway and Cindy the dispatcher had also been a licensed stylist before the nukes.

There were only about thirty people total at the church come one o'clock. For me there were friends from the Kaiserhof and the co-workers from the Gulag. Sarah had a few friends, mainly of the literary and poetic ilk. I recognized some from the open mic nights. Sarah's mother couldn't, or wouldn't, make it in from the western suburbs.

I wore a suit that I had bought specifically for weddings and funerals several years back. Nothing fancy, it was a conservative black suit that I wore with a bright white shirt and gray tie. I had no idea I'd be wearing it to my own wedding. People said I "cleaned up well." It felt good to be doing things in a simple, wholesome, throwback kind of way.

In accordance with tradition, the first time I saw Sarah that day was when she came around the corner at the first few notes of the processional. And when she started up the aisle, my heart almost stopped.

Gary Matherly, the old hippie and coffeehouse owner, escorted her down the aisle to give her away. He was tall and lean and looked distinguished in his dark suit with his gray ponytail neatly pulled back. He made a dashing accessory next to Sarah.

But, Sarah? She had her hair up and adorned with a small, simple veil. Perfect locks of hair wisped down and framed the sides of her face. She had a hint of makeup on which made her heart-wrenchingly beautiful. She wore was a simple white satin, sleeveless gown that stopped at mid-calf. She had on simple white shoes and a fine gold chain necklace around her graceful neck. That was it.

It was a standard small service. At our request, there was no mass or sermon. I had Ken Leland as my best man. Sarah and I exchanged vows, placed rings on one another's finger, kissed and were walking out the doors of the church as newlyweds in less than twenty minutes.

From there it was back to the Kaiserhof for our official reception. Jack and a couple others workers missed the wedding because they were back preparing for our celebration, not to mention guarding the joint. There was a table for the wedding party and the head of the larger of the two dining rooms. There was champagne on ice and the bar was open. Not being too fancy, our guests were allowed to sit wherever they chose. After all, most people knew each other to some extent or another.

Understandably, the menu selection would have to be limited when it came to the main course. No one was disappointed with the chicken and wild rice dinner that Sarah and I had chosen together. Wine, food, laughter and joy flowed like running waters all throughout the afternoon and into the evening.

After dinner, the festivities spread outside to the garden. I floated back and forth, trying to spend time with everyone who came to the wedding. There were two guitarists and a violinist playing in the back. There was bar service out there and people mingled and talked. Back inside, one of the larger tables had been covered with appetizers and desserts of all kinds. It was decadent and we celebrated late into the evening.

Sarah was busy talking and laughing with people, too. Several times I would just watch her; the way she'd throw her head back when she laughed, the way her mouth moved when she would talk, the way her eyes sparkled. After only a few seconds she would always look right at me, even from across the crowded room. Catching my gaze, she'd smile and wink. We were connected.

God, I love her.

As America staggered from her seven deadly blows dealt by the terrorists, I suddenly found my life more complete and together than it had ever been before. I wasn't a loner anymore. I had a wife that any man would have been lucky to call his own. I was proud to call myself a friend and co-worker to an incredible collection of brave souls who, unlike the majority of the population, stuck it out in a metropolis that was still a nuclear target as far as the federal government was concerned. I realized what a fantastic group of people it was that I associated with during that strange and tragic summer. People I never would have met had it not been for the bombs, including my precious new wife.

SEVENTEEN

I was a married man now. The very thought took me aback sometimes. I thought things would be the same but they weren't. Something changed. I lay there one morning up on one elbow with my head in my hand watching Sarah sleep, the way parents stare at their newborn babies, I suppose. I looked at the contours of her pretty face, her smooth skin. I silently watched her breathing, her chest gently going up and down ... the ring on her finger. It was my duty, I told myself, to protect and watch out for my wife.

There was a guy who came into town and was staying with one of our neighbors. His name was Dale something-or-other. He had fled the city after The Attack and had been staying in a small town in South Dakota. I wound up talking to him in the yard one evening and invited him inside for a beer and a sandwich. He told Sarah and me a little bit about life out of the city.

"It's really not bad out there, out there in the rural areas," he said. "It's a lot more peaceful. Gets hot, though. Not too much electricity, so no air conditioning. Groceries can be scarce sometimes. There's a lot of hunting and fishing going on. But it's not bad."

"That sounds alright," I said with a nod. I looked at Sarah. She didn't have much reaction on her face.

"Well, I'll tell you this; there's a shitload of folks out there," he said with a finger pointing off to the horizon, "who think you're a buncha crazy bastards."

"Whatta ya mean, 'cause of all the inner-city violence and stuff?" I asked.

"Inner city violence? Try an inner-city nuclear explosion. I pulled the short straw: I'm just back here checking on houses for a couple families and to grab whatever supplies I can."

"Are people really scared out there?" asked Sarah.

"Shit, man, I'm scared just sitting here. I wouldn't be surprised if I saw a nuclear flash right now."

I guess us city folks had gotten somewhat used to living in town. I thought it was a little strange that the outlanders were still terrified of more nukes. Maybe it I *was* us big-towners who were crazy, who knew? I thought about things and spoke to Sarah over breakfast few days later.

"So. Ever think about leaving town?" I asked.

"Oh," she said without missing a beat, "you've been thinking about that Dale guy, too?"

"Well, he got me thinking: What are we going to do with ourselves? With these lives of ours?"

"I know."

"And I feel like I have certain responsibilities that I didn't have before."

"Such as?"

"I have a new wife," I said, holding up my ring finger.

"Hey, I was taking care of myself before I met you, no offense."

"Fine. What if we get pregnant?"

"Pregnant? Slow down, buddy! Who's getting pregnant?"

"Sarah, I'm just telling you that I feel more responsibilities now. You are my family, baby. You're it. I want us to be together for a long time."

"Babe, I love you, you know that. I know you feel that way, about leaving the city. I understand and part of me feels it too. But, I love my house, for one thing," she said, gesturing about with her arms. "I'd hate to leave it. God, by the time we came back, it'd be full of horrible squatters. I couldn't take that."

I didn't feel like arguing. Besides, it was getting time for me to leave for work. Maybe we could bring this subject up again in a few weeks. Yeah, let the idea knock around in her head for awhile; gain a little foothold in some reality.

"Listen, baby, I'm leaving for work. Let's sorta think about moving out of town, though. I'm not saying make a decision this week, but let's think about it."

"Fair enough," she said as she walked me to the door.

"But I'd feel pretty shitty if we stayed and the terrorists did pop a nuke in Minneapolis," I offered in another one of my patented understatements.

"This is our house, Dallas, where we live. This is our *home*," she said. "Fuck the terrorists."

In late June, an earthquake registering 6.7 on the Richter scale rocked what was left of Los Angeles. Maybe this was the end of all things. Certainly, any humans left living in the Los Angeles area had to have felt as though they had been cast into Hades itself.

In an ironic twist, every clear night offered western horizons of beautiful flaming reddish-orange sunsets as the smoke of the unchecked and raging forest fires out west altered the sunlight coming through the dusky skies. The evening skies were simply spectacular that summer as fierce crimson moons rose over eastern horizons. But the stars had all but disappeared from the night skies.

People became more and more brazen about flaunting their violence. Thugs took pot shots at cop cars, less so at the Army Hummers. Police files were filled with cases of people being shot for no apparent reason other than sport. It happened only in certain parts of town but was nonetheless disquieting. It took nothing to send tempers over the edge and street arguments were a common sight. There were cases of murder that didn't seem to be robbery related.

The first of July was a foreboding day. Fifteen members of a Police/Community-Liaison Task Force were ambushed and killed by gangs near East Lake Street, southeast of downtown. The bodies were looted, stripped of their clothing and left to bake on the street in the hot summer sun. It was hours before they were recovered. Cop killings were fairly regular but the 15 murders were an ominous telltale sign: The civil situation was officially out-of-control.

The fourth of July started out as just another sultry summer morning in post-nuclear America. It was sure to be a hot and humid day. Sarah and I had real eggs with coffee and toast for breakfast. I was already showered and in my jeans and boots, Sarah was wearing comfy shorts and an oversized T-shirt. She said that she was going garden a little and then go out during the day and try to find a food dealer. It was good for her to have something to do but I worried about her.

We talked about nothing in particular. The electricity was on so we listened to the morning news as we sat at the table having breakfast. Nothing too new, we had Special Forces lurking about the Middle East flushing out suspected terrorists. CIA Predator drones were flying about and killing bad guys with their Hellfire missiles. Back here in America, recovery around the destroyed cities in crept along at a slow but steady pace.

"You be careful today," I said in what had become my standard departing words as I stood up and slipped on my vest.

"I will," Sarah said in what had become her standard reply. She accompanied me to the door. "I love you. Have a good day at work, my dear husband."

"I love you, too," I said as I kissed her sweetly on the lips. "I'll see you for dinner, my darling wife."

When I close my eyes I can still picture her standing there, seeing me off to work.

EIGHTEEN

Every day in the city brought serious incidents that could have turned into riot situations if it weren't for quick action by the peacekeepers. A lot of things that seemed benign, like a fight or altercation, could quickly snowball into something bigger. Police cruisers and Army Humvees were omnipotent and responses to unrest tended to be harsh and swift. Soldiers in tactical garb patrolled streets downtown, keeping safety and order for the comparatively few citizens who still went to work there.

The crime wave had been growing on a gentle upward slope for three months. People had removed all their cash from the banks. That meant that robbers assumed that any one person at random might have one, two, three thousand dollars on them, maybe a pocket full of quarter-ounce krugerands. Given the price gouging that was going on, it wasn't an unreasonable assumption. Being broke and having no money was not a guarantee that you wouldn't be the victim of an assault either. Residences and businesses were being broken into and pillaged quicker than we could possibly board them up. The feeling of danger was in the air.

Ken Leland and I were dispatched in one of our orange pickup trucks named *Wombat Wagon* to go around and put up public service posters on that particular day. These ones were a mix of warnings against violent crimes and another poster reminding folks not to hurt cats.

The Church had decried cats as agents of the devil back during the Middle Ages. It ordered cats slaughtered and, henceforth, helped bring about the black plague as rats propagated unfettered by their natural enemy. That was the lore passed onto us, at least.

Cats, if they weren't too fat and lazy, were natural urban predators and could be a big help in controlling the rodent population. CATS ARE YOUR FRIENDS. PLEASE DO NOT EAT THEM, the poster urged. There was a clever picture of a cat looking into the camera while pinning a rodent to the ground with one of his paws.

10:45 a.m.

"Have you noticed that our list of jobs is always getting bigger?" Ken asked.

"I was wondering if it was just me, but I didn't want to sound like I was whining," I answered. "I just signed on to this job to nail boards over windows."

"I hear that," Leland said. "Now we're putting up posters, putting up concertina, doing garbage disposal, shit-management. Shit."

We stopped and duct taped a poster to the plywood-covered window of an abandoned shop. It was one of those pro-cat posters. We got back in the truck and continued driving. Three Army choppers flew over in a loose formation.

"I don't even like cats," Ken said.

"Hey, cats are your friends," I responded. "Don't you read government posters?"

11:05 a.m.

We were driving around North Minneapolis, the mean streets. A loud metallic pop startled us. It sounded as if someone hit the truck with a rock.

"What the hell was that?" Ken said.

"I have no idea. Stop the truck."

Leland pulled the truck over and we got out to inspect the vehicle. I saw the damage right away.

"What the ... look here, Ken," I said pointing to what looked like a bullet hole in the front quarter panel.

He bent over to get a closer look. "If I didn't know better, I'd say that was a – "

BANG! SMASH!

A high-powered rifle round shattered the rear window of the truck and continued on through out the front of the windshield. The bullet hit the tree right next to Ken. It would have hit him in the upper torso if he had been standing straight up. We were under fire.

"Christ! Let's get the hell outta here!" We scampered back into the cab of the pickup as another shot rang out. I don't know where that round hit. Leland threw the truck into drive and floored it.

"*MOTHAHFUCKAAAAHHS,*" we heard someone yelling as we sped away. I dared not turn around to look and see who it was. I just kept slumped down low as Ken hunched over the wheel. Shattered glass was sprayed all over the inside of the pickup.

"You hit?"

"No," I said, feeling around my body. "I don't think so." I grabbed the mic: "Mayday Mayday, were are taking fire, over!"

"Who is this, over," the radio crackled back and I recognized it as Scheerer. His voice alone made me feel safer already.

"Leland and Burnette in the Wombat Wagon, over."

"Roger. Anyone hurt, over?"

"Negative, just scared shitless, over!"

"Roger that. Get back to the Gulag ASAP, over."

"What's going on?"

"We have a riot building northside. Just got word ourselves two mikes ago, over."

"Yeah, that's exactly where we're at!"

"Out."

Get back to the Gulag? That could be tough. You see, downtown Minneapolis is essentially an island: The only way you could get into downtown proper was over, or in a few controllable cases, under a bridge. The Mississippi River formed a natural border on the north and east sides while highways 35W and I-94 formed manmade barriers on the remaining sides. More than half of the bridges had been blocked off and barricaded by the government while the remaining open ones were heavily controlled by the guard. Downtown proper was pretty safe because police and guardsmen patrolled it heavily. That was where we needed to get.

Whether it was the heat of the day or the steadily increasing agitation of post-nuclear life, something had set off the violence. What started out as a small disturbance grew into a bigger disturbance and then, like a virus, separated, repeated and reproduced itself a block or two over. No one ever really knew exactly what the sequence of events was that led to the violence. A full-scale riot was in the making.

The Wombat Wagon careened through the low-income neighborhoods. Leland was a pretty good driver. The thin cardboard posters flew out of the bed of the pickup as we sped toward the tall buildings of the city. We could see them, tantalizingly close in front of us, visible over trees and houses yet it felt like they were a hundred miles away. There were bridges and train tracks and roadblocks and fences and rivers and violent mobs between haven and us.

We knew that if we could make it through to the industrial part of town with the huge warehouses and marshalling train yards, it would be a short trip from there into downtown. The trick would be finding a vehicle-accessible route. We decided to zigzag through residential neighborhoods as much as possible, avoiding busier streets and areas with stores. The hooligans tended to gravitate to those areas and wreak their havoc. We heard gunshots near and far and all of the compulsory sounds of urban violence; humans screaming, glass breaking, small explosions, unanswered burglar and fire alarms blaring and the roar of fires.

We would be in good shape if we could get to Broadway. Broadway Avenue had a wide, crested bridge spanning the Mississippi River leading to just off the western edge of downtown. We knew that it was a barricaded bridge but if we could just get there to the guardsmen, we could abandon the Wombat Wagon and make it to the Gulag on foot. I grabbed the radio handset.

"This is Burnette in the Wombat Wagon, over."

"*Roger, Wombat, go ahead.*" It was a different voice, one of the female dispatchers from the shop. I wondered where Scheerer was but asking about his whereabouts was low on the list of priorities.

"Yeah, this is Burnette. I have a crew of two, Leland and myself, up northside, over."

"Roger, we're aware. Be advised, Wombat, shop has several crews in or near riot areas, over."

"Understood. Wombat will attempt to get to Broadway Bridge."

"Roger, be advised, Broadway is barricaded, over."

"Understood, we know. Will dismount and cross on foot if necessary, over."

"Roger, Wombat, be careful. Out."

We had two long city blocks to go. After that we would take a quick right and the bridge would be there with its small detail of guardsmen manning the barricade. Ken whipped the truck around the corner and, to our horror, we saw that hooligans had overrun the little bridge outpost. Whether they took out the crew with weapons or the guardsmen deserted, we didn't know. Maybe the soldiers simply refused to fire their weapons on fellow Americans. Whatever the reason, our safest and most expedient route to safety was cut off.

Rioters were picking over the small outpost and we could clearly see two of them holding M-16s and firing them into the air. Others were holding boards or baseball bats and jumping around. It was clear that we couldn't simply drive up to them, identify ourselves as government workers and ask if we could pass on through. We were about 100 yards from them but they hadn't seen us yet.

"Put the truck in reverse," I whispered to Leland – as though whispering would matter – "and back the hell outta here."

Leland nodded. He quietly slipped the orange pickup into reverse and slowly backed up around the corner and kept going in reverse for another fifty yards before stopping. We were in between two long warehouses with no doors or windows facing us. We were safe for the moment.

"What in the hell are we gonna do now?" implored an exasperated Leland.

I grabbed the mic again; "Base, Wombat, over."

There was a few seconds delay. "*Go ahead, Wombat.*"

"Base, Broadway Bridge is overrun, National Guard troops have been taken out by hostiles, please advise on how to get back to friendly territory, over."

"*Wait one, Wombat.*"

"What do ya think?" I said to Leland.

"Well," he exhaled a long sigh, "we can make our way east, further up the river until we find a friendly access point. We really don't have any other options, do we?"

"*Wombat, base, over,*" the radio crackled.

"This is Wombat, over."

"*Wombat, make your way east to Hennepin Avenue Bridge, should be secure, acknowledge.*"

"This is Wombat, roger, make way to Hennepin Avenue Bridge, over."

"*Roger, Wombat, good luck. Out.*"

That would be easy enough. The Hennepin Bridge was only about a mile over heading east along the river. We started zigzagging through the streets trying to be as inconspicuous as two guys in an orange government truck could be. The north side of the bridge was located in an older part of town, a business area that included restaurants, shops, bars and liquor stores, many of which had been boarded up. It was a magnet for another horde of several hundred people intent on venting frustrations.

As we snaked up to the area in the Wombat Wagon, we could hear the sounds glass breaking and people shouting. We parked on the side a building several blocks away, got out of the truck and peered around from the back corner of an Asian dry-cleaning business. We had a limited view but could already tell that things were rapidly falling apart. There were mobs attacking Hmong-owned stores. The Asian shop owners were standing on rooftops and firing indiscriminately into crowds with guns.

"What do ya think?" I asked Leland.

"I wanna get outta this shit ASAP. I'm thinking maybe we could just drive around the main body of the mob like nothing is going on. Maybe no one will bother us."

"Hide in plain sight?" I rhetorically asked.

"Something like that."

"Sounds like a plan to me," I said. Safety was within a few hundred yards, so close we could feel it.

"You do know how to use that thing?" he asked nodding toward the pistol in my shoulder holster.

"I do," I said as I pulled it out. "But let's just be positive and focus on getting to friendly territory."

Firing a single handgun into a riotous crowd would make no more sense than intentionally rousing an angry hornets' nest. We peeled off our orange workers' vests. I took off my empty holster and threw it on the passenger-side floor of the truck. We hopped in the vehicle and I tucked the pistol right under my seat, out of sight but easily accessible. Leland threw the truck in drive and we proceeded.

We skirted the main body of the mob best we could and soon found ourselves within blocks of the bridge. There were people scattered loosely about, alone or in groups of two or three. We turned left and saw the bridge. Looking across the river we could see troops and police officers manning the downtown side of the bridge.

"Just drive nice and easy," I whispered to Leland. He nodded and crept along the river road at about 10-mph. We didn't want to come flying around another corner and run smack into peril like we did back at the Broadway Bridge.

People were eyeing us as we crept toward the bridge. Some of them held bats as weapons. Were these innocent civilians protecting themselves or the leading edge of the larger violent throng? Suddenly two men hustled out from the side of the street and situated themselves in front of our truck compelling Leland to stop short. A third man suddenly appeared from out of nowhere at my window. We were taken aback at how quickly the pedestrians had closed on our vehicle.

"Wazzup?" said a broad-shouldered young black man with a doo-rag on his head.

"Nuthin," I responded as cool as I could. "Just cruising around, you know."

Leland cleared his throat. I looked over to see more people filtering out of the side street a half a block up. They were intently interested in the goings-on at our truck and started moving toward us as though they had a mind of one.

"Looks like you mothafuckas been in th' shit," doo-rag man commented as he looked over our damaged vehicle and the broken glass inside the cab. More hooligans poured out from the side street and advanced toward us.

"Uh-huh." I looked in my rear-view mirror, it was clear behind us. *Anytime, Leland. You can throw the truck into reverse and floor it anytime now ...*

"You mothafuckas wit the government?" doo-rag scowled.

"We're just garbage men, man. We look like anybody important to you?" *Any fucking time, Leland ...*

"Wha'choo think, dog?" doo-rag said to one of the other men who was now standing at Leland's window. The crowd was denser now and just fifty dangerous feet away.

"I thinks we gots us a couple gov'ment bitches," he said as he reached back into his waistband. The front of the crowd started running at us.

Finally, Leland threw the truck into reverse and floored it. The side-mirrors of the vehicle hit both men, knocking doo-rag over. The other man pulled out a pistol and started shooting at our truck. I ducked down as far as I could into the footwell, pulled out my 9mm and peered over the dashboard.

THUMP, THUMP!

The radiator was hit and started trailing white smoke. I stuck my arm out the window and fired toward the crowd. I didn't know if I hit anybody and I didn't see anybody fall. In times of panic, inexperienced shooters tend to inadvertently aim too high in a firefight. That's probably what happened with me.

THUMP, WUMP!

The vehicle was absorbing more gunfire. Leland finally whipped the truck around a corner out of the line of fire and backed up quick into a driveway. We could hear the crowd approaching over the sound of the radiator hissing.

"So much for hiding in plain sight," I yelled.

"WHATEVER!" Leland screamed as he threw the truck into drive. We sped down the street.

"What the hell took you so long to get the fuck outta there?"

"Can we talk about this later?" Leland blurted as he concentrated on driving down the block.

A gaggle of rioters, maybe 30 or so, spilled out from the corner on our right we approached the intersection. Rocks and clubs pelted the truck and spider-webbed the windshield in front of me.

"SHIT!" Leland screamed as he cut a sharp left turn, clipping the curb. I grabbed the radio handset and keyed the mic – nothing. Our communication was dead. Leland floored the truck, which by now was making a loud knocking noise. We heading back through the neighborhood we had so recently and carefully negotiated, only this time as a big, smoking-generating noisemaker.

NOON

The police and guardsmen had been surprised by the quickly mounting trouble at first when the rioting first started, and then fell back to assume defensive positions on the downtown sides of the bridges. Some of the guardsmen panicked. Shots were fired indiscriminately into crowds, serving only to enrage the whole. Rioting soon broke out south and west of downtown as well. Dead bodies started to litter the streets. We were out in no-man's land. If we were going to reach safety, it would be totally up to us.

The Wombat Wagon limped into a quiet place to hide in the lot behind an innocuous old warehouse. It sputtered to a clunking halt as roils of steam curled up out of the radiator. The radio, upon further inspection, had taken a small arms round to the side. Judging by the bullet hole in my door, the projectile had miraculously just missed hitting the side of my knee. The left front tire rim had gotten slightly bent when Leland clipped the curb and developed a slow leak. It was now totally deflated. No matter, as the engine had clearly powered us into the lot with its final gasps of life. But the vehicle had delivered us from certain death.

You served us well, Wombat Wagon ...

A high chain-link fence topped with barbed-wire bordered the lot with industrial old railroad tracks down a rocky embankment on the other side. It was isolated and out of the traffic flow of the mobs. We were safe for the moment, but we were also farther away from the safety of downtown. I noticed that we were both breathing hard.

"Well. Whatta ya think?" asked Leland.

"We gotta ditch the truck."

"Uh-huh. Yup."

"Can't talk to anybody," I said.

"Nope."

"We'll have to hoof it on outta here."

"Yup."

We got out of the truck and Leland threw the keys under the driver's seat. There was a chance the vehicle could be salvaged after the riots subsided, whenever that would be. I retrieved the holster from the floor of the cab, put it back on and slapped in my second and last clip of ammunition. Leland threw his tool belt over his shoulder. There was nothing else of value that we needed to remove from the truck.

"Whatta ya think? How we gonna do it?" Leland said with a degree of hopelessness in his voice. I could see the skyscrapers of downtown far off in the distance over the trees and buildings. We had made it to within a rock's throw of a bridge to safety, only to find ourselves retreated to a position at least a mile-and-a-half from the river. It seemed so far, such a perilous trek to make on foot.

"One block at a time," I responded. "We'll just move one block at a time."

"Was that one big mob or a bunch of little ones … or what?" Leland asked, wiping his brow.

"I don't know," I said. If we were quiet, we could hear the sounds of violence off in the distance, hear the gunshots and screaming. Dark wisps of smoke were wafting to the sky in almost every direction. "You ready?"

"Let's roll," Leland said with a forced confident nod.

We scooted up to the corner of the warehouse and peeked around. There was nothing there except for a cat trotting across the street. This was a part of town that featured old warehouses, boarded up buildings and fallow train track beds. It had been a busy industrial area of decades gone by. We could take a chance holing up with some friendly civilians if we had been in a more residential neighborhood. We both knew the layout of the town and getting back to a quiet neighborhood meant crossing over busy streets, the kinds of throughways that were crawling with hooligans. The advantage to our present position was that an old industrial area like would be of no interest to the more violent elements of the population – I guess it's no fun destroying things of no value. We could move with relative safety for nearly a mile.

"Ready?" I said. Leland nodded. "Go!" He ran across the street and up to the next corner as I covered him with my weapon. After poking his head around the corner and ascertaining that it was safe, he motioned for me to follow. It was a bounding overwatch system that we quickly fell into, almost without even speaking to each other. Ken would run up the best secure corner or doorway he could find, never more than about a half a football field away. I would cover him and then run up to his position upon his non-verbal command.

So we went, block after neglected block, until we had covered over half a mile. We came to railroad tracks that were bordered by a fence on the north and a series of towering grain elevators on the south. To get across this scrap of terrain meant that we would be out in the open for at least a quarter of a mile. But we had been lucky so far. Aside from that cat, we had seen no one else up to this point. There was a small corrugated metal shed at the end of the elevators and beyond that there was a long stand of trees.

"I say we run together," Leland said. I nodded.

"Keep your eye on that shed," I said with a nod down the tracks. "If we get there, we can get to the stand of trees on the other side of the road and then figure out what we're going to do from there."

"Sounds good," he said, followed by a deep breath. "Ready, bro?"

"Let's do it."

We took off at something between a jog and a run along the fence. Halfway down we crossed over the tracks and ran in the shadows of the grain elevators. It seemed to take forever but we finally came up to the shed and slammed against it with our backs.

"See or hear anything?" I panted as my head swiveled around.

"No. Nothing. Cover me?"

I nodded in response. Leland looked around and then hustled across the street and disappeared behind some shrubbery. His torso popped back up, he looked around and then motioned for me to join him. I crossed the street and knelt beside him. We were both breathless, partly from the run and partly, I assume, from fear.

"I bet you're sorry you ever sat at my table that one day," I said in reference to our chance meeting at the Kaiserhof. He laughed a quiet but hearty laugh. It broke the tension and I laughed a bit, too. We took a short rest as we tried to figure out the best course of action to take next. An Army Blackhawk helicopter flew overhead at about 500 feet.

"I bet *they* have a nice view of things," Leland said half jokingly.

"Yeah," I said. I was looking back down the tracks when it hit me. I backhanded Leland on the arm. "You thinking what I'm thinking?" I asked as I eyed the grain elevators. Leland looked at them for a second before he knew what I meant.

"Shit. Why didn't we think of that before?"

A bird's eye view from one of the elevators would give us the best chance to properly assess our situation. We looked around and then ran back across the road to the first elevator. The doors were all padlocked and the exterior ringed utility ladders started 12 feet off the ground and were sheathed and secured with locked little tin hatches. But there might have been a route to the top as our eyes searched the structure.

There was an auxiliary silo for filling semi trailers off to the side. Up its side was a completely accessible ladder on the side going to the top of the mini-silo. It would be a simple affair to climb to the top of the silo and traverse the conveyer feeding system over to the main structure. Once over there, we could drop five feet onto the top of the maintenance shed roof. From there it would be an easy climb up the exterior zigzagging metal access stairs leading up the side of the massive structure.

We used the same system that we had in the streets: Leland went ahead as I covered him and then I followed as we made our way back to the elevator. The climb was as easy as we expected. We neither saw nor heard anybody, friend or foe, during our ascent and were 130 feet or so in the air in less than five minutes.

The horizons were laced with smoke in every direction as we looked out from our perch on top of the grain elevator. Whenever and however the riot had started, it had clearly spread far and wide. We had a good view of several strip malls and avenues lined with shops. We saw hundreds of inner-city denizens rushing out of stores and businesses that had been busted open, their arms full of whatever goods or appliances and boxes of who-knows-what that they could get their hands on. We squatted breathless on the uppermost part of the stairway that we could reach and thought aloud.

"I don't think we can make it to the river, let alone downtown," Leland said squinting in the sun and shaking his head.

I concurred. "We can head west. There's a railroad trestle we can cross," I said pointing to the narrow, iron bridge that was covered in graffiti. "We can make it to those residential neighborhoods less than a half mile away."

"Try to find some friendly civilians? Maybe use the phone?"

"Yup. Maybe even just hide out until morning. We can call the Gulag and I can call Sarah."

"I agree," Leland said, still trying to catch his breath. "Let's just get somewhere and not get shot at."

"Roger fucking that."

Leland and I had already suffered as the targets of numerous bullets, rocks, hurled debris and harsh language. We had no motorized transportation and no communication. Ducking into a friendly house sounded like the best thing we could do at this point. We looked around one last time then made our way back down to the ground.

We had done pretty good for ourselves up to this point, we thought, and were starting to get a little cocky. Upon getting back down to street level, we broke into a carefree jog towards the trestle, which was about another quarter mile down to the south. We ran right out onto the road without so much as looking right or left.

It was when we were in the middle of the road that it suddenly registered in my brain that there was a revving engine closing in on us. We turned at the same time to see the Army vehicle come screeching up to us. There was a man in the gunner's hatch handling the machine gun. A figure popped out of the passenger side and I recognized the young black NCO immediately: It was Sgt. Washington, the guardsman who had roughed me up when I was a little late coming back from the Kaiserhof a couple months back. He, in turn, did not seem to recognize me. I'm sure he'd roughed up more than one civilian in the months subsequent to our first meeting.

"You guys on your way home?" he asked.

"We're with the county," I said, raising my hands and turning so the servicemen could see the weapon in my shoulder holster. "We're trying to get over to the residential neighborhood so we can ride this riot out."

"You got some ID?" he said. The gunner had his weapon trained toward us.

"Yes," I said slowly moving my right hand to my rear pocket while keeping my left hand clearly in view. I threw the NCO my county ID and then Leland did the same. He seemed satisfied.

"We're going to make our way back downtown until we reach friendlies," Washington said.

"Damn, we already tried that and got our vehicle shot to hell," offered Leland.

"You boys weren't driving a Hummer and I'm betting you didn't have an M-60 machine gun either."

"That we didn't," Leland said.

"All right, then," Sgt. Washington said as he opened the back door of the Hummer. "You want a ride?" He didn't have to ask twice. We scampered into the back of the vehicle. There was a driver, in addition to Washington, and a young troop standing on the middle console manning the machine gun on top. We started rolling.

"Either of you guys hurt or shot or anything?"

"No, just scared shitless."

"Ya know, we saw you guys on top of that elevator from about three-quarters a mile away," the young NCO said turning around from his front seat.

"You're kidding," Leland said somewhat surprised. "I thought we were being downright sneaky."

"Hell no. You guys are lucky it's us who came up to you first. Anyway, what did you see from up there?"

"The further east you go, the more violence there is," I explained. "Like I said, we were just going to make our way to the west and find a place to hide out. How about you guys?"

"Right now, we're trying to make our way back to one of the bridges," Washington told us. "We were part of a three-vehicle patrol. We got separated. Now we just trying to get back in the city. Problem is, this side of all the bridges over the Mississippi are crawling with rioters."

"Then why don't you do what we were going to do?" I asked.

"Excuse me," Washington said as he turned in his seat. "I have a chain-of-command and you're not in it. Now tell me what else you know."

Asshole ...

"Okay," I said. "Hennepin Avenue Bridge is probably a no-go. That's where we got shot up. We were at the Broadway Bridge before that."

"How's that?"

"It's barricaded, you probably knew that. But there weren't that many guys there when we were there. But they were armed with M-16s."

"Ain't no match for a machine gun," Washington countered with youthful bravado. "You know how to use that piece you have?" he said to me.

"Sure do," I responded.

"Well, keep it in your holster and let us do all the shooting. I don't need no damn civilian getting all excited and poppin me in the back of the damn head."

"You got it," I said, perfectly happy to let the Army drive us back into downtown and do all the shooting on the way. Leland seemed fine with the arrangement, too. It struck me that we just all casually assumed that there'd soon be lots of shooting going on.

Washington seemed like a professional soldier and I respected him for that. But I thought that he was a little excessive with the macho testosterone act. I understand the need for police and military men to assume attitudes of control and authority. But it's a delicate line to walk; when does confidence cross the line into arrogance? When does authority cross the line into tyranny? I remembered back to when he slammed me into the ground that night when I was walking home from the Kaiserhof. How many people had he, and people like him, roughed up? Damn, I was one of the "good guys" and I sure as hell was on the receiving end of heaping spoonful of mistreatment. I wondered if that kind of daily behavior by government agents was a factor in swelling riot situation.

We drove back towards downtown and within minutes were back amongst the huge industrial warehouses where it all started for Leland and me. Washington was on the radio talking with some other units. From what I could hear, we were all by ourselves. We were the only Hummer in that particular part of town and word from Washington's higher-ups said it would be up to the five of us to get back to downtown on our own.

"That sounds familiar," I leaned over and whispered to Leland.

We were getting closer to the bridge and the closer we got, the more excited the driver became. I remember Leland's mistake of whipping around a corner and running smack dab into trouble. I was just about to lean forward and make a suggestion when the young Army specialist did the exact same thing.

The Hummer came around the corner of a warehouse real fast – there was a crowd of rioters at the bridge outpost. Rather than stopping and backing up, the driver just kept going. I guess his plan was to not stop just keep driving, take another quick right and duck back between warehouses. It was a good plan, except ...

It wasn't until we were way committed down the vehicle serviceway between two huge warehouses that we noticed that it was a dead end. There was a chain link fence down at the end, which we might have been able to break through except that there were pallets, boxes, dumpsters and debris piled up against it.

"Fuck!" the driver yelled as he slammed on the brakes. He cranked the wheel and threw the Hummer into reverse, then slammed in into drive and oriented us back toward the one and only exit.

Unfortunately, the crowd had followed us in there. The throng flowed around the corner and advanced toward us, many of them hold boards or clubs, some looking like they held firearms in hand. The din of their angry voices and menacing footfalls echoed challengingly off the walls of the buildings. We were cornered.

"STOP OR WE WILL FIRE ON YOU!" Washington ordered through the megaphone. He seemed pretty calm. The crowd advanced without a pause, intent on getting their hands on us. We were all government guys.

"Goddammit," Washington muttered. "Fire on my command, but shoot into the ground about 50 or 60 feet in front of them."

"Roger that," said the troop up in the gunner's hatch.

"Fire."

The gunner pointed the weapon downwards and pulled the trigger. The heavy weapon barked to life and M-60 rounds chewed up the ground and concrete before the crowd. Empty brass casings pinged off the roof of the vehicle and some of them spilled inside the passenger compartment, still hot and smoldering. Bullets disintegrated and whistled scatter-shot into the crowd along with tiny pebbles and bits of concrete. Washington fired his weapon, but I noticed that he was clearly firing too high to hit anyone. He was intentionally shooting over the heads of the crowd.

People dispersed like cockroaches, screaming, stinging and bleeding from non-lethal shrapnel. Some were limping as they disappeared behind boxes and barrels next to the buildings, or simply pinned themselves to the walls. Perhaps some of the bullets maintained enough mass to inflict grave injury, but I didn't see anybody go all the way to the ground. Even if that were the case, I was impressed at Washington's ability to disperse the mob without intending to inflict deadly harm.

"*Floor it!*" Washington ordered when there was a big enough gap for us to squirt through.

"Don't have to tell me twice," said the driver. He threw the army vehicle into gear and sped over the ground where the crowd had been menacingly advancing only seconds before. I heard a couple of guns discharging but I don't think we were hit. We spilled out onto the street and the driver pointed us toward the bridge. Again there was a large group of bad guys positioned at the bridge, again preventing our flight to safety.

"Shit!" Washington blurted. The driver drove across the median and we sped away in the opposite direction.

4:45 p.m.

Minneapolis and St. Paul – an entire double metropolis – buckled as block after block fell and the fires spread and multiplied. Houses burned and gunshots rang out. Lone cars filled with folks seeking safety from the mobs and the fires were bushwhacked as they tried to leave the inner city neighborhoods. Strangers pulled strangers from their cars and beat them and killed them. People went absolutely crazy, the metropolitan area was a giant mess.

Sgt. Washington decided against going to the residential neighborhoods. A Humvee parked in front of a house would be like a signal flare for hooligans to come and mess with us.

"We're with the government, all of us," Washington said. "Ain't no need to involve civilians in our sorry-ass troubles." Maybe he was right.

We came across a wrecked Minneapolis police car a few blocks down. It had been pretty well smashed up by the rioters. The tires were slashed, the windows were blasted out, there was a lot of blood on the street and no sign of the officers but, curiously enough, the shotgun was still in the car.

The shotgun in modern police cars sits upright between the driver and passenger seats and is secured by a magnetic lock. Whoever destroyed the car obviously didn't know where the release mechanism was. Washington did: There were five white buttons in a row on a little console underneath the weapon. The middle one released the magnetic lock for three seconds. Washington leaned in the car, hit the button and effortlessly pulled the shotgun out of its rack.

"*Dumb-ass civilians,*" he chuckled to himself. "If the motherfuckers had any smarts, they'd have just unplugged the battery."

We made it back to the industrial area. The Hummer was backed up down an alley and around into a little nook between two burned out old factories. We were invisible to anybody out on the streets: We were safe. Our present position was probably less than half a mile away from where Leland and I had abandoned the Wombat Wagon.

The gunner, whose name I finally learned was Vogelgesang, had removed the M-60 from the swivel-ring and set up a defensive position in a pile of garbage and debris. The weapon had its own built-in bipod at the end of the barrel. The driver, Fifield, had made his way to the roof via an exterior ladder on the eastern building and was keeping watch as best he could. Washington manned the radio. The good news was that we had communication. The bad news was that a single Humvee and its crew were low – very low – on the Army's priority list of concerns.

"We 'sposed to keep our heads down and wait."

"Wait for *what*?" Leland asked.

"Shit's going down everywhere, man," Washington said. "As long as we're safe, they say sit tight for the moment."

"Any chance of notifying our home base?" I asked.

"I can't even talk with the damn police on that radio. It operates in a secure, scrambled military net. Ain't no way I can raise some damn civilian construction crew."

"Did you tell them about us?"

"Yes. Whether they pass on the word, I don't know. Everybody's got their hands pretty full right now."

"So *now* what?" I asked.

"We sit here and wait, that's what."

"Got anything to eat?" Leland asked.

"Yeah, we got five or six MRE's in the back. Why don't you guys find a place to get comfortable. We're just gonna ride this thing out from here for now."

Sgt. Washington showed us how to work the M-16s during our first hour down that alley; how to lock and load, where the safety was and so on. I didn't tell him I already knew, I just wanted him to carry out all his duties as seamlessly as possible. He wanted us to know, he said, in case one of them went down and we had to use that guy's weapon. He also wrote down our full names, social security numbers and the department where we worked. He didn't say why, but I guess that was in case we got killed.

We were relieved to be in relative safety, but I was also going crazy wondering about my wife. Was she unharmed? Was she at home when the riots broke out or out with friends? If she was, did they make it to safety? I was quietly going nuts. We could hear the sounds of helicopters near and distant. I was growing familiar with the feeling of safety being so close, yet so impossibly far away. But I only cared about one thing:

God please let Sarah be safe.

1:45 a.m.

I sat with my back against an alley wall, pulled my knees up and pillowed my head on my arms. I managed to doze off into a dreamy state. I dreamt it was two or three years down the road: America was still healing but things were much better. By that time, there would be less violence and more order. Yes, less violence and more order in society.

Sarah and I would throw a huge summer party at our house. Guys from the Gulag and the Kaiserhof would be there. It would just be all us who made it through the riots. There would be T-bone steaks and potato salad and beer. Lots of beer. The story-telling would begin later in the evening. Guys would take turns telling about their adventures on that one July fourth when all hell broke loose.

Then it would come to Leland and me. People would get real quiet and gather 'round as we told our story. If one of us missed a part, the other would chime in with the missed details. *"Oh yeah, how'd I forget that?"*

After awhile I'd get to the part about a brash young National Guard NCO who scooped us up off the streets in the middle of the riots. I'd nod over to Jerrell Washington, who'd be standing off to the side of the group in his civvies and holding a cold beer in his hand. He'd nod to the group and smile a humble smile.

Surely we'd be good friends by then.

Vogelgesang and Fifield had switched off duties between manning the machine gun in the alley and keeping watch on the roof. They switched top of the hour, every hour. I guess that prevents boredom and gets a fresh set of eyes on an observed position or some military crap like that. I asked Washington if I could go up on the roof with Fifield. I couldn't sleep and it wouldn't hurt to have a second pair of eyes up there. He said okay.

Fifield seemed like a competent soldier a smart enough guy. He was in his early- or mid-twenties, about 6'1", 175 pounds with blond hair. He was a good-looking kid, with one hell of a jagged scar running from his right temple to his lower right jaw. Other than that, he seemed like just a regular civilian who happened to be wearing Army clothes.

We had a fairly decent view from up there: We could se the main avenues of approach if any bad guys started coming our way and we could see around the city a bit. Fires glowed here and there. The lights of the city were out; probably another black-out. There was the occasional gunshot and far away yelling. We were fairly safe and out of sight.

"Pretty exciting, huh?" Fifield quietly said.

"Oh, yeah. Barrel of fuckin monkeys."

"So you from here?" he asked.

"Yup. Minneapolis. I sold sandpaper before."

"Sandpaper? Really? That sounds boring."

"It was. How 'bout you? You been in the Army long?" I asked.

"Me? I was in the 1st Cavalry for a two-year hitch after high school. I fought in Iraq then got out and joined the Guard. I grew up right … *over there*," he said pointing to a neighborhood off to the northeast. I pretended I could see exactly where he was pointing.

"I was a diesel mechanic before all this shit happened," he continued.

"You were in Iraq, huh?"

"Yeah. Got my vehicle blown up, not once, but fuckin *twice* by those damn roadside bombs, those IED's."

"Really?" I said.

"Yeah, really. That's where I got this," he said with a casual gesture to the angry scar running down the side of his face. "Scarier than shit, man. And *loud?* Whew …"

"I bet," I said, and then changed the subject. "So, tell me; how's Washington?"

"Sergeant Washington? A little cocky, but he knows his shit. He's a good soldier."

"Think he can get us all out of this jam?"

"Shit's quieted down some …" He never really finished the thought or answered the question. It wasn't the ringing endorsement that I was looking for. We talked for awhile longer and soon enough, it was 3:00 a.m. and it was Vogelgesang's turn on the roof.

4:05 a.m.

We spent a fitful night in that alley – nobody really slept. We heard the sounds of violence, sometimes nearby, but no one seemed to have noticed us squirreled away between those two buildings. Washington manned the radio and was in the truck most of the night talking in hushed tones every now and then and writing things down using a flashlight with a red lens. Apparently he and his superiors had worked out a plan. When he came out, he stopped Fifield from going back up on the roof.

"Huddle up!" he said in a real loud whisper. We all gathered around. "Alright, here's the deal: We're going home, over the Hennepin Bridge."

"When?" asked Fifield.

"Right goddam now," answered the young NCO.

"What's the catch?" said Vogelgesang.

"There's a good chance there's gonna be shootin and probably some teargas," Washington said casually, then turned to Fifield and me. "You guys ever been gassed?"

"No," we both said, wide-eyed and a little scared.

"You guys don't have NBC masks, we do. We have to wear ours 'cause we got a job to do, understand?"

We nodded.

"You'll be in the Hummer, so you won't get the worst of it, but there will be gas coming down through the open gunner's hatch. Okay? I don't know if it will be horrible or just plain old bad, but you'll be okay when it's all over. Got it?" He said, trying to be reassuring while not putting a glossy face on things at the same time.

"Okay," we said simultaneously.

"These dipshit civilians can't shoot for shit ... sprayers and prayers."

We nodded nervously.

"Now if by some stroke of shitty luck the vehicle gets taken out and we get killed, you'll have to dismount and try to make it on foot. There's gonna be a password. Okay?"

We nodded again, eyes wide. *Holy shit!* This was the real deal: This was real live Army stuff: Getting back through enemy lines, passwords, live gunfire, casualties. It was nowheres *near* as fun as I always thought it would be. This crap was downright, your-last-day-on-Earth scary.

"Okay," Washington continued. "Approach friendly forces with your hands visible and yell, 'Manitoba!' Got it?"

"Password is Manitoba. Got it."

"That's only until 6:00 a.m."

"What happens then?"

"If you get delayed in your crossing for whatever reason, the password changes at six in the morning. After six, the password changes to 'Yorktown.' Say it."

"Yorktown."

"If one of us gets killed, take our weapon and take our gas mask. Use them both, understand?"

"Yes," we said. I was impressed with the young Sergeant's contingency planning.

He turned to his men. "You hear all that?" They were on the roof of the Hummer remounting the machine-gun and nodded affirmative. "You guys ready to rock?"

"Let's go home," Fifield said, matter-of-factly.

"Let's go, gentlemen," Washington calmly said. We all piled in the Hummer. Vogelgesang and Fifield put their protective masks within reach, Washington kept his at the ready on his lap. Since he was driving, Fifield got the shotgun – Washington still didn't trust us civilians with weapons. Leland and I hunkered in the back seat.. The Hummer rolled out of the alley and Leland and I began our *fourth* run at getting back to safety.

We snaked through the early morning darkness like a ghost ship. Streetlights were out and the Hummer's dim tactical lights were the only light pollution generated by us. Every now and then we would see the glowing remains of some building or house.

Soon enough, we got to the little business district on the riot side of the Hennepin Bridge. There was debris, burning cars and dead bodies strewn about. Through the building we could make out the bridge through the darkness and we could even make out the soldiers on the other side, silhouetted by a few dim lights. Snipers had harassed the government troops so they kept their distance. We were idling about three hundred yards from the bridge, all but home.

"Wha'choo think, Fifield?" Washington said to the driver.

"Let's go, Sarge. I don't see nobody."

"Roger that," Washington said, donning his mask. "Proceed to the bridge," came his order, muffled through the NBC mask. Fifield put the Hummer into drive and we moved forward. Two-hundred and fifty yards ... nothing. Two-hundred yards, still nothing. Closer ... closer ...

"Six, three-one," Washington lifted his mask and called in. "You should have us in sight, over."

"Roger, three-one, over."

Closer ... closer ... I felt like we weren't alone ... one-hundred and fifty yards ... I first sensed, then saw figures in the darkness, in the windows ... one-hundred yards ... closer ... across the dark intersection ... *WHAM! CRASH!*

Something big hit the Hummer from the side: A civilian car with its lights off T-boned us from the right, throwing the Army vehicle into the wreckage of a burned out car. We didn't even hear it coming and we were all roughed up. My shoulder and head hurt like hell. The side of the machine-gunner's ring caught Vogelgesang in the ribs and he was hurt but stayed in his position. Gunfire rang out from everywhere; corners, windows, doorways ... from the very darkness itself.

"Get the hell outta here!" Washington ordered.

"I'm trying," Fifield screamed. "She won't start!"

"VEE, FIRE!" Vogelgesang painfully swung the machine gun barrel toward the large civilian sedan – I don't know the make, maybe a Crown Victoria – and opened up. The car was having trouble starting back up itself and Vogelgesang thoroughly raked the passenger compartment with point-blank machinegun fire. There was no way anyone could have survived. He then turned his attention to the rest of the street and sprayed wildly. Washington had his weapon out his window and was firing one round at a time, carefully aiming before squeezing off each shot.

"Get this fucking thing outta here."

"Got it," Fifield cried as the engine roared back to life.

"We're in the shit now, Just go for the bridge."

"Roger," Fifield said as he backed the Hummer out of the wreckage and then slammed it back into drive, skirted around the wrecked car that had hit us and headed for the bridge. Bullets pinged off the vehicle and then smoldering shell casings rained down from the gunner's hatch as Vogelgesang's M-60 answered back. Out of nowhere, dozens of screaming figures appeared in the street ahead between the bridge and us. Some were firing at us with small arms; others were throwing bricks and stones at the Hummer. Fifield was blasting suppressive fire out of his window with the shotgun, quickly taking his both hands off the wheel to re-pump and then firing again.

A volley of teargas canisters arced into the crowd from unseen soldiers on the bridge. We could barely see as it was because of the darkness. Within seconds, we were driving through a blinding white smoke. Sure enough, some of it swirled in through the top hatch just like Sergeant Washington said it would.

WUMP! WUMP! – we heard the sounds of bodies hitting the Humvee as the blind vehicle tried to drive through blinded pedestrians.

At first the gas wasn't that bad – *I can take this,* I thought. But after several more seconds, the agony began. My eyes stung and watered worse than I could ever remember in my life. Then my throat started burning and I had trouble breathing. It was pure hell. I was blind but could hear gunfire and military chatter through the radio. I remember hearing Washington yelling muffled orders through his mask, *"Slow down! Watch out! Right, turn right! RIGHT!!"*

CRASH!

I was thrown forward – I assumed everybody was. Fifield couldn't see very well through the darkness and the teargas cloud and we hit the bridge abutment. I was pretty banged up and sore – I'm sure we were all feeling about the same. Fifield immediately tried restarting the Hummer. It was dead.

"Un-ass this goddam vehicle," Washington ordered. Leland and me were gasping and coughing. My eyes watered, and the more they watered the more they stung. I felt Vogelgesang slinking by us on his way out, lugging the heavy machine along with him and cracking me across the knees in the process. I think it was he who then turned around and grabbed me. I heard the pops of shitty civilian weapons and could hear distant voices of soldiers yelling; "*C'mon, run for it! This way! C'mon ...*" Next thing I know, we were running, all five of us arm-in-arm. I was blind and was just trusting that we were headed to safety and that nobody would guide me over an open manhole.

"*MANITOBA! MANITOBA!*" Washington and Fifield were screaming.

"Leland?" I yelled between wheezes.

"(cough) *Yeah?* (gasp)." I heard him. He was two guys over to my left.

"Just checkin (gasp)."

We kept running, waiting for a final bullet to rip into one of our spines. The run to safety seemed to take forever. Finally we were past the midway point and some soldiers grabbed us. Still blind, I could hear weapons firing from both directions. As we got to the other side I heard Leland puking. We were hustled a block or two back into downtown to some little tactical command post next to the post office and administered first aid. First we had our eyes flushed with saline. Sight painfully returned.

"You shot or anything?" an Army medic asked each one of us.

"No." Leland and I were fine except for the gas. I was a sore from being thrown around the Army Humvee but not enough to say anything about it. Leland had a foot-long string of pure snot hanging out of his nose as he sat recovering hunched over with his elbows on his knees.

I wasn't in any better condition: I suddenly realized how exhausted my mind and body were and I just sat on cement retaining wall, my head and arms hanging down in surrender to fatigue. I sat there aware of the tear-gas stink wafting off my body and could barely form a thought outside of the lizard brain. I suddenly became aware of a string of snot hanging out of my nose too. I thought about wiping it off but my arms continued to hang there. This is who I am, I thought. This is me; stinking, tired, festooned with snot.

I came back to the world after a few minutes and started thinking coherently. We were a little banged up, yes, but we were okay. Vogelgesang was a different story. He had some badly broken ribs as result of the couple of crashes we were involved in. He was one tough guy, though. He'd be okay, too.

Washington did it. The young Army sergeant got his crew and two dumb-ass civilians back to downtown alive. I wanted to thank him, but he was already gone. Fifield was gone, too. I asked if they were okay. The medic said they were fine, just had to go report in somewhere. Just another day on the job for those guys, I guess.

Dusk was breaking to another cloudless sky, surely to give rise to another hot day. I looked at the moon, which was burning in crimson red low on the western horizon. We took another ten minutes to collect ourselves and then headed out.

NINTEEN

We had made it back to the Gulag on foot less than fifteen minutes later. There were two Army guys guarding the front gate and we had to show our ID. Our noses were running and we still reeked of teargas.

The first thing Leland wanted to do was sit down and slam a Coke. The first thing I did was run up to the office and try to phone Sarah. No answer. I called at least five times, hanging up when the voicemail kicked in and re-dialing. I couldn't get ahold of her. Maybe she left an email, I thought. I asked one of the dispatchers if I could hop online quick. It was no big deal; there was a computer online almost all the time in the dispatch office. I checked my email. Nothing.

Shit.

I had to get home. I went back down outside. One of our trucks was parked with a body in the bed. I saw a worker's boots and lower legs sticking out from under a tarp.

"Who is that?" I asked one of the engine shop guys walking by.

"Boone," he answered casually.

"Boone?" I asked in surprise. "Are you sure he's dead?" I said moving to uncover him.

"Don't," he said grabbing my arm. "You won't like what you see under there. Just trust me, he's dead." I nodded.

Damn. Boone was a good man and a good worker. He wasn't my best friend or anything, but we got along pretty good and it was a shock to hear that he was killed.

I made my way out onto the street where my car was parked. A Humvee stopped next to me as I was digging my keys out of my pocket. Fred Zampoli poked his head out of the window.

"What the hell you doing?"

"Can't find my wife. I gotta go home."

"You know it's still dangerous out there, right?"

"I don't care. I'd rather die than lose Sarah."

Fred paused for a thoughtful second and then reached into the rear of the vehicle. He pulled out an M-16 and handed it to me. "You know how to use that. There's a thirty-round clip in there. That's yours from now on."

"Thanks, Freddy," I said as I put the weapon in the back seat. "You won't get in trouble?"

"Trust me, our supply and organization is so screwed right now, no one will miss it."

"You're a good guy, Fred."

"You stay alive, you bastard," he said with his Long Island brogue and a slap on my arm.

"I will, buddy."

Fred respected me as a man with a mission and he didn't try to dissuade me from going out to look for my wife. I, in turn, respected him for that. I started my car and headed south, out of downtown. There weren't many people out on the street but there was some debris a wrecked car.

Our house was about a ten-minute drive from the Gulag. The scenery went from peaceful to war zone as I crossed out of downtown proper and into the inner-city residential area. My heart was pounding as I got closer and closer to home. The drive seemed to take forever but finally I screeched to a stop in front of our house. Miraculously enough, it had remained unscathed during the riots and her car was parked on the side street.

I grabbed the M-16 from the back seat and circled the house slowly. I didn't want to burst through the front door and catch a perpetrator's gunblast upon entry. I was looking for broken windows, signs of forced entry, anything that would denote violence. Nothing. The house looked secure from the outside. Our windows were still papered over so I couldn't peek inside. I unlocked the door with my key and stepped inside. "SARAH?" There was no response. The house was very much as I remembered it when I'd left almost twenty-four hours earlier.

"*SARAH?*" No response. I began frantically searching the house. She simply wasn't there. I was looked for an address book or anything that would have phone numbers written down, particularly those of her parents. I couldn't find anything. Sarah's cell phone had stopped working shortly after The Attack and she said that she threw it away – it certainly would have had a treasure trove of phone numbers in the memory. *Dammit!*

She never mentioned which city in Texas her dad lived in. I tried an internet search but there were hundreds of Penningtons listed in Texas. But she said something about her mom living in Minnetonka, which was an affluent suburb west of Minneapolis. With any luck, the mom kept her last name. I grabbed the directory and the landline phone in the kitchen and began calling. There were only about twenty

Penningtons listed in the whole Minneapolis phone book and only three of them – all young married couples – lived in Minnetonka.

Frustrated, I made one last sweep through the bedroom. Something caught my eye – a small electronic box to the rear on the mid-level shelf of the nightstand. It was a caller ID box – how I'd never seen it before I don't know. I guess it was a testament to our whirlwind marriage. I rushed to it, hoping that there hadn't been a power outage that might erase any numbers stored on its electronic recent calls list. There were calls stored on it, mostly from or to me.

One number stood out as I scrolled down. Minneapolis was in the '612' yet one number registered as a '952' area code number – the area code for the Minnetonka area. I called the number and it just kept ringing and ringing. No person or answering machine ever picked up. I wrote the number down and stuffed it into my pocket. While I was there I took off my reeking work shirt and quickly threw on a clean oversized sweatshirt.

There was no note indicating Sarah's whereabouts. *What did she say she was doing yesterday?* I thought. She said she was going out looking for a food dealer. That's it, that's all I knew. That was my one and only clue. I left a note telling her to call me and leave a message at the Gulag and I left.

I felt hopeless. I had no clue where to even begin looking for my wife. I felt like a caged tiger, constricted by a force that was totally out of my control. I got back in my car and drove towards Uptown. It wasn't very far away; maybe she had hunkered down with some of her poetry friends. I parked in front of *The Word* coffeehouse. I ran down the stairs into the dark venue. The stage lights were dimly lit and there was a small office lamp on behind the bar. That was it for illumination. I squinted trying to make out if anyone was actually in there.

"Hello?"

"Hello, Dallas," came a man's voice from the darkness.

"Gary?" I said as my eyes struggled to adjust to the dark.

"I'm right here, right in front of you," said the old hippie and establishment owner. His voice was sullen.

Suddenly I saw him – my eyes having crossed the threshold into nightvision – sitting alone at one of the small round tables. A tiny ceramic cup and saucer sat neatly before him.

"Oh, there you are," I said and walked over to him.

"Would you care to sit?"

"Sure," I said. "But just for a minute. Have you seen Sarah?"

"Sarah? No, is she missing, too?"

"What do you mean, 'too'?"

"The riots, they scattered people. I've kind of been 'central command' for our little group here. People are missing. Now you're telling me that Sarah is gone, too? She would make six missing." He looked down at the floor and whispered, *"Sweet Sarah ..."*

"What's your number here?" He wordlessly handed me a card from his shirt pocket. "Here's my numbers," I said handing him a card of my own. "Can you please call me if you hear anything from Sarah?"

"Of course I will, Dallas. I'll do anything within my power to help you find Sarah."

"Thank you, Gary. I'm running out of places to look."

"It's a terrible mess. All of it, everything." He was speaking quietly, philosophically, almost as if he were in a trance or meditative state. He seemed somewhat depressed and I wasn't sure if he was under the influence or not.

"I just want to find my wife. That's all that matters in the whole world to me."

"I understand."

"Just call if you hear from Sarah."

"You know I will. Be careful out there, young man," he answered. And with that I left and went back to the Gulag.

I got back downtown, parked on the street right outside the Gulag and walked into the compound. The yard was abuzz with activity; damaged vehicles parked haphazardly and workmen criss-crossing the grounds. Lebenze was sitting on a stack of cinder block bricks smoking a cigarette. His head was down and he was staring at the ground. It was the first time I'd seen him since the riot and I was glad to see that he was alive.

"Henri!" I said as I approached him.

"*Oui, mon ami*," he replied like a man who'd been through a wringer.

"What are you still doing here?"

"Orders. We were told not to leave since yesterday when we got back."

Now that I was up close to him I saw that his face was cut and bruised up.

"What the hell happened to *you*?"

"I got beat up."

"Yes, I figured as much. I guess my question is how'd you get back here alive?"

"Stubbs," he replied.

"Stubbs? What about Stubbs?"

"We were out on crew *togezzer*, Stubbs was our leader. We were out checking on recent projects. *Zat* was our detail for *ze* day, yes? Just to drive around and see if people had broken into *ze* buildings, *oui?*"

"*Wee* ... go on."

"Stubbs was our leader. He dropped us off to work on a building, very light work, and says he *iz* going to check on a different building, not too far away, yes?"

"Then what?"

"While he *iz* gone, me and a new guy – I don't know his name – start working on *ze* building. Next thing we know, we are surrounded by a bunch of *peessed*-off people. *Zen zay* start to beat us up. Suddenly, Stubbs *iz* pulling *ze* angry people off of us and telling *zem* to leave us alone."

"And they stopped?"

"*Oui!* Stubbs *iz* a large black man and *zay* do what he says. But while he *iz* helping us, some bastard steals *ze* truck! *Sacre' bleu* ..."

"Shit, which vehicle was it?"

"*Rolling Blunder.*"

"Damn. So how'd you get back here then?"

"*Zat iz* something, let me tell you. Stubbs stands us up, puts an arm around each of us and *zen* walks."

"Walks?"

"*Zat's* right. We walk two kilometers and *ze* riot raging all around us. But Stubbs *wiss hiz* arms around us? It *iz* a magic bubble of protection. It was like we were invisible. No bad people fucked *wiss* us anymore. For two kilometers, he walks *wiss hiz* arms around us *ze* way a father protects *hiz shildren'*. He never took *hiz* arms from around us.

He walked us right into downtown, right up to *ze* soldiers." Henri took a long and thoughtful drag from his cigarette. "I will never forget what Mr. Aaron did for me. *Never.*"

I had always liked Stubbs and now I saw him in an even better, nobler light. He risked his own life putting his arms around two white men and walking them out of the riot zone. He didn't have to but he did it. For two kilometers – a mile-and-a-half – he did it. My eyes scanned around the compound until I saw him. He was sitting on the gate of a pickup, leaning back an elbow and drinking a can of Coke. Between sips his face was cocked up to the late morning sun, his eyes closed in quiet meditation. I felt like going up and saying something to him but decided to let him have his peace.

"*Holy fuck!* Did you hear about Scheerer?" Brian proclaimed with a combination of youthful exuberance and vulgarity when I bumped into him in the maintenance bay about ten minutes later.

"No, what?" I asked.

"He saved our lives! Me, John and Boone got caught out in the riots about two miles east of where you and Leland were."

"Yeah?"

"Yeah. So we're working and all the sudden there's these people out in the street talking shit, threatening us. We just keep working, we don't know what's going on, right?

"Go on."

"More people come, and then more. Next thing we know, dispatch is on the horn telling us to get back to the Gulag, there's a fucking riot going on. No sooner do they tell us that than our truck starts getting pelted with rocks and shit. We hop in, Boone floors it, runs over about two or three guys and we're on the run, right?"

"Yeah ..."

"We drive around, the fucking bridge is blocked by assholes and they're throwing shit at us. John swears he heard gunshots. We heard you and Leland taking fire over the radio."

"Keep going."

"Yeah, long story short, we hole up in this building, some abandoned store or something. People are freaking shooting at us. They were trying to kill us, like, for real! They're screaming and yelling, they light our truck on fuckin fire. Boone has a pistol and two clips. He was firing into the crowd, holding people off. We were like Butch Cassidy and that Sundance dude, you know that movie where they're surrounded by the Bolivian army?"

"Yes, I know the movie."

"So we're surrounded by a hundred people at least, I shit you not. Boone has like one bullet left, our truck is burning, we're screwed, right? Suddenly, freakin Scheerer comes tear-assin around the corner with his truck, runs over about ten assholes, shoots another five dudes or so with an M-16 and tell us to run for it."

That explained why Scheerer was on the dispatch radio when Leland and I first called in and then was gone. He went out looking for his workers. By himself.

Brian continued with his story; "The crowd falls back for a few seconds 'cause of this crazy white guy is fucking up their shit, so we run for his truck. All the sudden Boone gets shot in the leg and falls down. Scheerer gets out and comes over to help us. He empties his clip into this crowd of assholes, throws the rifle in the back and then runs and picks up Boone like he was a little kid and throws him in the bed of the truck. John hops in the back and I hop in the front. Just as Scheerer was running back to get in the truck, this asshole motherfucker comes outta nowhere and swings at him with a fuckin two-by-four. Scheerer ducks, pops back up, and chops the guy in the throat with the edge of his hand."

"Holy *shit!*"

"Yeah, then as the guy is grabbing his throat in pain, Scheerer grabs this fucker's head from behind and snaps it around a hundred-and-eighty degrees. He snapped the dude's neck as easy as you or me would crack a chicken bone. The whole freaking deal took about three seconds, then this guy is laying dead on the ground looking like an owl with his head pointing in the wrong direction and his eyes bugging out. It was incredible!"

"Then what?" I said, mesmerized by the account.

"Scheerer gets in the truck and we drive off," Brian said with a shrug.

"Then what the hell happened to Boone?"

"Oh, that. We got about a block down when this volley of freakin bullets rips into the truck. Boone was poking his head up at the time. He took a bullet in the face. Man, it was bad. He was dead, like, instantly," Brian's cheeks puffed out as he exhaled, his eyes wide.

"Shit," I whispered as I shook my head.

"Yeah, so Scheerer got us back here. He didn't get so much as a goddam scratch. He tried to go back into the riots but the Guard wouldn't let him back out of downtown. But he saved our lives, man. *He saved our lives.*"

I patted my young friend on the shoulder and told him I was glad he made it. I talked with John later. He pretty much told me the exact same story.

TWENTY

Dozens of riots broke out in many urban centers across the United States on that day, not just in Minneapolis and St. Paul. Some were limited to certain neighborhoods within a city, others were rolling waves of destruction. The Minneapolis riot was more on the violent end. No one knew exactly what started them, the violence was nothing more than a case of spontaneous combustion, a Big Bang of malfeasance. It was as though a collective and evil consciousness took over and drove people insane. Thousands of citizens died that day across the country: Americans, for the vast most part, at the hands of other Americans. Now, in addition to potential nuclear detonations, there was another calamitous reason to stay out of the big cities.

The mayor of Minneapolis came to the Gulag to give us a pep talk and to say thank-you the next day. Everyone, the shop workers, field crews, supervisors and dispatchers were up in the briefing room. I was sitting in the way back with some of the other field guys. One of his aides introduced the youngish Democratic mayor. I hadn't voted for him, but from what I'd seen and heard of him I thought that he'd stood up well in a time of national crisis. Everyone stood and applauded politely as the mayor took his place in front of us. He was dressed casually wearing a dress shirt with rolled-up sleeves and no tie.

"Thank you, thank you. I just wanted to stop by very informally and relay my profound gratitude for all the work you and people like you have done. I know when you workers are out there sweating bullets and working, you have to wonder sometimes if it's all worth anything, right?"

Some of us kind of nodded and grunted.

"As your mayor, I am here to confirm to you that your work *is* important. I'm around, I know what's going on, I see you guys out there even if you don't know it. I know you guys are out there pounding nails, picking up garbage, doing whatever – excuse me – *shitty job* comes down the pike. But you people hang in there and tough it out. That makes you champions in *my* book, everyone of ya," he emphasized with a thrust of his finger.

"And if that weren't enough, then came the riots. Helluva a way to celebrate the national birthday, huh?"

Again, nods and grunts.

"I've heard the stories. I heard how some of you got trapped out in the war zone during the riots. I heard how some of you were back here directing traffic as best you could over the radio. I heard how some of you tangled with some of the rioters and I heard how some of you risked life and limb to save your fellow workers. And how some of you paid for it with your lives. I salute you, all of you.

"The police and military guys did their jobs, but that's the point: Fighting the riots *was a part* of their jobs. You people are just the working salt-of-the-earth, the backbone of Minneapolis. You didn't sign up for gunfights and riots, but that's what you got. And you were out there fighting and helping people. I couldn't run my city if it weren't for people like you. Sometimes I get misty-eyed and I thank

God, I really do. If the citizenry of this town were here, I'm sure they'd tell you the same thing. To paraphrase Winston Churchill, 'never have so many owed so much to so few'."

Lebenze leaned over and whispered, "*I sink perhaps he iz talking about our tab at ze bar, oui?*" Leland's face reddened and his cheeks puffed out as he tried containing his laughter. I admit, I thought it was pretty witty too.

The mayor continued; "I know things sometimes seem to be pretty dismal, folks. I'm not gonna give you a bunch of Pollyanna rah-rah bullcrap. But I will say this; April first we *the* worst day for us as a country. July fourth was *the* worst day for us as a city. We've survived both and now it's time to work for tomorrow. I know it may be hard to believe, but things *are* getting better every day. We *are* on the upswing.

"So, in closing, let me just say this; I couldn't do my job without you. Keep swinging those hammers, keep driving those trucks around the city, keep putting up signs and keep picking up trash. You're work does not go unnoticed. God bless you, everyone." And with that, the mayor left the room.

We stood and applauded and cheered heartily as the mayor walked out. It was a helluva speech. Under his orders, we got three days off. The shop guys had to keep working – broken trucks wait for no one – but the mayor thought that the city needed at least a few days to cool down so there would be no field work.

Detainees had to be processed in the aftermath of the riots. They would be dealt with harshly under martial law and would, at the very least, be charged with sedition. Dead bodies had to be collected before they could foster disease and pestilence. In a sweeping stroke of efficiency, uninjured rioters who had been arrested were put to work on dead body removal detail.

I drove toward my old apartment building. Minneapolis looked like a war zone: Debris lay strewn everywhere. Houses stood burnt out and fallow with telltale charring swooping up from blackened windows. The ambient stench of death was as strong as ever. The crews from the Dead Body Hotline were busy. I was glad that I never got stuck on *that* duty. I had driven by not less than seven dead bodies in the street twisted in dramatic poses of dying agony by the time I turned onto the block and parked where the apartment stood. As I got out of my car, one corpse seemed to mock me with a ghastly rictus frozen on his face, his dead eyes "looking" right at me.

The apartment building was smoldering and thoroughly burned out. It looked as if a five-alarm fire was simply left to consume the structure at its leisure. The roof had collapsed in and the sky was visible as you looked up into the windows of the top floor apartments – through my apartment. It was no use to check if there was anything left that might have been salvageable, it was clear that the destruction was thorough and complete. There was no sign of Lee or the wacky neighbor dude, Ellis. I hoped they were okay but I haven't seen them since. The rest of the neighborhood was dotted with destroyed houses and smoldering buildings. What causes one human to destroy that which another human has built?

There had always been threats from the government about recalcitrants being treated "in the harshest of terms." I think most people just considered the comments as fulminations from Big Brother that would never really ever come to fruition – we found out differently.

The Guard carried out dozens of hasty "trials" followed by summary firing-squad executions in the first week after the riots. These were allegedly "the worst of the worst." Having been fully documented in most cases, the bodies of the executed were shuttled immediately to the crematoriums.

The Kaiserhof had survived the riots. The employees and a handful of regulars – all armed with semi-automatic weapons – had manned the rooftops two of the four corners of the intersection and kept order in that one little pocket of the near-inner city during the riot.

I stopped in a few days after the riot and people were surprised to see me. Several of the regulars came over to slap me on the back or give me a hug. Derek Juravek was in his usual spot down at the end of the bar with a foamy beer in front of him.

"Burnette!" cried Jack as he emerged from the kitchen through the swinging doors. "We thought you were dead!"

"I'm still alive," I said in a statement of the blazingly obvious.

"What do you want, my friend? Anything."

"You got a Coke?"

"You got it, on the house," he said happily.

"So where you been, young man?" asked Derek.

"I was trapped in North Minneapolis during the riot. Me and Leland." A few people gathered around.

"And you guys survived?" Jack asked as he set a sweaty can of Coke in front of me, already opened.

"Apparently so," I said. "Leland hasn't been by yet?"

"No, you're the first one we've seen from the Gulag."

"Yeah, everyone is kinda decompressing and taking their time getting their shit back together, myself included."

"Is everyone okay?" asked Derek. He'd gotten to know some of the guys pretty good over the previous five or six weeks.

"No, Boone is dead. A few other guys got hurt bad," I told him.

"Boone? Aw shit. That's too bad. He was a decent guy," he said with a shake of his head.

"Listen guys, anyone seen my wife, Sarah?"

"No. What, she's gone missing?" Jack asked surprised.

"Yes. I don't know where she could have gone."

"When's the last time you saw her?" Derek asked with concern.

"The morning of the riots."

Jack and Derek looked at each other.

"Don't even go thinking that," I warned. "Our house is fine, it's still standing. She's not dead."

"Nobody said anything, buddy," said Jack.

"It's just not like her to up and split without leaving me a note or anything."

"I got your phone numbers. I'll certainly call you if I hear anything," Jack said.

"I appreciate that," I said. I took one more sip of my Coke and I left the bar. Under normal circumstances, it would have been a time for backslapping, drinking and story-telling. I certainly had a barnburner to tell of how we escaped the riots, but my mind wasn't on self-congratulatory adulation. The only thing that mattered to me was finding Sarah.

Where could she have gone?

While life in the city was dangerous, leaving the city was no guarantee of safety either. After the initial mass exodus, some people had tried to sputter out of town on their own. Radiological and military checkpoints were further out of the big cities, starting twenty miles or more. That meant that the bad people could set up ambushes right outside the fringes of metropolitan areas. Marauding bands sometimes picked off fleeing families, the females raped and the men killed. I was terrified that if Sarah tried to leave town on her own she would become one of those casualties.

That was my main concern about Sarah – that she had fallen victim to lawlessness. The good news was that I hadn't heard anything. That was also the bad news. The riots had been over for two days and I still couldn't find her. I knew that some people had bugged out of town because of the riots, but I couldn't believe that she wouldn't have left a note or a message. Hell, we'd agreed to email each other in the case of an eventuality just like this.

I had some good digital photos of Sarah and I made a detailed "missing" poster using Photoshop. I printed off hundreds of them and handed them out everywhere I went, even while at work. I even made some laminated ones and duct taped them to the side of my car. I spent many hours on many days driving around, cruising the streets hoping to find her. No luck.

TWENTY-ONE

After the fourth of July, police and military interventions became more and more sporadic as their members fled, were killed, or in some isolated cases, joined or started their own survival groups. Gangs started to run more and more rampant and there was a fundamental moral breakdown in society. Rape, robbery and murder continued their ominous, steady rise. Human culture and behavior regressed at an alarming pace.

Turns out that the peacekeepers in the Twin Cities restrained their reactions better than those in other cities: Guardsmen on Chicago's Southside opened up on crowds with heavy machine-guns killing hundreds of people. Same thing in Detroit. Hundreds and hundreds of people were killed by the government. Were the soldiers right? Were they wrong? To this day, I can't answer that question, I wasn't there. Trying to keep a lid on unrest was like using ten fingers to plug a rain barrel that had 25 leaks.

The remaining peacekeepers were frustrated and overwhelmed. Commensurately, warnings from the police and military increased in severity. Citizens now risked drawing gunfire if they were witnessed looting or committing any act deemed "harmful to society" by the peacekeepers that were left. It was an open-ended provision that tested the judgment and maturity of every person who had a weapon and was charged with maintaining law and order.

In the city, life went on for the crew and me. We lost seven vehicles to the violence on the fourth. Leland told the wrecker guys exactly where to find the Wombat Wagon and that he had left the keys under the front seat. They went out, found it, and towed it back to the Gulag. It hadn't been torched or suffered any more damage after Leland and I abandoned it. It needed a new engine, radiator, radio, windshield, back window and left front tire & wheel, other than that it was in good shape. The bullet holes in the body would just be a permanent reminder that she'd carried her previous occupants from harm's way.

The smell of death was now constantly in the air. God only knows how many houses and apartments held decaying murder and suicide corpses that hot summer. Dead bodies were also tucked away in bushes and behind garbage dumpsters. The summer's heat caused them to bloat to the point that many corpses looked like ridiculous comical mannequins. The stench was not so comical. Dead Body Hotline vehicles were omnipresent.

The only monetary-oriented things that held value were liquid cash, bonds and CD's. Sex, cigarettes, food and drugs became the commodities of the street. Most folks had maxed-out their credit cards on cash withdrawals soon after The Attack, so credit card commerce was pretty much a thing of the past. Some of the more wealthy folks were bartering, in varying degrees of success, with junk silver, krugerands, Swiss francs or St. Gaudens gold pieces, trinkets that had been tucked away in safety deposit boxes or buried in mason jars.

I took Brian out for some beers on Friday afternoon ... *I think it was a Friday* ... in order to self-medicate. John and Brian moved into the Marriot downtown after our apartment building burned down. Rooms were starting to get a little short so they were roommates – again. We parked at my house and decided to walk to the Kaiserhof for a little change.

"What's John up to today?" I asked.

"He's working on that song."

"Ah," I said, not wanting to continue. I knew what Brian was talking about: John was putting the finishing touches on a tune he wrote called, *"All My Shit Seems to Disappear (Whenever You're Around)."*

A hearse casually rolled by us as we made our way to the bar. The driver and his assistant had the windows open and were trying to get as much fresh air as they could by tilting their heads out of the windows. It looked like three bodies inside, best we could tell.

"Bring ou'cher dead! Bring ou'cher dead!" Brian said in a cockney British accent. All I could do was chuckle. Death had not only become meaningless, but also the fodder of stupid, immature jokes.

"Who in the hell would volunteer to do that job?" Brian asked rhetorically.

"I dunno," I said.

What we didn't know at the time was that Executive Order 11000 allowed the government to mobilize civilians into work brigades under government supervision and that the poor schmucks picking up stinky bodies were conscripts.

A skinny young woman, maybe in her mid-twenties, approached us as we made our way down the city sidewalk. She had striking blue eyes and looked like she might have once been a nice-looking girl, but she was now gaunt and dirty looking. Her hair was stringy and I could see fleabites on her ankles. There was desperation in her voice as she stepped in our way and spoke.

"You guys got any money I can borrow?" she asked. Her voice was rough liked she'd drunk too much whiskey and smoked too many cigarettes in her short time. "I'll pay ya back as soon as I get back on my feet," she said with a wipe of her nose.

"No, we got nothing," Brian said as we tried to skirt around her.

"I'll give you a blowjob for twenty bucks," she said. It was a highly untantalizing offer.

"No thanks," Brian answered for both of us.

"Ten bucks. How 'bout a blowjob for ten bucks? *Please*?"

"No."

"*Pleeeaaasse?*"

"Oh, Jesus Christ!" I finally said reaching into my pocket. I pulled out a crumpled ten and threw it at her.

"Here. Now leave us alone." We turned and continued on to the bar.

"Oh, thank you, sir! Thank you *so much*, sir! Thank you! Thank you, sir. I'll pay you back when I get back on my feet, sir ..." We heard her whiskey voice fading behind us as we walked away. She was dirty and disgusting, but she was a human being, too. It struck me as being very sad and dreary that she was willing to do ... *that* for ten lousy bucks. Brian had his own take:

"Judging by how skinny that bitch was, I'd say blowjob sales are down."

We spent several hours at the Kaiserhof. Nothing too spectacular going on, just talking and drinking. Finally I just left Brian there and walked home by myself. I hated the feeling of walking up to that house, the house where I'd so recently experienced so much joy.

I unlocked the front door, trudged over the threshold and secured the deadbolt and lock behind me. The house was dark and empty, silent. *"Sarah?"* I called out, as was my new habit. I stood motionless for several seconds with my head cocked into the air – no answer. It was always worth a try. I put on an instrumental CD and lit incense in an attempt to create some kind of atmosphere in there. I guess it was my way of trying to keep Sarah current, keep her in the present.

Easing into a living room chair, I gazed about the room. Right here, right in the middle of this very room we danced and didn't care how silly we looked. Over there in the kitchen, cooking and laughing … *how many times?* That one Saturday morning making love on the couch and on the chair … and on the rug … and, and …

Dear God, please return Sarah to me.

TWENTY-TWO

I was downhearted most of the time. I still had heard no word from Sarah. Certainly by now she could have emailed and told me where she was, where she had fled to. I could tell her that she could come back if only she would reach out and contact me. I even summoned the courage to call the Dead Body Hotline. They hadn't registered anyone under the name of Sarah Pennington or Sarah Burnette.

Between the death and destruction that I'd witnessed recently, the ongoing strain of post-nuclear holocaust life and Sarah disappearing, I could feel my soul oozing out of my body. I was becoming an empty shell, robotically going through the motions of my life, lacking any sense of humor or frivolity.

I showed up to work early the next day and dug out the number that I'd copied down from Sarah's caller ID, got onto the internet and went to a criss-cross directory. I entered the number and waited. It only took a few seconds for the entry to come back – Katherine Greene-Pennington. Not only did the search engine give the exact address in Minnetonka, there was an option icon called *print map* that spit out a precise pictorial road-guide to the front door of the house.

I had called out to the house several times over the previous days and never gotten and answer, but the phone didn't appear to have been disconnected. I decided to drive out to the house right after work. I had to go through several check-points but things went smoothly when I explained that I was with the county and that I'd be coming back the other way pretty soon.

The map was good. After getting off of the main highway, I had to snake around a two-lane country highway for a few miles and then get off that road and drive through some spendy-looking estates. Finally, I parked in front of a gated property that looked as if it might be abandoned. I got out of my car and went to the callbox. I was surprised when the buzzer actually worked and even more so when a voice answered through the intercom.

"Who are you? What do you want?" an older woman's voice crackled out of the speaker.

"Is this the home of Katherine Pennington?"

"None of your business," came back an angry response. *"Go away or I'll call the police. Somebody will come and shoot you."*

"Ms. Pennington, my name is Dallas Burnette … I'm a county deputy. I'm here about Sarah. Sarah Pennington?"

"What about Sarah?"

"Is she your daughter? I'm a friend." There was no response for several seconds. "Hello?"

The woman responded after another several seconds. *"Are you alone?"*

"All alone, ma'am," I responded. The gate buzzed and unlocked. I stepped inside the grounds and closed the door securely behind me. It was about a fifty-yard walk up the drive to the front of the house. There was a slender woman looking to be in her mid-fifties with bleached hair and dark roots standing on the elegant stone steps when I reached the house.

"Good day," I said with my county ID already at the ready. She looked at it and seemed to approve its authenticity. I held out my hand.

"Katherine Greene," she said as she limply shook my hand. "I dropped the Pennington. Would you care to step inside, Mr. Burnette?" Her speech was ever so slightly slurred as though she'd been drinking. She led me to a tastefully appointed solarium at the side of the house and motioned for me to sit. There was a mostly empty bottle of wine and a wineglass stained with lipstick sitting on the table next to her.

"You're with the county?" she asked tersely.

"Yes," I said.

"And you're here about Sarah?"

"Yes," I said. She breathed in and exhaled heavily with her hands lying flatly upon the tops of her thighs. She looked to the ceiling and I saw her eyes get even glazier yet.

"Okay. I'm ready."

"Ready for what?" I said slightly confused.

"You're here to tell me that my daughter has been killed, aren't you?" The words alone made my heart beat faster.

"Oh, no, not at all, ma'am. I'm … I'm Sarah's husband."

"Oh," she sighed. "You're *that* fellow."

Yeah, you would've known that if you showed up her your own daughter's wedding ...

"Yes, that's me. I'm here because I can't find Sarah."

"God, I thought you came here to tell me that my little baby had gotten killed in the city." She exhaled audibly with her hand over her chest.

"No, no. The problem is that I just can't find her," I repeated.

"Could I get you something to drink?" she said standing up, still a bit shaken. "I have almost everything."

"A Sprite if you got one."

I heard the sound of a refrigerator opening and closing. She came back with another near-empty wine bottle in one hand and handed me the Sprite.

"You don't mind if I have a drink?" she said as she sat back down and poured the remainder of the wine bottle into her glass.

"No, ma'am," I responded.

"And stop calling me 'ma'am,' call me Katherine."

"Okay." She looked as though she might have been a pretty woman when she was younger but now her face was defined by harsh, thin lips and lines in the face that I surmised were borne more of hostility than age.

"So, what's the story with Sarah?" she said as she leaned back and crossed her legs.

"Well, Katherine, as you might know, there was quite a riot in Minneapolis on the Fourth of July."

"Yes," she answered, "I know. I was afraid of something like that. I told that girl a thousand times to come live out here with me but, *nooo* … she has a stubborn head like her father."

"Well, I've tried calling you but the phone just rings and rings," I explained.

"I turned off the ringer and the answering machine, there's not too many people I want to talk to," she said with a gulp of her wine. "Me and Sarah's father don't get along at all. I can't say that Sarah and I have the best mother/daughter relationship in the world. Then her father went and bought her that awful house in the city. Sarah isn't happy about my drinking or the way things ended with Donald and me."

"Uh-huh. Do you have any idea where Sarah would have gone?" I said, trying to get the conversation back on track. "We were very close and it just wouldn't be like her to disappear and not tell me where she went."

"Off with her father maybe."

"I thought about that but it doesn't fit. She wouldn't just leave the city without telling me. She certainly wouldn't just up and leave and drive all the way to Texas."

"Are her purse and keys gone?"

"Well, yes, but there aren't any spare clothes or jackets gone."

"I saw on the news that people fled the city during the riot. Maybe you weren't as close as you thought and she ran off with another fellow," she offered with a slurp of her wine.

You mean old drunk rich-bitch ...

"I don't think so, Katherine. Trust me, she just disappeared."

"People do that," she said, suddenly seeming ambivalent about her own daughter's fate. "So what do you want me to do?"

"Well, for starters maybe you could turn your phone back on. She might call here, she could be calling right now for all we know."

"I can do that. What else?"

"I have your number. Here's mine," I handed her a card with my name and the main office number at the Gulag. "I also spend some time at Sarah's house, you can try there at night. But call me anytime of day or night if you see or hear from her."

"Will do," she nodded and carelessly put the card on the table next to her. "You know, I don't get too many visitors. Would you care to sit a bit longer? Have something to drink? I have beer, wine, hard liquor."

"No, no, I have to leave. I have things to do in the city yet."

"Suit yourself," she said, looking away as though I'd offended her.

I felt sorry the woman in a way. She was, indeed, all alone and drinking herself silly as Sarah had told me the first night we met. But, then again, there was a harshness about her that made me understand why Sarah wasn't close to her. I left and drove back into the city.

TWENTY-THREE

The Kaiserhof remained the place where I could relax and lose myself in my thoughts. Having gone virtually unscathed during the riots, it maintained its allure as a safe haven. The place never seemed to run out of beer or edibles. I don't know how they did it, but it was a mystery I was thankful for.

There was a little oddity about the place that I haven't mentioned yet. There was a strange, bullet-ridden art piece on one of the bar walls over between the restrooms. It was a huge five-foot by six-foot photograph shot by a famed photographer named Richard Avedon. He was famous for trying to capture the inner truth of his subjects so he often surreptitiously shot them before they were actually ready for the shoot to officially begin.

This particular piece was called "The Daughters of the Generals of the American Revolution." It showed a group of matronly older women pouting and preening and thrusting their multiple chins about. It was a B&W print that was originally shot in 1964. While on sabbatical at the nearby art institute in 1970, the artist often stopped in the Kaiserhof to wet his whistle and he fell in love with the place. He gifted the portrait to the bar before he left town. But that's only part of the story.

Now fast-forward to October 17, 1985. It's about five minutes after one in the afternoon. Tables are toppled, drinks are spilled and patrons are trying to dig holes in the wooden floor with the buttons on their shirts. A whacked-out 38-year-old Vietnam vet named Robby Gerbach has just popped off a couple rounds from a .357. There are two smoldering holes in the portrait: One a head shot and the other right in the heart. Two of the subjects in the picture received mortal wounds. The bartender was frozen in place thinking that, surely, this was his last day on planet earth.

Robby turns to him, barrel still smoking, and screams, "I CAN'T STAND THEM! I HAD TO SHOOT THEM! YOU UNDER-STAND, DON'T YOU?" Robby re-holsters the weapon and walks out. He even holds the door open for a couple of older folks walking in for lunch. He reportedly walked directly to the nearest police station and turned himself in. They upped his dosage and sent him to the county pokey for a stint and that's the last anyone saw of him.

The artist Avedon himself got wind of the story and thought the whole yarn was pretty cool. He was appreciative that his work could emote such a response. So with his blessing the bar let the piece hang, bullet-holes and all. The Kaiserhof was *exactly* the kind of place you could fall in love with. It was an odd combination: the peaceful venue and its violence-related art centerpiece.

I was able to get ahold of a roll of concertina. With Jack's blessing, Brian and I strung it up along the top of the iron fence out in the garden of the Kaiserhof. We took our time and did a nice job, making sure that it was nice and even and symmetrical. We had to wear thick metal and canvas gloves that went almost all the way up to the elbow. We still got nicked up a little bit handling the wire. Once the razor wire was in place, we took a roll of thick .042 safety wire and secured it to the fence with little pigtail knots about every three feet. I was glad to have a constructive little project to do to take my mind off things, if only for a little bit. It looked real nice, too.

TWENTY-FOUR

Hitting Atlanta was a brilliant stroke by al Qaeda; those guys were not stupid. Not only was it home to CNN, one of the most watched news channels around the world – ergo, information dispersal venue – but it was also home to the United States Centers for Disease Control, the CDC. In fact, Ground Zero for the Atlanta nuke was in Druid Hills, roughly equidistant between CNN Center and the CDC, almost as if trying to assure that both would be rendered useless – they were.

I used to see T-shirts with pictures of giant cartoon mosquitoes on the chest with "Minnesota State Bird" captioned underneath. While known for its cold winter months, the Minnesota climate is also capable of reaching tropical conditions during the summer months, a perfect breeding and living climate for mosquitoes.

It was humid and damp that summer, but it rarely rained – a truly odd combination. It was as though God had decided to make life just as miserable as possible in all ways, big and small. As result of The Attack, government resources were stretched so thin that duties like mosquito control, a lower-level governmental function, had fallen by the wayside. Mosquitoes were, after all, just a minor pest that would be a nuisance as you tried to sit on your deck and enjoy a summer's sunset. At least up until The Attack.

With the continuing emergence of West Nile Virus and the maladies of brought with it, the pests had become the mice that roared. West

Nile virus, a mosquito-borne disease, was never reported in the Western hemisphere before the late 1990's. By 2005, cases were fairly common even as the CDC was making great strides in controlling the disease. Birds are the natural hosts for this virus, which can be transmitted from infected birds to humans and other animals through mosquitoes. The disease could be transmitted through blood transfusions, mothers' breast milk, organ transplants … it was a villain.

The rainy and damp spring followed by a sultry, hot summer aided the breeding of the mosquito species *culex pipiens*, which plays a major role in spreading West Nile. Lack of significant rain wiped out darning needles, dragonflies and amphibians, which destroy mosquitoes and are their natural enemies. A lack of water also aided the spread of infection by drawing thirsty birds to the few pools and puddles where mosquitoes breed. The hot weather itself played a role, too. Warmth increases the rate at which pathogens mature inside mosquitoes.

I'm not an expert in the field or anything, I learned all this from another class given to us by one of the feds from the CDC.

The risk of severe disease is higher for persons fifty-years and older with a disease like West Nile Virus usually. We took a lot of garlic pills as a personal anti-pest measure and used a lot of Deet. The local government made some common-sense changes, too. Folks were allowed to burn trash and yard waste in the city, something that had been outlawed by county ordnance back in the seventies. The smoky haze would be a good pest deterrent. Someone even came up with the idea of breeding bats in the city. A bat can eat 600 mosquitoes in one hour – an efficient ally. Lord knows, there were enough empty buildings where bat shelters could be constructed.

The good news was that there was no evidence to suggest that West Nile virus could be spread from person to person or from animal to person unless their was a direct exchange of bodily fluids. Most people who become infected with West Nile Virus will have either no symptoms or very mild ones. But, battling mosquitoes was an increasingly serious affair because, on rare occasions, West Nile infection could result in a severe and sometimes fatal illness known as West Nile encephalitis – an inflammation of the brain.

Ken Leland was bitten by an infected mosquito and contracted encephalitis despite the fact that he was a healthy and robust 34-years-old. My friend, my buddy, the guy with whom I survived the Fourth of July riots, the Best Man at my wedding – fell sick. Ken's nightmare with the illness happened very quickly.

Three days prior to his diagnosis he began running a high temp. Thinking it was just a fever he just took Tylenol. That night he continued to get worse. By the next morning, he was hardly able to walk without running into every wall. We went to the doctor, and he was admitted to the Hennepin County Medical Center for possible brain damage because his eyes were going from side to side real fast, something called a *nystagmus*. A spinal tap was done, and he was told he had meningitis. His temperature hit a high of 105.6 later that day. He then suffered a seizure and spent six days in ICU with an ice water blanket on him. He was disoriented for a few days and didn't know where he was. He had three more seizures in those first days.

Encephalitis is colloquially called the "Sleeping Disease." Infected people are very tired and sleepy all of the time and lose mental sharpness. Ken was very tired and couldn't remember things very well when he was conscious. One day he curled up into a little ball and started crying and the nurses called the doctor.

The next day, he quit breathing, and was put on a ventilator. He was put into an induced coma with some kind of medication, and was left on it for a couple of days. When he was taken off of that medication, he went into a coma on his own. At this point the doctors said his chances of survival were very slim. If he lived, he would have to endure a lovely drug called Dilantin, as well as Klonopin and Diazapan. But the Klonopin was the wildcard; it would throw his mood swings all over, the doctor warned us. *If* he lived.

A week passed by with no improvements, so they decided to go ahead with the brain biopsy. A week after the biopsy, he came out of the coma. He was unable to move any part of his body. He lingered for a few days, suffered several more violent grand mal seizures and then passed away. In less than three weeks after the first time he noticed a fever, Ken Leland was dead. The man survived thousands of insane rioters and hooligans only to be felled by a common mosquito.

I wrote a nice letter to his children.

TWENTY-FIVE

I was sitting in the Kaiserhof. My crew leader had cut us loose around 3:30 due to the heat. As if life wasn't unbearable enough, that August was sweltering. Temperatures were in the upper nineties and the humidity was tropical. The bar's central air conditioning system had permanently failed in early July, but the joint was kept relatively cool with the use of two window air conditioner units. The structure's thick stone walls and stained glass windows that did a fairly good job of keeping solar radiation heat out. The Kaiserhof became my home-away-from-home and I treasured my times sitting there, sipping pilsner and chatting with members of the exclusive club that frequented there.

The drunker people got, the more they loved to tell funny stories of things that had happened to them in the past – High School football stories, Navy shore leave stories, buddy road-trip stories, relationship stories. People would get lost in their own words as they recounted joys from the past, and then … delirious smiles would melt from their faces as they came back to real life and remembered where they were. You could count on it. It was sad.

I stepped out of the bar a few hours later and immediately almost tripped over the dead body of a white male who looked to be thirty-ish. He was gripping his gut and his face was frozen in agony. How he died, I don't know. Maybe he was shot or stabbed a block away and almost made it to the bar in a vain search for life-saving assistance. He wasn't stinking yet so I assumed he had died quite very recently. I thought about going back inside to tell someone, but instead, I simply stepped over him and kept walking, sure that somebody else would call the Dead Body Hotline. I wondered, but only lightly, about how such a thing that would have been an extraordinary event in my pre-April Attack life could now be so mundane now. Life had become surreal.

I had been checking the email at every possible convenience for correspondence from Sarah – nothing. I continued handing out missing posters as I cruised the streets in the evenings, optimistic and hopeful that we'd serendipitously cross paths out on the street.

I had pictured it already: We would scream ourselves into delirium and nearly hug the life out of each other. Tears of joy would stream down our faces. Then she'd tell me that she was hiding out with friends and didn't have access to communication. I'd tell her how I survived the riots that horrible day and that our house was okay. Our faces would hurt from the beaming smiles that we couldn't control and wouldn't want to anyway. Then we'd go home.

I'd draw her a bath and cook her the best meal I'd ever cooked in my whole life. She would repose in the tub with a glass of red and we'd talk the whole time as I sautéed veggies in the kitchen around the corner. We would eat and drink wine and talk and laugh. I would tell her how much I truly loved her, how much she meant to me, how sad I was when I thought that she was gone forever. Then we'd hold each other for about three days straight. Everything would be right again, yes …

But I never saw her out on the street.

Of the dozens of times that I had called Sarah's mother she had answered only three or four times, never with any positive news to relay. She was a useless ally in my quest for Sarah. Gary Matherly hadn't heard anything, either. I had exhausted every avenue I could think of and I was going crazy. I was starting to feel like a rabid dog.

I was walking down the street early one evening. Someone was walking behind me. That made me a little nervous, but I had my Baretta tucked in the back of my jeans, out of sight under the tail of my untucked shirt. The guy behind me was dragging his feet on the sidewalk, making an obnoxious scraping sound with his stupid shoes. He was also slurping a can of cheap soda. I stopped and stood off to the side so he could pass. He was tall, scruffy and wearing a dirty T-shirt. He sneered at me as he went by, his feet still dragging across the sidewalk. How much goddam effort does it take to lift your feet when you're walking? I didn't know him, but I hated the guy.

I let him get ten feet ahead and then started walking again, trying my best to ignore him. He finished his can of soda and let out a loud, sickening belch. Then he carelessly flipped the can end-over-end off to the side of the sidewalk. Then the fucker stopped to light up a cigarette.

My eyes widened. I couldn't take anymore.

"Pick up that can," I said as I strode up even with him, keeping about an eight-foot gap between us in case he lunged.

He looked me up and down. "Fuck you, motherfucker." He kept walking.

I looked over at the can that he had just discarded. These were *my* streets; I drove them, I cleaned them, I worked on them … only to have this useless piece-of-shit throw his soda can off to the side so I could pick up after him next week? I strode after him.

"Hey, asshole," I called.

He turned around with anger and hatred in his eyes. I didn't even wait for a response – I pulled my 9mm out, assumed a two-handed firing position and cocked the hammer.

"Get your fucking hands up, cocksucker," I hissed through clenched teeth.

His hands went up, his eyes went wide and the cigarette tumbled out of the corner of his mouth. He started trembling.

"I try to keep this fucking town running and you throw a soda can on the sidewalk? *In my town?"*

"I-I-I—" he stammered.

"SHUT THE FUCK UP!"

He jumped and his hands went a little bit higher.

"You're gonna pick up that fucking can now, aren't ya?"

"Y-y-yes, sir," he stammered.

"Move."

He carefully walked back to his discarded soda can and picked it up. He did his best to keep his hands up and visible the whole time.

"Now pick up that damn cigarette and put it in the can." My weapon remained trained on him. My eyes burned wild with hatred.

"But ... that's my last ciga—"

"SMOKING'S BAD FOR YOU! PUT IT IN THERE!"

I felt my finger putting pressure on the trigger. I wouldn't have been surprised, or disappointed, if the 9mm discharged. He walked over to the smoldering cigarette and put it in the soda can. I heard it hiss out.

"Into the alley," I said.

He turned like a man going to gallows. I followed him around the corner and into the alley. He looked at me and I jerked my weapon towards an already-packed dumpster.

"Cram it in there," I ordered.

He jammed the can in and slowly turned around. His eyes were wide with fear and his hands were trembling.

"Today's your lucky day, asshole. Pick a number between one and ten."

"Wha—"

"Pick a fucking number," I said with evil coolness. "If I have to repeat myself, I'll shoot ya and stick ya behind this dumpster." I kept my two-handed grip aimed at center-of-mass.

"S-s-seven," he stammered.

"When I tell you, you got seven seconds to be out of my sight. If I can still see you when I get to 'seven,' I'm going to kill you. Understand?"

"Y-y-y-es."

"GO!"

He took off without hesitation at a fast sprint and disappeared around the corner. I started counting out loud; "ONE ... TWO ... THREE ..."

I suppose if he had picked 'one' or 'two' as his number, I would have had to shoot him right then and there in that alley. A man's gotta make good on his threats. Right?

I fucking hate litterbugs.

Fred Zampoli had given me rudimentary instruction on zeroing and firing the M-16 on the makeshift shooting range back at the compound back about the middle of June, a couple weeks before the riots. He started me out by having me shoot while resting the weapon on sandbags. What if I'm in the field and have no sandbags handy, I sarcastically queried. He explained that we had to 'zero' the weapon; I had to learn how to acquire the same sight picture each and every time I put a bead on target.

He told me to squeeze, not pull the trigger. He showed me how to correct for windage. The rear sight of the M-16 had a tiny little wheel that clicked over micrometers at a time, and with great difficulty so that a shooter couldn't accidentally throw his own weapon off sight. The front sight post clicked up and down, also in microscopic increments. After about three blocks of instruction, I got to be pretty good. Shooting the weapon was pretty easy, once you got the hang of it. Then Freddy gave me that M-16 right after the riots and now I had a rifle for myself.

I was frustrated and angry. My emotions were on a hair-trigger. I almost killed a guy for throwing a can on the sidewalk – and I liked the feeling. I had no idea where Sarah could have gone to and that's a feeling I didn't like. I got in my car and started driving north, towards Columbia Heights – towards Erik Johnson's house.

Since falling in love with Sarah, my plans of committing the first-degree murder of Erik Johnson had disappeared from my mind. But now the plans were back. I don't know why, I guess it was just at least something under my control. Telling myself that the murder of Johnson was a positive entry in the cosmic ledger books placated me. As long as I couldn't find Sarah, my worse angels were telling me, might as well take care of some other business.

My car turned onto his street after about a twelve-minute drive up Central Avenue and over a couple blocks. The road veered of to the east by about 25 degrees on the north end of his street to account for the curve of the railroad tracks about a block over. It was perfect. By parking right at that bend, I had a clear line-of-sight down and across the street to his yard and even his front door. It would be about a 75-yard shot, I guessed. It was getting to be dusk and I could see the mild glow of a light on in the house. He was still in town apparently. All I would have to do is to get him outside somehow and then take the shot.

But how to get him outside?

I had it. I remembered a little trick from high school. If one pours the contents of a bottle of Drano into an empty plastic two-liter bottle, like the ones that soda pop come in, and then tosses in about twenty little balls of rolled-up tin foil and screws the cap down tight, it will cause quite an explosion. The chemical reaction causes gases to form and expand. The bottle itself will become huge and almost perfectly round until the plastic can't hold anymore, and then ... *BOOM!* The process would take about ten minutes and the loudness of the explosion is far more impressive than the potential damage it can cause. But it would be more than enough to get someone's attention, say, that of a homeowner.

I looked up and down the street and saw two more house lights on further beyond Johnson's house. Down by the bend where I would park, I saw nothing. The houses looked abandoned. But there were overhead streetlights, one on the corner and one directly over my shooting spot. I would have to take care of them. I drove home for the night.

I knew that I had a .177 caliber pellet gun that was kicking around somewhere in one of the boxes of stuff I'd brought from the apartment over to the house. I found it and a box of blunt-end pellets. I drove back to Johnson's street at about the same time the next night and backed up into the driveway of an apparently abandoned house. From that vantage point I could hit both streetlights.

I pumped the pellet gun's handle its requisite ten pumps and loaded a pellet. I discreetly looked around and took aim out of the driver's side window at the corner light first. There was no sound but crickets just starting to chirp. I gently squeezed the trigger ... *POP!* I thought the light might shatter and cause noise but it didn't. Apparently the projectile had penetrated the thick, outer glass shell of the unit and found its mark – the light went out, quietly and immediately with just a minimum of sound. I looked around and stayed still for at least a full minute. Nothing.

I reloaded and re-pumped the weapon and slid over to the passenger side window. I took aim at the other light and squeezed the trigger. This time there was a loud clang and the sound of some glass breaking – and the damn light didn't go out. The glass shell came loose and swung down like a pendulum, squeaking back and forth. *Dammit!* I reloaded as quickly as I could and re-aimed. *POP!* I hit the bulb directly this time and it popped and shattered, raining little glass shards down upon the street. It was a little noisy, but I had knocked out both lights. I slid back over to the driver's side, looked around and started the car. As best I could tell, no one had noticed my nefarious activities. I drove home and watched TV for a couple hours and then went to bed.

My car was parked on Johnson's street for the third night in a row, same time, same place: At the bend in the street. This time it was dark.

I was wearing my regular work boots and jeans but I had on a black windbreaker. I didn't want to look *too* para-militaristic and raise suspicion in case the police or the Guard stopped me.

I backed my car into the driveway one house closer to Johnson's from the night before. I thought about parking in the street and shooting from the back seat, resting the weapon on the driver's seat and out the driver's window at and angle. But I thought it would be better to be sitting in the driver's seat so I could kill him and then get the hell out of the area as quickly as possible. From the driveway vantage point, I could comfortably rest the weapon out the passenger window, fire off a shot and then get out of the neighborhood fast.

Reaching into a gym bag, I pulled out an empty plastic jug, a bottle of Drano and a baggie filled with tin foil balls that I'd rolled that afternoon. Down the street, light glowed from Johnson's house. I poured the Drano into the jug and then got out of the car. Once again most of the street was dark. There were no lights or signs of inhabitation between my car and the little bastard's house.

I crossed the street and scampered through the front yards of houses finally reaching the shrubbery at the edge of my target house. I could ever so faintly hear the sound of a television or stereo coming from inside and his car was in the driveway. He was surely home.

I took a large handful of tin foil balls, poured them into the jug and then screwed the cap down as tightly as I could. I sneaked over to the shrubs under the living room window and gently placed the bomb on top of one of the bushes. It wasn't that heavy so the shrub cradled to plastic bottle like an egg in a bird's nest. I ran back through the darkened house yards bent over at the waist like an infantryman running through a battlefield. I was breathing heavy by the time I got back in my car. I was nervous. I could almost hear my own heart beating.

If memory served correctly, it would take about ten minutes for the Drano bomb to reach critical pressure and burst. I picked up the M-16 from the floor of the back seat. I had a twenty-round clip locked-and-loaded with ten rounds, safety on. I looked at the dashboard clock – it was 9:48 p.m. It would take about eight more minutes, I figured. My stomach tightened as I raised the weapon up to shooting position with my thumb on the safety. I had watched Scheerer shoot and kill a man and it didn't look too hard. *I can do this*, I thought to myself.

9:52 p.m.

I felt the urgent need to piss, but there was no way I could step out of the car now. I had to be ready to shoot seconds after the explosion. With my luck, the Drano bomb would explode while I was in mid-pee and my plans would be ruined.

9:55 p.m.

Nothing.

9:56 p.m.

The only change was that I had to piss even worse.

10:02 p.m.

Still waiting. *What in the hell?* I had been looking down the sights of the M-16 for fourteen minutes now. *Did I do something wrong? Was there a crack in the plastic bottle that I didn't see? Why wasn't there an—*

BOOOOM!!!!

Even though I was expecting the blast, I still jumped. The decibel level of the Drano bomb was unbelievably loud. It hurt my ears and I was a good distance down the street. The front window of Johnson's house shattered and I saw the curtains puff inward from the concussion. I clicked the M-16's safety to the 'fire' and took up position.

C'mon out, you bastard ...

There was no movement from Johnson's house, but three other house lights came on, two of them between the target and me. *Damn it.* I heard a voice from the darkness, then another one. Neighbors were slowly poking their heads out of doors, wondering what had just happened and eking out into the yards. I dared not take my sights off of Johnson's front door.

Finally, I saw his curtains move. The front light came on next to the door. This was it – he would be in my sight-picture in seconds. Another exterior house light came on, this time just two houses away from me on my side of the street. *Shit!*

Somebody wandered into Johnson's front yard, a neighbor, and then another. Finally, Johnson came out and stood on his front stoop to inspect the damage, pistol in hand. I took a breath and took aim. He was right there, right in my sights. His life was mine for the taking.

But now porch and house lights illuminated the street far more than I had planned and there were potential witnesses, also unplanned. *Center-of-mass in sight picture ...* I could hear the din of people talking but couldn't actually make out what anybody was saying. *Breathe in ...* It was now or never. *Breathe out, slowly ...* Johnson was an easy stationary target ... *squeeze, don't pull ...* I felt the resistance of the trigger against my finger ...

And then backed off.

Surely, someone would see the muzzle-flash coming out of my car if I fired. They'd all hear the direction the shot came from and would get an accurate description of the vehicle and maybe a partial license plate number. An oversight; why didn't I drive someone else's car and duct tape other license plates over the car's own? Abandoned vehicles were all around; it would have been no problem to procure plates.

Situations in life-equations are composed of variables and constants: In planning an operation of any sort, the goal is to remove as many of the variables as possible and work with the purest set of constants attainable. I thought that I had planned my little operation out to the last detail but I wasn't even close. Nowhere near close.

Bloody Hell ...

I clicked the weapon to 'safe,' put it in the backseat, started the car and departed at a low-rate of speed with the lights off, not wanting to attract attention. I don't know if any of the bystanders took notice of my car or not. Once I was about four blocks away I pulled over in the middle of a darkened residential block and took a much-needed piss. When finished I got back in my car and continued on home. My opportunity had come and gone, and there would be no more attempts.

I felt a sense of guilt, but not about planning to kill Erik Johnson. In fact, the only thing that I felt guilty about was *not* feeling guilty. I came within a second of being a cold-blooded killer and didn't think twice about it. Oh, well.

The best laid plans of mice and men.

TWENTY-SIX

Though they happened any day of the week, Sunday had become the traditional day of suicide among the more organized of the remaining population. I guess people felt a little closer to God if they took their own lives on a Sunday morning. Jumpers included the sick, the lonely, the heartbroken and the depressed. The Tenth Avenue Bridge near the University of Minnesota had become an informal gathering spot for the big jump. It was one of the bridges shut down by the government and had an anti-vehicle barricade at the north end. But it was easily accessible by pedestrians, especially coming from the downtown side. At first the authorities tried to stop people, but they eventually just looked the other way.

The bridge was high enough to ensure, if not death, at least unconsciousness upon impact that would allow the jumper to drown without agony. I thought about doing it from time to time. The most common thing now was a solitary person making the decision and planning his or her own death and bringing a friend or two down for morale support. Sometimes, whole families were rumored to jump hand-in-hand.

By the time I found out about the new "tradition," someone had taken an acetylene torch and removed a section of heavy railing between two concrete supports near the middle of the span. Over a short period of time, the sidewalk in front of the jump area of the bridge had been lavishly painted and decorated. The railings were adorned with flower boxes and conical rose holders. On Sundays, carpets and ornamental chairs were arranged. On the very few rainy days, a small canopy was put over the jump site so the soon-to-be-departed could give their final words in dignity. People gathered as if they were seeing a loved one off at the gate of an international airport.

Observers gathered on the banks of the river on Sundays. At first they were quiet, but after a couple weeks they started hooting and hollering, goading people with chants of, "JUMP! JUMP!" They cheered when a body hit the water and booed veraciously when someone chickened out. They were soul-less animals.

TWENTY-SEVEN

Word came through government guys and then on the internet; the feds had located four more nuclear bombs on U.S. soil. One was a dud found in a semi in Pittsburgh. It had apparently gone through its detonation sequence but simply failed to explode. Another dud was found in a moving van in the outskirts of Houston. Two others were found, of all places, in a barn out in the country north of Defiance, Ohio. They appeared to have been abandoned, almost detonation-capable but not quite. Damned Kleinhoffer was right: There were more nukes scattered around the country. Finding them was good I suppose. Maybe like finding half a worm in an apple you just took a bite out of.

Minneapolis was quickly becoming a ghost town come August. What was left of the population was eking out day-by-day, week-by-week. Men would often come slinking back into town to check out if it were safe to move the family back, only to find houses burned or ransacked.

Citizens and peacekeepers were killed nearly every day. Anything left of hope or relative happiness deflated out of the general community consciousness like air going out of a punctured tire. There wasn't much in the way of good news coming from the central government and supporting one's self in traditional way became ever more unrealistic. Opening or running a business of any sort was merely an invitation to getting robbed and killed.

And, of course, suicide was one more factor that thinned the herd. The government started cracking down on the bridge jumpers. Decaying bodies were hell to pull out of the river and created somewhat of a health crisis as well.

I spent several hours after work putting up posters and asking around about my wife; there were still no sign or clues about Sarah. Frustrated again, I went home and tried to get some sleep. It was a horribly hot and oppressive evening. About ten o'clock, the power went out; no AC, no TV, no electric fan. I just lay on the bed and sweltered. Outside the moon glowed red again. I could hear the distant whining of Humvee engines racing through the city streets and crickets chirping. Gunfire. A dog barking. There was no breeze. Just oppressive, oppressive heat and heavy air. I decided to assume one position and tried not to move. I would just lie there and marinate in my own sweat and misery, waiting for some level of unconsciousness to wash over me. Maybe I could fall asleep and this hellish night would be over all the sooner.

I awoke with a start. I didn't know if I had been asleep for three minutes or for three hours. I looked out the window and the moon had moved through the sky – it was now hanging off the *west* side of the tree outside – and it was lightly glowing in a brownish-red hue. It was then that I noticed that the AC and fan were on as was the TV, casting that eerie glow that a snowy television screen does in a dark room at night.

There was a man in a suit talking into the camera. I tried changing channels but nothing else came in with any discernable clarity. I was awake now so I settled back on the channel with the man in the suit.

He spoke:

"God's end-times prophecies are coming into clearer focus, it is important that this major subject of the book of Revelation is not ignored or misunderstood. The world power, which precedes the kingdom of the Antichrist, is painfully obvious. America is the New Babylon."

I felt alone, like I was the only other person on the planet and the man on the TV was speaking directly to me. I was feeling that middle-of-the-night feeling of anxiety and sharpened sensibilities. He continued.

"The Bible tells of a sign on the hand: That the day when a mandatory sign on the right hand would be a sign of the end. Many have speculated if we were destined to bar code our hands or implanted chips. But the answer is clear: The sign has always been there. It's our fingertips, or more specifically, our fingerprints.

"Governments started using fingerprints as crime solving tools at first, and it evolved into a method of cataloguing citizens. Cashing a check at the bank? Surrender your personal sign, your right thumbprint. Applying for a driver's license? Surrender your right thumbprint. Get charged with a crime by the government? Surrender ALL of your fingerprints. The point, my friends, is that the sign prophesized in the bible has always been with us, it's only modern technology that allowed us to realize its existence. The Bible is time-locked, its mysteries revealed as man gains knowledge. Now I'd like to talk about references to modern America in the bible.

"The scriptures that mention Mystery Babylon by name are Revelation 17 and 18. As a man of God I believe that all of biblical prophecy is God-given and one hundred percent correct. I believe we can safely apply the Old Testament prophecies that were directed at Babylon and remain unfulfilled to the Babylon of the end-times, that is, "Mystery Babylon," and these prophecies combine to give us a very clear description of that great power.

"The new Babylon would be a major port city, as well as the greatest and wealthiest city, and it would be a city of Jewish exiles. New York City was undoubtedly the most important port city in the world, as well as the wealthiest: Half of the world's capital was located in New York City. This means that half of the world's money was in New York. The money of the IMF and the World Bank was located here, as well as the New York Stock Exchange, and many other international banks. Regardless of the truth of this statement there was not another city in the world that could come close to equaling New York in wealth, and in total wealth the USA is by far the richest nation on earth.

"What may not be known is that when a ship approaches the New York City harbor from the south, in order to properly conform with the shipping lanes it must aim due north straight for a municipality on Long Island named Babylon. A tall water tower on the shoreline is used as a reference point for navigation and when a ship reaches closest to shore before turning west to enter the harbor, the name Babylon, written on the tower in big bold letters can be easily read.

"The community of Babylon was a predominantly Jewish community of over 250,000. Babylon was so named by early Jewish immigrants because of their study of the scriptures and their belief that Ancient Babylon would be relocated west of the Nile. It was the only inhabited and functioning community in the world that is known as Babylon. There were more Jews living in New York City than in any other city on earth, and there were more Jews living in America than in Israel and Russia combined. Clearly America is the home of Jewish exiles.

"Mystery Babylon is represented by a woman, we read in Revelation 17:1, ' ... I will show you the punishment of the great prostitute, who sits on many waters ... the waters you saw, where the prostitute sits, are peoples, multitudes, nations and languages.'

"Let me show you how America in general, and New York City in particular, fit the biblical descriptions of Mystery Babylon: The New Babylon is represented by a woman: America's most famous landmark is the Statue of Liberty. Studies make a solid case that our Statue of Liberty is in fact a reproduction of the Babylonian goddess Ishtar. Ishtar was at the top of the Babylonian pantheon of gods, and like the 'progressives' and 'open-minded' thinkers of the modern West, her cult promoted the notion of personal freedom and liberty to pursue a wild hedonistic sexual lifestyle of immense promiscuity: 'If it feels good, do it.' Central to her cult was the practice of prostitution for religious purposes, thus the scripture of Revelation 17:5, '... The Mother of Prostitutes ... '

"America's most profitable export is sexually and violence-charged entertainment. We had young female pop stars, idolized by even younger girls, who dressed and acted like prostitutes-in-training.

Pornography was a multi-billion dollar industry. There are several scriptures that point out the immorality of Babylon, especially the sin of adultery, which is celebrated and promoted all over the world through our unparalleled entertainment industry. California, ergo America, was the worldwide capitol of porn production.

"The 'Mother of Prostitutes' of Revelation 17-18 is a literal representation of the ancient Babylonian goddess Ishtar, whose cult demanded prostitution as a form of religious service. In former times she was known as Inanna to the Sumerian civilization and later she was worshiped as Venus and Libertas by the Romans. At one time Liberty was worshiped at a temple that was dedicated to her on Aventine Hill in Rome, and coins were even minted with inscriptions of her image and her name.

"The Statue of Liberty was conceived of, funded by and created by men who were intimately involved in the occult organization known as the Freemasons. Edouard Laboulaye was the chief fundraiser and Frederic August Bartholdi was the head sculptor. These men, and the freemasons in general, idealize the pagan gods and goddesses of ancient Rome and Greece. It is a well-known fact that Bartholdi intended the Statue of Liberty to be a representation of the Roman goddess Liberty, also known as Inanna and Ishtar. The likenesses between the two are eerie.

"On October 28th, 1886, President Grover Cleveland accepted the Statue of Liberty on behalf of the United States. In the ceremony, which celebrated the unveiling of this ancient pagan deity, he spoke these words, 'We will not forget that Liberty has here made her home; nor shall her chosen altar be neglected.'

"Follow me, my friends, as I outline my beliefs and I hope that they will become clear to you. Descriptions claim that Mystery Babylon is the lone Global Superpower. We read in Revelation 17:15, "The waters you saw, where the prostitute sits, are peoples, multitudes, nations and languages." And in Revelation 17:18, "The woman you saw is the great city that rules over the kings of the earth." Revelation 18:7, "In her heart she boasts, 'I sit as queen; I am not a widow, and I will never mourn.'

"America in the global superpower in three ways; economically, militarily, and politically. First, is there any doubt that America was the Economic Superpower of the planet? We repeatedly see biblical references to the "merchants of the earth" and the "the world's great men." In a 21st Century context, when we spoke of the "merchants of the earth" we could only have been speaking of Global Corporations and their officers. It was the corporations, which had all the money, and New York City was the engine that ran the economy of the world and it was the home of the majority of the world's wealthiest corporations. New York was the home of the World Trade Center and was also the home of the New York Stock Exchange where corporations reaped their unscrupulous wealth.

"With the demise of social security, the common people of America, the bewildered herd, were tricked into gambling their future on the well-being of these global concerns as well, through 401k Plans, stocks, and mutual funds. Hyper-inflated stock and company values and book cooking in the billions of dollars dealt crippling blows to the American – Babylonian – economy. And when it crashed it was not the banks or the mega-corporations that suffered or the orchestrators of "self-made" wealth – they insured that they would win either way – it was the bewildered herd. Driven by greed or envy, people placed their trust in the false idol of speculative economics, and betrayed their families in the process.

"Retirees, committed employees who gave their adult lives to false gods – the companies they worked for and the promise of economic security – were left with little or nothing. Or it was the young family man who trustingly placed his faith and his money in the hands of corporations. These were predicted.

"In Revelation 18 we read, ' ... and the merchants of the earth grew rich from her excessive luxuries ... ' and, 'The merchants of the earth will weep and mourn over her because no one buys their cargoes any more.' And a bit later we read, 'Your merchants were the world's great men. By your magic spell all the nations were led astray.'

"Secondly, it is undisputed that America was the dominant military superpower. There can be no doubt in anyone's mind that, even now, America possesses the world's most powerful military. The question then is, has America used it in an oppressive and relentlessly aggressive manner that is described of Babylon in the scriptures?

"Jeremiah 50:23, 'How broken and shattered is the hammer of the whole earth!' and, 'You are my war club, my weapon for battle—with you I shatter nations, with you I destroy kingdoms,' and Isaiah 14:4-6, '... How the oppressor has come to an end! How his fury has ended! The Lord has broken the rod of the wicked, the scepter of the rulers, which in anger struck down peoples with unceasing blows, and in fury subdued nations with relentless aggression.'

"Of course being the engine to the world's economy and possessing the world's most powerful military guarantees that America is a political superpower as well. However, the scriptures are pointing to something else that Mystery Babylon possesses. Jeremiah 51:44 mentions that at one time, before its demise, the nations of the world streamed to Babylon. Revelation 17:18 tells us that the city of Babylon rules over the kings of the earth. In Revelation 18:9-10 we see the kings of the earth declaring that Babylon was the "city of power."

"New York City fulfills these scriptures by being the home to the governing body of the Planet Earth: The United Nations. This fact alone makes it the most important city on the planet. It is from here that deals are made, boundaries are drawn, and lives are bought and sold as read in Revelations. It appears that after the sudden and catastrophic destruction of the city of Mystery Babylon that the Antichrist and his forces attack the remainder of this once great power.

"This is recorded in Revelation 17:16-18, 'The beast and the ten horns you saw will hate the prostitute. They will bring her to ruin and leave her naked; they will eat her flesh and burn her with fire. For God has put it into their hearts to accomplish his purpose by agreeing to give the beast their power to rule, until God's words are fulfilled.' And then goes on to say, 'The woman you saw is the great city that rules over the kings of the earth." Revelation 18:9-10, "When the kings of the earth ... see the smoke of her burning ... they will stand far off and cry: 'Woe! Woe, O great city, O Babylon, city of power! *In one hour your doom has come!'*

"And on April First, this prophecy came true. The new Babylon would be home to a large population of Jewish Exiles. Jeremiah 51:45, 'Come out of her, my people! Run for your lives! Run from the fierce anger of the Lord.'

"The above descriptions are just a few of the many biblical indicators that, I believe, point unequivocally and obviously to

America as the great power known as Mystery Babylon, and New York City as the specific city destined to fall in Revelation 18.

"After examining the conspicuous lack of pronouncements on the cultural evils of the West, such as Hollywood, pornography, drugs or homosexuality, we may conclude that the Jihad on the United States is intended as a political war, not ideological. And they may actually have been unwittingly playing out prophecies predicted in the Bible. My friends – "

The TV screen went black and the electricity in the house went back out leaving only the sound of chirping crickets from outside. Quite some time had gone by as I listened to the man on the TV.

It's always lonely in the middle of the night and people tend to be a little more receptive to new ideas in the wee hours of the morning. That's why infomercials used to play all night long. The scary thing was that the TV came on and no other channels would come in. It was as though the man came to speak to me and me alone. I lay there sweating and thinking; I was never a big Christian sort of person, but that bible stuff always scared me.

TWENTY-EIGHT

Good news was hard to come by but it was easy to hear of the bad everyday. It seemed as if the entire world had turned into a cauldron of misery. The world economy had all but collapsed and natural disasters reared their spiteful heads as allies of the terrorists ensuring that life was difficult everywhere. North Korea was starting trouble with South Korea and China threatened Taiwan. A crippled America could do little but sit on the sidelines like the superstar football player observing the game from crutches.

The combined forces of several countries attacked Israel. Her fight with Lebanon had grown to crescendo. Now with America immersed in her own problems, Israel was a tempting target for long-time anti-Semitic regimes. Scud missiles and Katyusha rockets rained mercilessly down upon her daily as armored forces pecked away at outlying settlements. The IDF fought well. They didn't roll over and most of the country was embroiled in battle of one sort or another twenty-four hours a day.

Meanwhile, some people eked back into the city from their rural hideouts. The numbers were negligible as they simply replaced some of the dead. Usually it was men coming back as forward scouts, as it were, to check out if things were okay. Sometimes they came home to an untouched house but in too many cases they returned only to find looted or burned out hulks of what was once their family home. Some stuck around, some got back behind the wheel and puttered heartbroken back out of town.

I was out on crew with Stubbs and three other newer guys on garbage detail north of downtown. We had been working all morning in the hot sun and took a break. I leaned up against the pickup talking with the other guys while Stubbs stretched himself out on an empty bus bench. We were all just hanging out, shooting the shit the way guys do. There was no one else around, no civilians or anything.

"Man, you know what?" Stubbs said.

"What's that?" I said.

"I've been saving up some money and keeping in touch with my kids over the 'net."

"Yeah?"

"Yeah. I think I'm gonna drive myself on down to *Chi-town* before winter set in. Start makin a life down there."

"I didn't know you had little kids," I said.

"Little kids? Man, my children be adults! Aaron Junior be twenty-four, my daughter Alicia be twenty-two."

"Damn," I said with a shake of my head. "Ya think ya know someone ..."

Aaron chuckled his baritone chuckle to himself and laid his face back up to the sun. Suddenly a dirty-looking homeless man came out of a building foyer and marched over to the bench.

"Hey motherfucker. That's my bench," he said to Stubbs. The man looked and acted like the street-crazies we'd seen a thousand times before.

Stubbs arched an eyebrow and slowly opened an eye. "I *know* you ain't talking to me."

"I'm looking right at your ugly ass," said the vagrant. "Get off my bench."

"Hey bitch, move your meat, lose your seat."

Well, shit, nobody had been there for awhile now. This guy seemed like just another street flake, right?

"You motherfucking bastard ..." the hobo mumbled as he reached under his coat. Before any of us could react he pulled out a .357 Magnum. Stubbs never saw it coming: The street-crazy calmly aimed at Aaron's head and squeezed off a powerful and loud round, blowing the top of Stubbs's head off in one impossibly quick and frightening seism. There was no question about the need for medical care. A significant part of Stubb's skull was missing and his brains were splattered all over the sidewalk. His eyes were wide and the last pumps of his heart were squirting obscene geysers of blood into the street.

The killing seemed to simultaneously last five minutes and last a nanosecond. There was no time for thinking, only reaction. The other guys and I ran up and tackled the bum before he could turn and take aim at us. I was intent on grabbing the revolver but the new guy who I only knew as Gardner grabbed it first. He snatched the gun and without pause or time to reflect simply jabbed the barrel into the assailant's abdomen and blew his stomach out of his back, killing him instantly.

That's how Aaron Stubbs died.

Weeklong celebrations sometimes preceded a jumper's death. It was now general knowledge amongst the Kaiserhof regulars that Derek had decided to end his life. When he told me over a beer at the Kaiserhof, it was as though someone had told me that they decided to by a Ford over a Chevy.

"So have you heard?" he asked one afternoon as I started to park my ass on a stool.

"Heard what?"

"I'm taking the plunge. Tenth Avenue Bridge."

"What? Is that a joke? Am I missing the punch line?" I asked, sure that there was some pun buried in his phraseology.

"No, buddy. You heard me right." He was serious. I was shocked.

"You're not really ... the kind of person ... *get the hell outta here!*" I was still unconvinced that this wasn't some sort of tasteless joke.

"I'm serious. Most everybody else knows. You're a good guy and I thought it was important that I told you in person before you heard it through the gossip mill."

I was starting to believe him. I looked at Jack, who was bringing me the pilsner that he'd started pouring when he saw me walk in. I looked at him and his non-verbal language told me that Derek wasn't joking. He was intent on taking his life.

After ten more minutes or so of talking, I was convinced of his sincerity. It was just a decision, nothing more than that. I stuck out my bottom lip and nodded in feigned understanding. For him, I figured, Derek had simply reached the point of understanding that life held no more promises and simply wasn't worth the effort anymore. If all went according to plan, he would kill himself on the following Sunday. "Life is unbearable, but I'm going out in style," would become his mantra for that week.

With Jack's help Derek planned a huge party for himself at the Kaiserhof. He had always struck me as a stand-up guy, and now he was facing his own demise with unflinching grit. He was actually quite upbeat all that week and, come Saturday night, was the star of his own party. It was as if he were about to take a long trip to Europe or something – there was no sense of sadness or doom in the air. We all just rolled with it, knowing that some dark sort of death probably awaited us all. At least he was calling his own shots and aware of his own destiny.

Derek had hired armed guards to watch the outside, so there wasn't a danger of hooligans breaking up the party with a spray of gunfire and looting. There was a guy with an M-16 on the roof diagonally opposite the restaurant and two more on the street corners. A couple people ran some food and soft drinks out to the guys every now and then.

Back inside the restaurant, people gathered, talked and ate appetizers. Jack had been able to order and procure a small truckload of alcohol and food. There was a buffet with chicken, ribs, potato salad, rolls and pastries. There was a near constant din of the clinking of glasses as people drank and got drunk. Beer was abundant, harder alcohols less so.

There were ten guys from the Gulag there. I strayed close to Henri Lebenze on my way to the restroom and, like clockwork, heard him discreetly whispering into the ear of a female guest who I'd never seen before. He was drinking a concoction invented by John called "The Pan-Galactic Gargle Blaster." (He stole that name from *A Hitchhiker's Guide to the Galaxy* but I didn't let on that I knew).

There were times when you could just hang out and talk with people and forget about the apocalypse. Those were times to savor and that evening was one of those rare times. It wasn't that long ago that the place was packed with mostly the same group of people celebrating my marriage. Now the occasion was bittersweet. The proximate cause of this particular celebration was itself, macabre in nature. In spite of that, we drank and celebrated. Derek totally blew what was left of his cash.

"Can't take it with ya!" he said with a wink. "Ya gotta spend that shit, move it around. Doncha think, Dallas?"

"I suppose," I mumbled.

"I mean, what am I shootin' for? A solid-gold coffin? I think not." He raised his drink and whispered to himself, *"Closer to God,"* and he drank.

I wondered if Derek would change his mind. I got him alone off in a corner at one point during the festivities. We were both fairly buzzed so the words flowed freely.

"So, Dallas, no word on your wife, eh?"

"No. I don't know what else to do."

"Stay positive. Keep looking."

Stay positive? From a man who was on the brink of killing himself?

"Derek, listen, are you sure you wanna do this bridge thing?" I said.

"I'm sure ... don't worry about it, okay?"

"Look, man, life goes on," I said sweeping my arm out. "There's still good people all around, there's still reasons to live."

"You don't understand," Derek shook his head and took a swig of beer.

"Sure I do. You don't think I've thought about blowing my head off? I can't find my wife, the only woman I ever wanted to really be with."

"You're young, you have your health," he said with a slap on top of my shoulder. "And you'll find your wife. Mark my words, you'll find her. What's more, you'll figure out something to do with your life."

"Yeah, I'm not putting boards over windows from here till eternity, that's for sure. But, listen … it's not like you're not young, you're in your, what … mid-forties? Late-forties?"

"Yeah …"

"And you've got your health …"

"No, Dallas, I don't have my health."

"What are you talking about?" I asked.

"About a month before The Attack, I went in for a checkup."

"Yes, and?" I said as I looked intently at my friend.

"I was diagnosed with a moderately advanced case of colon cancer."

I was dumbfounded and took a few moments to comprehend Derek's last statement. "Can it be treated?" I asked.

"I was beginning my regimen of non-surgical treatment in the last week of March and then," he made an explosion sound with his mouth and gestured a blossoming mushroom cloud with his hands, "April first. No more treatments."

"So you're just giving up?"

"You don't understand, Dallas. It's getting worse, not better. Cancer has a way of doing that."

"I …"

"Don't try, my friend. I'm in a fair amount of discomfort most of the time. I eat these pain-killers like they were M&Ms," he said as he pulled a prescription bottle out of his pocket and shook it like a baby rattle, "and it's why I took up drinking so much again. This suicide thing, this is what I want to do."

"It just seems like a … *waste*," I protested.

"Listen, Dallas. I used to run a successful business. I used to be in command of my life. I used to be worth several million dollars. Now, I've got nothing. I've truly got nothing."

I began to understand my friend and realized that I was slowly nodding in agreement with him as he spoke.

"The only thing I've got now is a say in how I go out and when I go out. Will you do me a favor and leave me that?"

I nodded and then slowly held my glass up for a discreet toast. He clinked his mug to mine.

"You'll be missed," I offered.

"As will we all," he said as he smiled and then drank.

I was no longer the sort to even *try* to figure out life's little mysteries anymore and I merely nodded in agreement and then changed subjects.

I'd like to be able to say that Derek went out with dignity. I had pictures in my mind of a tear-jerking farewell speech delivered at the edge of the bridge, followed by a glorious life-ending plummet into the Mississippi river. *"Well, that man went out on his own terms, he did,"* we would mutter in sad admiration as we ambled back to the bar for drinks.

But, no. After talking with Derek at the bar that night, I continued drinking. The rest of the evening is a splotchy patchwork of blurry memories. I woke up on the living room floor of Jack's apartment the next morning. Jack was having coffee.

"Looks who's alive," he teased.

"Yeah," I said. I didn't feel too good. The mid-morning sunlight beaming through the windows hurt my eyes all the way to the back of my head. It took me a few moments to remember the night before.

"Oh, did Derek jump off the bridge?" I groggily asked, worried that I missed the final farewell.

"Nope," Jack replied flatly.

"Oh, good," I said relieved. "So is he around?"

"You don't remember, Dallas?"

"Shit, I was fucking ripped last night man. Remember what?"

"Derek called the Dead Body Hotline about one in the morning. He didn't say anything to anybody. Right before they showed up, he just stepped out onto the sidewalk, put a gun in his mouth and blew the top of his head off."

Oh, yeah. How did I forget that?

TWENTY-NINE

Scheerer came up and joined me the next day as I sat on a pile of lumber after a day's work. He was usually busy doing something – prioritizing work orders, figuring out crew assignments, bugging the shop guys to get this vehicle or that vehicle up and running. It was a little strange for him to come up and just talk. He sat down.

"How's it going, troop?"

"Same shit, different day," I answered.

"Any luck with your wife?"

"None," I said. "I'm losing a grip, man."

He shook his head in commiseration. "I'm sorry."

"Shit, I almost shot a guy awhile back because he was littering. I mean, I'm really losing it."

"It's a tough, tough world. You're one of the good guys, you deserve better."

"I don't know if I'm all *that* good," I shook my head.

"What's on your mind?" he asked, getting to the root of it. All things seemed minor compared to my anguish over Sarah's unknown whereabouts, so I spilled the beans.

"Well, not too long ago, I went out and … I tried to kill a man in cold blood." There, I said it.

"You tried to kill a man?" he asked, somewhat surprised.

"An old enemy, a civilian from my past. It was just an impulse that I acted on. I know better."

"What were you going to do, shoot him?"

"Yup, sniper-style."

"Why didn't you?" he asked.

"Too many witnesses showed up. That's the one and only reason. Other than that, I was ready to do it."

"How many men have you killed?" Scheerer asked casually.

The question took me aback. "You mean since the nukes?"

"I mean ever."

"None that I know of," I said. *What kind of question was that?*

"Do you know how many men I've killed?" Scheerer asked.

"How many?"

"At least eighteen. I'm talking Americans here in this city. I never killed any enemy soldiers as an Army Ranger but I've killed eighteen fellow Americans as a civilian maintenance supervisor. Probably more than that. And now you're self-conscious because you almost killed *one*?"

"I'm self-conscious because I planned it out, it was going to be a murder. It wasn't self-defense or saving someone else's life like with you. The only reason I was going to do it was because I could get away with it. Once the risks outweighed the benefits, I scrubbed the mission." I liked speaking in military-lingo from time to time.

"Okay. Anything else bothering you?"

"Well," I said looking off to the distance and scrinching my nose, "I feel like … I've failed … as a … husband." It was as though my throat was made of velcro and the words barely crawled out of my mouth. "I was married a couple of weeks … and then it was, *Whoops, where'd my wife go?*"

"You have no responsibility in that, Burnette. That was the most screwed up day ever."

"So I shouldn't feel responsible for the welfare of my wife? That was implicit in the deal, wasn't it? That I would take care of her safety?"

"You're piling a awful lot of guilt on yourself and that's perfectly normal. In fact, I'd be worried if you didn't feel guilty. But let's be logical; what could you have done? It started out as a normal day, you were out working on the other side of town and then all hell broke loose."

"I just don't feel good about myself. Not now."

"Stay strong. Be positive. She could be on her way home as we speak."

"Thoughts like that are the *only* thing keeping me going," I said.

"I hope you find your wife soon, Dallas. I really do," he said with a firm slap on my knee. That was the first time he ever called me Dallas, not Burnette. "Just make sure she has something to return home to." He got up and walked back into the maintenance building.

THIRTY

I drew a peculiar assignment one day in late August.

We had to go secure several broken windows at the armory downtown. The very armory that was in service as a body identification and disposal station. This was where they brought bodies when people called in on the Dead Body Hotline. We only had a crew of three guys and the job took us less than an hour. I was the crew leader. I told the guys to take a break upon completion of the job and brought the paperwork in to be signed off on.

"I'm looking for Dr. Bill Peterson," I said to the first person I saw inside.

"Yes, that's me," answered older man in a lab coat with white hair and reading glasses perched on the end of his nose.

"Hi, Dallas Burnette from the county," I said. "We cleaned up and secured three windows on the south and east sides of the building per the work order. Was there anything else you needed?"

Peterson looked through the paperwork quickly and then signed off. "No, sir, that should do it."

"Okay," I spun around to head for the door but stopped, acting on a quick whim, and turned back around. "Dr. Peterson?" I was nervous.

"Yes?" he answered turning back to me.

"If someone were missing … I'm missing someone, a woman. If she were … killed …"

"If she were picked up, we'd have her on file here. Are you talking about a relative?"

"Yes, my wife. Sarah Pennington," I answered, using her maiden name.

"Okay, sir, we do have a data base. Whenever we get an unidentified body— "

"I work for the county," I interrupted, "I know how it works."

"Okay, sir. Follow me."

Dr. Peterson led me to an office filled with desks and files. We sat down across from each other at one of the desks with a computer. We waited as the computer booted and then Peterson went to the appropriate application. Sarah had been missing for almost two months now. This was one of the first places where I should have checked but I tried to remain as positive as I could and checking here would have been a surrender to the worst-case scenario.

"Okay. Name of the missing person?" he asked clinically.

"Sarah … Pennington."

"Is that first name with or without the 'h'?" he said as he starting tapping away on his computer keyboard.

"With," I said wiping my nose.

"And 'Pennington' just like it sounds?"

I nodded. If she'd had any identification on her it would most certainly be in the name of Pennington.

"Middle name?"

"Renee," I said. I could feel my heart beating.

He tapped in the information and we waited a few seconds. "Sometimes bodies come in with a drivers license or some other form of ID."

I nodded again.

"Okay, no one named Pennington, Sarah or otherwise, has been identified by us here. That doesn't mean that she didn't come through here, just means we didn't identify her."

"I understand." I felt a slight wave of relief.

He clicked over to a different screen. "Can you describe the missing person to me?"

"She's, uh, five-seven, about a hundred-thirty pounds, dark shoulder-length hair ..."

"Approximate age?"

"Twenty-eight."

"Any tattoos or other identifying marks?"

"Yes, she had a flower tattooed on her left ankle."

He tapped on the computer. "When is the last time you saw this person?"

"The morning of July fourth."

He nodded knowingly. After ten seconds or so he removed his glasses and looked at me. It was that horrible look that doctors give family members in waiting rooms when the news isn't good.

"Are you a tough man, Mr. Burnette?"

"Tough in some ways, I suppose," I said. "Maybe not so tough in others."

"I have a preliminary match to the description you gave me. Are you prepared to make a photo ID of the body?"

I simply froze. I literally felt a painful sensation as the muscles in my lower back contracted in fear.

"Sir?" Dr. Peterson said.

I could feel my pulse on my neck and was sure that the throbbing was visible. I took a long breath and let it out slowly. After several seconds I slowly rolled my chair around to get a better view of the screen.

I recognized Sarah instantly. Tears welled up at the corners of my eyes.

"Sir? Can you identify this body?"

I sat staring at the screen. There were three pictures of her face – front, side, and oblique – and one of the tattoo on her ankle. Her hair was messy and gooey with thick, semi-coagulated blood on the back, her lips were blue, her mouth was grotesquely ajar and her eyes were slightly open. Her face was a little scuffed up as though she'd been in a fight and she looked as if she were in the early stages of post-mortem bloating. But she was still my Sarah.

"Sir, I know that this may be difficult, but can you identify this person?"

I nodded affirmative. "Yes … that's her."

"You're quite sure?"

I nodded. He hit a few more keystrokes.

"Do you know how she … died?" I asked with a trembling voice.

Peterson scrolled down until he found the appropriate paragraph and began reading: *"Female victim found July four, nearest cross street 24th & Lyndale Avenue, partially clothed, no ID found on or near the body, body processed and recorded at 5:30 p.m., victim estimated to be dead five to eight hours at that time of arrival."*

"Was she raped?" I fearfully asked with my hand over my mouth. The beat of my heart thumped in my inner ear.

Peterson could tell this was hard on me and he sighed. "Does it really matter, sir?" he asked with compassion.

"Just tell me. I'll deal with it."

He read on: *"Victim found partially clothed, one sock, short sleeve shirt, bra and panties."*

"So she wasn't ..."

"No sign of forced sexual assault. But there was some significant skin residue under her fingernails. My guess is an *attempted* sexual assault, but she fought the bastard off. Your wife was a tough little lady."

I was trembling and took a difficult breath before I responded. "How how was she killed?" I asked, not sure if I really wanted to hear the answer.

"Close range pistol blast to the head, through-and-through," Dr. Peterson said without even looking at the computer screen.

I put my face in my hands and he put his hand on my knee in an attempt at condolence. I was crying. Who in the world would want to put a gun to Sarah's head and end her life? *Who?*

"If it's any solace, I processed the body," Dr. Peterson said. "That's why I remember her. She – Sarah was handled with dignity and care when she got here."

"Thank you," I said, fully crying. My voice was high and I'm sure that I sounded like a child. "Do you ... do you still have her here? Do you think I could see her?" It was a foolish question: My mind knew better but my heart had to ask.

"I'm sorry, she was cremated right after processing. It's very standard procedure."

My head dropped and I cried even harder. Peterson waited a few seconds before speaking again.

"Sir, I know this is hard but we have to have you do some paperwork for us. It will just take a moment."

"Why?" I challenged, still lingering in the stage of denial.

"Frankly, you could be killed in a street robbery two hours from now. Sarah needs to be officially declared as identified for her family's sake, sir. Sooner or later somebody else will come looking for her. She needs to be taken from … 'Jane Doe #2,398' to 'Sarah Pennington.' You understand, don't you sir?"

I nodded.

I could have come to the armory weeks before then and discovered Sarah's disposition. I had made some tepid phone calls searching for her by name, but not as a Jane Doe. Some folks are afraid of getting checked for cancer, as if the news of sickness would be worse than the disease itself. I think that's how I felt about exhausting any search that had the possibility of disclosing that my wife was dead. Ignorance *is* bliss, and as long as I was unaware of her death, there was the possibility that Sarah would come walking through our front door. My wife was now officially dead.

I signed her out as 'Sarah Burnette.'

THIRTY-ONE

The world had become a living nightmare. Lawlessness ran amok. Beautiful buildings were vandalized; houses and dwellings were burned or filled with nasty squatters. My own apartment building lay in charred ruins and my possessions destroyed. I had lost friends and coworkers to bullets, disease, suicide and mishap. Teenage daughters of good people were raped and killed. People could be pulled from cars and beaten at any time, or randomly shot. Pestilence and filth were omnipresent. The scummy, chronically criminal elements of society actually seemed to enjoy the new world. After all, the playing field was level: The millionaires, corporate officers and wealthy entrepreneurs were now basically the same as the poverty-stricken. They, too, were powerless nobodies with wealth and carefree comfortable retirements absent from their futures. A rich man died just as easily as a poor man and both were accorded the same indignities in death. These were the realities of humanity.

I cut the crew loose after I identified Sarah and just walked until I found a place to sit. I sat on an old bus stop bench in the late afternoon, surrounded by urban debris and awash in sorrow. I stared at the asphalt out in front of me. After some time, I realized that my fingers were absentmindedly spinning the wedding band on the marriage finger of my left hand. Crows squawked their annoying squawk. Every now and then a piece of garbage would blow by like tumbleweed through an old western town. Last spring seemed like twenty years ago. I'd lost more friends in one spring and summer than most people lose in a lifetime. I'd lost most of my possessions.

And, of course, I lost my Sarah.

Everything was a surreal adventure in the beginning right after The Attack, terrifying and exciting all at the same time. But post-nuclear holocaust society had slowly degraded into a vast emptiness of difficult existence. My soul wandered in the hopeless purgatory of not wanting to live and not wanting to die. Infinite sadness was a millstone around my neck. It must have showed.

A cordial elderly gentleman was shuffling by when he stopped and looked at me. He thought for a reflective moment before saying something;

"Anyone can see beauty in the ruins of a church. But no one can see beauty in the ruins of a man."

He smiled a kindly smile, nodded gently and then continued on his way. I don't know if he thought he needed to say that or if I needed to hear that, but I was somehow glad that he did.

An unseasonably cool wind stirred, whispering a vague threat of colder months to come. Soon it would turn into autumn, and then autumn would turn into winter. Diesel generators would be useful until the fuel was depleted. As any truck driver could tell you, diesels idled at such a low rate of fuel consumption that you could leave a truck idling all night long if you had to leave it outside on a cold winter's night. A battery system with solar panels for recharging would be a more practical solution for long-term recovery. Wood or coal burning stoves and fuel storage would be apart of every county emergency system. Coal would store well if it were placed between a straw blanket and covered with dirt. I'd been studying for cold weather survival on the internet, see.

Whatever.

Such are the things that weighed on the mind as September neared. A cruel sibling of time, the seasons were without a flyspeck of concern if you were prepared or not. A harsh winter would separate the weak from the strong, the prepared from the unprepared.

What started out as a nightmare turned into an adventure, and adventure turned into a mindless, soul-sucking hell. I was in a situation way over my head. Fate, God, Allah, terrorists – whatever entity was, it had beaten me. I tired of this life. Living only to live? What's the point?

Nothing lasts forever. I guess just about everyone would agree with that.

My name is Dallas Burnette. I'm 35-years-old and a native of Minneapolis. I used to sell sandpaper but now I nail boards over windows. I'm a scoundrel, a near-murderer – and a widower. I don't know why I was put here on this Earth, why I'm still alive as people better than I die all around me. I don't even know why I'm sitting on this bench. Maybe I'm paying for a life not well-lived and this existence that I'm experiencing is merely Erebus, the dark place through which the dead must pass before entering hell.

FINAL CHAPTER:

A SOCIETY OF GOOD MEN

In a culturescape where obtaining food and dodging random death were daily challenges, the things people used to fight for and about – universal health care, social security, civil rights, environmentalism, campaign finance reform, corporate tax-breaks – all of these things had become silly in comparison. Concerns about such things as credit card debt and rotten love lives evaporated into nonexistence.

A man used to be measured by his portfolio, bank account, job and status. Now a man knew he was a winner at the game-of-life if he simply woke up in the morning. Breathing and relative health were the signs of a blessed person. Compared to the carnage and inhumanity that I saw every day, I had it very good. I had food, shelter, and a job. Hell, I even sat in a bar and drank pretty good beer on a regular basis. Yet, I thought of taking my own life almost constantly. Derek had the courage to do it, why couldn't I?

Scheerer called me into his office one day in early September. Through everything that had happened to me in the previous months, Dan Scheerer had been a solid rock of stability. It was of little wonder to me that he was alive and thriving as a human being, all things considered.

He told me that he was sorry, very sorry about Sarah. He knew that her loss was an on-going source of great sadness for me. Then we had a little friendly small talk before getting down to business.

"Our mission has been reduced to doing anything and everything at the whim of government minions higher on the food-chain than us," he said. One thing was clear; trying to be the stewards of a dying city was a losing battle. "We're just rearranging the deck chairs on the Titanic, I think you know that."

"Yeah, I guess," I replied.

"The meek may indeed inherit the Earth, but I can tell you that shitbags have inherited the city of Minneapolis," he said.

I'm not sure but I think that was the first time I heard Dan Scheerer use a cuss word.

"If you want to stay," he continued, "that's up to you. You'll still have a job with the county. God knows, metropolitan areas need guys like us. But if you decide to leave, I won't stop you and I won't report you as deserting."

"Thanks, Dan, but why are you telling me this?" I said. "Where the hell am I going to go?"

"There's a man in town, I guess you'd call him a recruiter," Dan said.

"A recruiter?" I said surprised. "I'm not joining the Army!"

"Get serious. What I'm telling you is in the strictest of confidence."

"Okay," I said, somewhat intrigued.

"There are more nukes in America."

The mere utterance of the phrase made my heart skip a beat. After staring at Dan for a few seconds, I managed to speak. "How do you know?"

"You're going to have to trust me on that one, I have my sources." Scheerer's honesty was beyond reproach and I believed him. He continued; "There's a man looking for people to help start a new community, a new society, far from any urban area. I recommended you. If you're interested, go to the community center tonight at ten o'clock. It'll be after sundown so nobody but a few government folks will be there."

"You're not telling everyone? Just me?"

"The people I'm recommending find out one-on-one from me. You understand this is strictly confidential?"

"Of course, I do. But, why in the hell would you pick me?"

"Don't be so hard on yourself. You're a better man than you think you are."

"Thanks," I said.

"Get outta here for now, Dallas," he said with a fatherly hand on my shoulder. I nodded, left his office and went out on duty for the day. Yet I was curious. I had no idea what this recruiter was all about or what he could want from the straggling remnant population of a dead city.

I finished out the workday and went down to the bar. A peaceful beer at the Kaiserhof was one of the few things in my life I could count on. I talked with no one as I nursed two pilsners over several hours and then headed out.

I showed up at the community center on time along with some other people and we were led as a group to a room in the basement. There were about fifteen men in the room, mostly folks from other departments of the government. There was a tall, rugged man standing in the front of the room with his hands on his hips waiting for us to get situated. He was a light-skinned African-American with an air of dignity and intelligence about him, even as he stood there motionless. He wore a clean denim work shirt tucked into pressed khaki pants with cargo pockets and clean, but well-worn hiking boots. A gold wedding band shined on his left hand and a large ring – *Annapolis?* – gleamed on his right. Next to him was a cart with a TV and DVD player hooked up and ready to go. I wondered what he would have done if the power had been out on this particular evening, as it appeared he was ready to give us a media presentation. People settled in and he spoke.

"Ladies and gentlemen, thank you for venturing out to meet with me tonight, my name is Boscoe Williams. I'm a former U.S. naval aviator and I used to work for the federal government as a nuclear physicist, before the The Attack. I was the nuclear search team leader in San Francisco on April first. We disabled that bomb. Nowadays, I guess I'm what you'd call a consultant to the feds.

"What am I doing here? I drive around the upper Midwest looking for just a few men and women to hear a proposal. I have a DVD to show you, which I think will be self-explanatory. I'll take all of your questions afterwards, so please save your thoughts for now."

With that, he pointed the DVD remote at the machine, hit the start button and stepped to the back of the room. The first thing we saw was white letters on a black background:

This presentation is sanctioned by the government of the United States of America and exists under EXECUTIVE ORDER 11004 which allows the Housing and Finance Authority to relocate communities, build new housing with public funds, and designate areas to be abandoned, and establish and sanction new locations for populations.

After ten seconds or so the screen started showing scenes of pre-April Attack society with a soothing male voice-over narrating;

"Do you remember what life used to be like? Do you remember the simple joys of life? Do you remember having a general feeling of safety and a hope that life held treasures and dreams yet to be realized? Life may never be the same since the nuclear attacks of April, but good people in this world can still find life, liberty and happiness in communities of shared philosophies.

"Who are we? We started as a group of concerned fathers and husbands. We have come to the firm resolution that our lives will go on. Our lives will go on in peace and tranquility. While sanctioned by the government, we are not a part of, nor are we directly linked to the government.

"If you decide to join us and are accepted, we expect you to bring your talents, your resources, and your optimistic belief that life and everything about life is precious. Every nail you hammer, every broken hinge you fix, every flower you nurture, every bit of knowledge or expertise that you pass along – from teaching someone how to dress a freshly-shot buck to teaching someone a new chord on the guitar – every single thing you do is important for now, and for the next generation.

"A person brought into the society is expected to maintain the highest standards of good community behavior: A member of the society is not expected merely to exist, but to share and contribute and be a clear asset to the community on many levels. Everyone must perform assigned duties. There are no wealthy passengers along for a free ride to be served by others. There are many limitations to personal freedoms such as contraband materials. There will be no recreational drugs or alcohol. All firearms and weapons will be placed in a common armory and will not be released except under orders from a commanding authority. There will be no private stocks of foods because under survival conditions this can lead to social disorder.

"We believe that we are strong when we live and function as one: No individual has the personal resources that a group has. However, if it is a large group then there are numbers of people available to continue to give support. Just like there are numbers of people available to maintain 24-hour security, or to dispatch well-manned convoys to go after necessary supplies. One more prepared and equipped individual added to such a group is an asset. One more unprepared and unequipped individual is a liability. A successful society will be completely homogeneous regarding economics, values and future expectations. Still, the society is not a democratic community anymore than is a ship or an airliner.

"Neither is the society a democracy in the sense that there must be much more stringent rules regarding behavior. Malfeasance of any sort will not be tolerated: Order will be kept. And, lest there be any confusion, we are not survivalists or supremacists. Racially motivated violence or killings will be dealt with harshly and swiftly. Information is shared between like-minded communities and the banished will find themselves wandering in a wilderness of the evil; the roving bands, the gypsies, the robbers and the killers.

"The nuclear attacks of the first of April were a birthing process, and all birthings are painful. Natural progression demands catastrophe as catalyst. And as we shift into a new way of life – a new brand of human being – we become more complex, gain a higher level of consciousness and gain new freedoms. These are simple laws of nature and natural progression. To quote Kahlil Gibran, *'When you have reached the mountaintop, then shall you begin the climb.'* Welcome to the mountaintop, my friends.

"Tough? Yes, anything worth having is tough. But not nearly as tough as the conditions of survival will be for those who are not prepared.

"We are in a fight to preserve any semblance of a good and a free society. We don't know what the future holds, but we will give our descendants the best chance they can get. We will do this by starting over and creating a society with templates of good and decent behavior, and by seeking the simple goals that founded our American country many years ago; life, liberty, and the pursuit of happiness.

"Please remember: Destiny is not a matter of chance, it's a matter of choice. Thank you."

The television screen faded to black and the lights came back on. I was awestruck. For the first time in months, I had a feeling of optimism. Hands shot into the air as people tried to ask Mr. Williams questions about this new society, this society of good men. For me, there was no question: I was behind the wheel of a pickup full of supplies and leaving Minneapolis before sunset on the very next day.

-THE END-

A WORD FROM THE AUTHOR

The inspiration for this novel had actually been in my mind for quite some time; what would modern American society do if the world went through a traumatic event that threatened a potential apocalyptic outcome? And what sort of event would cause such a circumstance? An Earth-crossing asteroid would be one. Global thermonuclear war would be another. Worldwide plague, either natural or manmade would be yet another. But in the opening few years of the third millennium, it is clear that terrorism poses a threat on a potential global scale. I wrote "A Society of Good Men" originally as a 7,ooo word short story and couldn't resist the urge to expand it into novel form.

When I was a young US Army intelligence officer circa 1990, we were told as a part of our coursework that there would, in all likelihood, be a catastrophic attack on a major American city within twenty years. It took less than twelve. Now there are those who say that, no matter what we do, there will be a day when a nuclear device will be detonated in a major American city – probably within twenty years.

Unlikely? Probably. But America thought that it had wiped out airline hijackings by the late seventies, only to wake up one beautiful fall morning in 2001 and find four of her ships commandeered by terrorists and three of them flown into iconic buildings of the country. It wasn't very likely, but it most certainly happened.

Rather than focusing heavily on high-level government goings on, the novel mostly deals with the relationships of regular people left in an unattacked metropolis. Written in the first-person, past-tense, the reader gleans information along with the main character, Dallas Burnette, from hip-pocket discussions with federally employed scientists from CDC or the Department of Homeland Defense. Other novels and other novelists can concentrate on super-secret CIA internal protocols and military actions by characters that graduated as one of the top students from Annapolis or West Point. Dallas Burnette is just a regular civilian, an Everyman caught up in enormous events.

In any case, if a near Apocalypse were ever to transpire I always thought that the best and most moral would come together and form "a society of good men." The society would protect not only their immediate families, but also humanity and its ideals in the difficult years surely to come.   *RPM*